THE LION TAMER'S DAUGHTER

and other stories

PETER DICKINSON

Delacorte Press

Published by
Delacorte Press
Bantam Doubleday Dell Publishing Group, Inc.
1540 Broadway
New York, New York 10036

Library of Congress Cataloging-in-Publication Data

Dickinson, Peter.
  The lion tamer's daughter and other stories / Peter Dickinson.
      p.   cm.
  Contents: The spring—Touch and go—Checkers—The lion tamer's daughter.
  Summary: Each of these stories touches on the idea of a twin, a ghostly double of a live person, or a secret self.
  ISBN 0-385-32327-1
  1. Supernatural—Juvenile fiction.   2. Children's stories, English.
  [1. Supernatural—Fiction.   2. Short stories.]   I. Title.
PZ7.D562Li   1997
[Fic]—dc20   96-20022
                                                                   CIP
                                                                   AC

The text of this book is set in 14-point Perpetua.
Manufactured in the United States of America
May 1997
BVG   10   9   8   7   6   5   4   3   2   1

CONTENTS

THE SPRING

When Derek was seven Great-Aunt Tessa had died and there'd been a funeral party for all the relations. In the middle of it a woman with a face like a sick fish, some kind of cousin, had grabbed hold of Derek and half-talked to him and half-talked to another cousin over his head.

"That's a handsome young fellow, aren't you? (Just like poor old Charlie, that age.) So you're young Derek. How old would you be now, then? (The girls—that's one of them, there, in the green blouse—they're a lot bigger.) Bit of an afterthought, weren't you, Derek? Nice surprise for your mum and dad. (Meg had been meaning to go back to that job of hers, you know . . .)"

And so on, just as if she'd been talking two languages, one he could understand and one he couldn't. Derek hadn't been surprised or shocked. In his heart he'd known all along.

It wasn't that anyone was unkind to him, or even uncaring. Of course his sisters sometimes called him a pest and told him to go away, but mostly the family included him in whatever they were doing and sometimes, not just on his birthday, did something they thought would amuse him. But even those times Derek knew in his heart that he wasn't really meant to be there. If he'd never been born—well, like the cousin said, Mum would have gone back to her job full-time, and five years earlier too, and she'd probably have got promoted so there'd have been more money for things. And better holidays, sooner. And more room in the house—Cindy was always whining about having to share with Fran . . . It's funny to think about a world in which you've never existed, never been born. It would seem almost exactly the same to everyone else. They wouldn't miss you—there'd never have been anything for them to miss.

About four years after Great-Aunt Tessa's funeral Dad got a new job and the family moved south. That June Dad and Mum took Derek off to look at a lot of roses. They had their new garden to fill, and there was this famous collection of roses only nine miles away at Something Abbey, so they could go and see if there were ones they specially liked, and get their order in for next winter. Mum and Dad were nuts about gardens. The girls had things of their own to do but it was a tagging-along afternoon for Derek.

The roses grew in a big walled garden, hundreds and hundreds of them, all different, with labels. Mum and Dad stood in front of each bush in turn, cocking their heads and pursing their lips while they decided if they liked it. They'd smell a bloom or two, and then Mum would read the label and Dad would look it up in his book to see if it was disease-resistant; last of all, Mum might write its name in her notebook and they'd give it marks, out of six, like skating judges, and move on. It took *hours*.

After a bit Mum remembered about Derek.

"Why don't you go down to the house and look at the river, darling? Don't fall in."

"Got your watch?" said Dad. "OK, back at the car park, four-fifteen, sharp."

He gave Derek a pound in case there were ice creams anywhere and turned back to the roses.

The river was better than the roses, a bit. The lawn of the big house ran down and became its bank. It was as wide as a road, not very deep but clear, with dark green weed streaming in the current and trout sometimes darting between. Derek found a twig and chucked it in, pacing beside it and timing its speed on his watch. He counted trout for a while, and then walking further along the river, he came to a strange shallow stream which ran through the lawns, like a winding path, only water, just a few inches deep but rushing through its channel in quick ripples. Following it up, he came to a sort of hole in the ground, with a fence round it. The hole had stone sides and was

3

full of water. The water came rushing up from somewhere underground, almost as though it were boiling. It was very clear. You could see a long way down.

While Derek stood staring, a group of other visitors strolled up and one of them started reading from her guidebook, gabbling and missing bits out.

". . . remarkable spring . . . predates all the rest of the abbey . . . no doubt why the monks settled here . . . white chalk bowl fifteen feet across and twelve feet deep . . . crystal clear water surges out at about two hundred gallons a minute . . . always the same temperature, summer and winter . . ."

"Magical, don't you think?" said another of the tourists.

She didn't mean it. "Magical" was just a word to her. But yes, Derek thought, magical. Where does it come from? So close to the river, too, but it's got nothing to do with that. Perhaps it comes from another world.

He thought he'd only stood gazing for a short time, hypnotized by the rush of water welling and welling out of nowhere, but when he looked at his watch, it was ten past four. There was an ice-cream van, but Dad and Mum didn't get back to the car till almost twenty to five.

That night Derek dreamed about the spring. Nothing much happened in the dream, only he was standing beside it, looking down. It was nighttime, with a full moon, and he was waiting for the moon to be reflected from the rumpled water. Something would happen then. He woke before it happened, with his heart hammering. He was

filled with a sort of dread, though the dream hadn't bee.
nightmare. The dread was sort of neutral, halfway between
terror and glorious excitement.

The same dream happened the next night, and the next,
and the next. When it woke him on the fifth night, he
thought this is getting to be a nuisance.

He got out of bed and went to the window. It was a
brilliant night, with a full moon high. He felt wide awake.
He turned from the window, meaning to get back into
bed, but somehow found himself moving into his getting-
up routine, taking his pajamas off and pulling on his shirt.
The moment he realized what he was doing he stopped
himself, but then thought why not? It'd fix that dream, at
least. He laughed silently to himself and finished dressing.
Ten minutes later he was bicycling through the dark.

Derek knew the way to the abbey because Mum was no
use at map reading so that was something he did on car
journeys—a way of joining in. He thought he could do it
in an hour and a quarter, so he'd be there a bit after one.
He'd be pretty tired by the time he got back, but the roads
were flat down here compared with Yorkshire. He'd left a
note on the kitchen table saying "Gone for a ride. Back for
breakfast." They'd think he'd just gone out for an early-
morning spin—he was always first up. Nine miles there
and nine back made eighteen. He'd done fifteen in one go
last month. Shouldn't be too bad.

And in fact, although the night was still, he rode as
though there were a stiff breeze at his back, hardly getting
tired at all. Late cars swished through the dark. He tried to

think of a story in case anyone stopped and asked what he was doing—if a police car came by, it certainly would—but no one did. He reached the abbey at ten past one. The gate was shut, of course. He hadn't even thought about getting in. There might be ivy, or something.

He found some a bit back along the way he'd come, but it wasn't strong or thick enough to climb. Still, it didn't cross his mind he wouldn't get in. He was going to. There would be a way.

The wall turned away from the road beside the garden of another house. Derek wheeled his bike through the gate and pushed it in among some bushes, then followed the wall back through the garden. No light shone from the house. Nobody stirred. He followed the wall of the abbey grounds along toward the back of the garden. He thought he could hear the river rustling beyond. The moonlight was very bright, casting shadows so black they looked solid. The garden became an orchard, heavy old trees, their leafy branches blotting out the moon, but with a clear space further on. Ducking beneath the branches, he headed toward it. The night air smelt of something new, sweetish, familiar—fresh-cut sawdust. When he reached the clear space, he found it surrounded a tree trunk which had had all its branches cut off and just stood there like a twisted arm sticking out of the ground. Leaning against it was a ladder.

It wasn't very heavy. Derek carried it over to the abbey wall. It reached almost to the top. He climbed, straddled the wall, leaned down, and with an effort hauled the ladder up and lowered it on the further side, down into the darkness under the trees that grew there, then climbed down and groped his way out toward where the moonlight gleamed between the tree trunks. Out in the open on the upper slope of lawn he got his bearings, checked for a landmark so that he would be able to find his way back to the ladder, and walked down in the shadow of the trees toward the river. His heart was beginning to thump, the way it did in the dream. The same dread, between terror and glory, seemed to bubble up inside him.

When he was level with the spring he walked across the open and stood by the low fence, gazing down at the troubled water. It looked very black, and in this light he couldn't see into it at all. He tried to find the exact place he had stood in the dream, and waited. A narrow rim of moon-shadow cast by the wall on the left side edged the disk of water below. It thinned and thinned as the slow-moving moon heeled west. And now it was gone.

The reflection of the moon, broken and scattered by the endlessly upswelling water, began to pass glimmeringly across the disk below. Derek could feel the turn of the world making it move like that. His heartbeat came in hard pulses, seeming to shake his body. Without knowing what he was doing, he climbed the fence and clung to its inner side so that he could gaze straight down into the water. His own reflection, broken by the ripples, was a squat black shape against the silver moonlight. He crouched with his left arm clutching the lowest rail and with his right arm strained down toward it. He could just reach. The black shape changed as the reflection of his arm came to meet it. The water was only water to his touch.

Somehow he found another three inches of stretch and plunged his hand through the surface. The water was still water, but then another hand gripped his.

He almost lost his balance and fell, but the other hand didn't try to pull him in. It didn't let go either. When Derek tried to pull free the hand came with him, and an arm behind it. He pulled, heaved, strained. A head broke the surface. Another arm reached up and gripped the top of the side wall. Now Derek could straighten and take a fresh hold higher up the fence. And now the stranger could climb out, gasping and panting, over the fence and stand on the moonlit lawn beside him. He was a boy about Derek's own age, wearing ordinary clothes like Derek's. They were dry to the touch.

"I thought you weren't coming," said the boy. "Have we got somewhere to live?"

"I suppose you'd better come home."

They walked together toward the trees.

"Who . . . ?" began Derek.

"Not now," said the stranger.

They stole on in silence. We'll have to walk the whole way home, thought Derek. Mightn't get in before breakfast. How'm I going to explain?

The ladder was still against the wall. They climbed it, straddled the top, lowered the ladder on the far side, and climbed down, propping it back against its tree. Then back toward the road.

There were two bikes hidden in the bushes.

"How on . . . ?" began Derek.

"Not now," said the stranger.

They biked in silence the whole way home, getting in just as the sky was turning gray. They took off their shoes and tiptoed up the stairs. Derek was so tired he couldn't remember going to bed.

They were woken by Cindy's call outside the door.

"Hi! Pests! Get up! School bus in twenty mins!"

Derek scrambled into his clothes and just beat David down the stairs. Dad was in the hallway, looking through the post before driving off to work.

"Morning, twins," he said. "Decided to have a lie-in?"

They gobbled their breakfast and caught the bus by running. Jimmy Grove had kept two seats for them. He always did.

Very occasionally during that year Derek felt strange. There was something not quite right in the world, something out of balance, some shadow. It was like that feeling you have when you think you've glimpsed something out of the corner of your eye but when you turn your head it isn't there. Once or twice it was so strong he almost said something. One evening, for instance, he and David were sitting either side of Mum while she leafed through an old photograph album. They laughed or groaned at pictures of themselves as babies, or in fancy dress—Tweedledum and Tweedledee—and then Mum pointed at a picture of an old woman with a crooked grinning face, like a jolly witch, and said, "I don't suppose you remember her. That's Great-Aunt Tessa. You went to her funeral."

"I remember the funeral," said David. "There was a grisly sort of cousin who grabbed us and told us how handsome we were, and then talked over our heads about us to someone else as if we couldn't understand what she was saying."

"She had a face like a sick fish," said Derek.

"Oh, Cousin Vi. She's a pain in the neck. She . . ."

And Mum rattled on about Cousin Vi's murky doings for a bit and then turned the page, but for a moment Derek felt that he had almost grasped the missing whatever-it-was, almost turned his head quick enough to see something before it vanished. No.

On the whole it was a pretty good year. There were dud bits. David broke a leg in the Easter hols, which spoilt things for a while. The girls kept complaining that the house wasn't big enough for seven, especially with the pests growing so fast, but then Jackie got a job and went to live with friends in a flat in Totton. Dad bought a new car. Those were the most exciting things that happened, so it was a nothing-much year, but not bad. And then one weekend in June Mum and Dad went off to the abbey to look at the roses again. Cindy and Fran were seeing friends, so it was just the twins who tagged along.

The roses were the same as last year, and Mum and Dad slower than ever, so after a bit David said, "Let's go and look at the river. OK, Mum?"

Dad gave them money for ices and told them when to be back at the car. They raced twigs on the river, tried to spot the largest trout, and then found the stream that ran through the lawn and followed it up to the spring. They stood staring at the uprushing water for a long while, not saying anything. In the end Derek looked at his watch, saw it was almost four, woke David from his trance and raced him off to look for ices.

A few nights later Derek woke with his heart pounding. It was something he'd dreamt, but he couldn't remember the dream. He sat up and saw that David's bed was empty. When he got up and put his hand between the sheets, they were still just warm to the touch.

All at once memory came back, the eleven years when he'd been on his own and the year when he'd had David. The other years, the ones when he'd been growing up with a twin brother and the photographs in the album had been taken—they weren't real. By morning he wouldn't remember them. By morning he wouldn't remember David either. There was just this one night.

He rushed into his clothes, crept down the stairs and out. The door was unlocked. David's bike was already gone from the shed. He got his own out and started off.

The night was still, but he felt as though he had an intangible wind in his face. Every pedal stroke was an effort. He put his head down and rode on. Normally, he knew, he'd be faster than David, whose leg still wasn't properly strong after his accident, but tonight he guessed

David would have the spirit wind behind him, the wind from some other world. Derek didn't think he would catch him. All he knew was that he had to try.

In fact he almost ran into him, about two miles from the abbey, just after the turn off the main road. David was trotting along beside his bike, pushing it, gasping for breath.

"What's happened?" said Derek.

"Got a puncture. Lend me yours. I'll be too late."

"Get up behind. We'll need us both to climb the wall. There mayn't be a ladder this time."

Without a word David climbed onto the saddle. Derek stood on the pedals and drove the bike on through the dark. They leaned the bike against the wall where the ivy grew. It still wasn't thick enough to climb, but it was something to get a bit of a grip on. David stood on the saddle of the bike. Derek put his hands under his heels and heaved him up, grunting with the effort, till David could grip the coping of the wall. He still couldn't pull himself right up, but he found a bit of a foothold in the ivy and hung there while Derek climbed onto the crossbar, steadied himself, and let David use his shoulder as a step. A heave, a scrabble, and he was on the wall.

Derek stood on the saddle and reached up. He couldn't look, but felt David reach down to touch his hand, perhaps just to say good-bye. Derek gripped the hand and held. David heaved. Scrabbling and stretching, Derek leaped for the coping. He heard the bike clatter away beneath him.

David's other hand grabbed his collar. He had an elbow on the coping, and now a knee, and he was up.

"Thanks," he muttered.

The drop on the far side was into blackness. There could have been anything below, but there seemed no help for it. You just had to hang from the coping, let go and trust to luck. Derek landed on softness but wasn't ready for the impact and stumbled, banging his head against the wall. He sat down, his whole skull filled with the pain of it. Dimly he heard a sort of crash, and as the pain seeped away worked out that David must have fallen into a bush. More cracks and rustles as David struggled free.

"Are you OK?" came his voice.

"Think so. Hit my head."

"Where are you?"

"I'm OK. Let's get on."

They struggled out through a sort of shrubbery, making enough noise, it seemed, to wake all Hampshire. Derek's head was just sore on the outside now. Blood was running down his cheek. David was already running, a dark limping shape about twenty yards away. His leg must have gone duff again after all that effort. Derek followed him across the moonlit slopes and levels. They made no effort to hide. If anyone had been watching from the house they must have seen them, the moonlight was so strong. At last they stood panting by the fence of the spring. The rim of shadow still made a thin line under a wall.

"Done it," whispered David. "I thought I was stuck."

"What'd have happened?"

"Don't know."

"What's it like . . . the other side?"

"Different. Shhh."

The shadow vanished and the reflection of the moon moved onto the troubled disk. Derek glanced sideways at his brother's face. The rippled, reflected light glimmered across it, making it very strange, gray white like a mushroom, and changing all the time as the ripples changed, as if it wasn't even sure of its own proper shape.

David climbed the fence, grasped the bottom rail, and lowered his legs into the water. Derek climbed too, gripped David's hand, and crouched to lower his brother—yes, his brother still—his last yard in this world. David let go of the rail and dropped. Derek gripped his hand all the way to the water.

As he felt that silvery touch the movement stopped, and they hung there, either side of the rippled mirror. David didn't seem to want to let go, either.

Different? thought Derek. Different how?

The hand wriggled, impatient. Something must be happening the other side. No time to make up his mind. He let go of the rail.

In the instant that he plunged toward the water he felt a sort of movement around him, very slight, but clear. It was the whole world closing in, filling the gap where he had been. In that instant, he realized everything changed. Jackie would still be at home, Fran would be asleep in his room, not needing to share with Cindy. Nobody would shout at him to come to breakfast. His parents would go about their day with no sense of loss; Jimmy Grove would keep no place for him on the school bus; Mum would be a director of her company, with a car of her own . . . and all the photographs in the albums would show the same cheerful family, two parents, three daughters, no gap, not even the faintest shadow that might once have been Derek.

He was leaving a world where he had never been born.

Touch and Go

1. About Me

My name is Cyril Batson. I am a bookseller, aged sixty-five. I have a little shop in Chelsea, London, and two rooms above where I live with my cat. I have never married. Don't be put off. Most of this story is about stuff that happened when I was twelve, but first I've got to explain a few things.

My father was in the Merchant Navy, but he wasn't a real sailor. He was a ship's cook, working on the Union Castle line, the big ships that took passengers out from England to South Africa and back. Nowadays almost everyone goes by air, but it was ships then. Liners, they called them. My mother used to take me to see my father's ship come in. It had three red funnels with black bands round the top.

Each of his trips lasted almost six weeks—eighteen days out, four days there, and eighteen days back. Then he had three days at home with us and one day to go and see his mother. She was a cook too, in a big house in London, but my mother didn't get on with her so I hadn't seen her since I was small. Then my father would have another six weeks away.

In the end my mother couldn't stand it anymore. She fell in with a man called Maurice who lived somewhere up north, and while my father was away she ran off with him. Before she left she took me up to London, to a square with a garden in the middle and large white houses all round. She made sure I knew which was the right one and then we walked along to the next corner and stopped. She gave me a letter and told me to go back to the house she'd shown me and go up the steps and ring the bell, and then give the letter to whoever opened the door and wait there.

I did what she said, only before I went up the steps I looked back to make sure she was waiting for me, and she was. A maid came to the door and told me to go to a different door, in a little dark yard down some stone stairs. As I came down the front steps I saw my mother wasn't waiting for me anymore. I ran to the corner to look for her, but she was gone. I never saw her again except in dreams.

I went back to the door the maid had told me about and rang and someone came. I showed her my letter and she took it in. I waited. Then my grandmother came and told me in a cross voice to come in. She was a short fat woman who limped from a bad hip. She took me into a big kitchen and told me to sit down and gave me a mug of milk and a slice of bread and dripping, much nicer than we had at home. Then she told one of the maids to go and ask if she could have a talk with the lady who owned the house.

The lady wasn't pleased about me, any more than my grandmother was, but they both did the best they could, by their lights. My grandmother was a good cook and the lady didn't want to lose her. She let me stay in the house for a couple of days until they found a place for me in an orphanage not too far away. The lady said she'd pay the fees until my father came home and made arrangements. (My grandmother told me all this later.)

My grandmother came to see me on her afternoons out—just one afternoon a week she had. It wasn't easy for her because of her bad hip. My father didn't find out what had happened until his ship came in several weeks later and he went home and found the note my mother had left him. I expect he was upset but he didn't say anything when he came to see me. He took me to Madame Tussauds. And he saw the lady who owned the house and they sorted out about the orphanage fees and decided I'd better stay on there.

All this sounds very bad, the sort of thing nobody ought to do to a kid, and I didn't like it at the time, but pretty soon I was really glad it had happened, because there were several ways the orphanage was much better than South-ampton. The first was that there were no real bullies there. I was the sort of boy bullies seem to pick on, small, a bit fat, a bit oily, no use at games and so on—nobody would ever have taken one look at me and decided they wanted me for a friend. There were three boys who used to wait for me in the school yard. Day after day I'd have to go off, knowing they were going to be there.

Another good thing was the women at the orphanage found out about my eyes. At Southampton they'd decided I was stupid, but it was because I couldn't see the blackboard. These women gave me some spectacles. They didn't take me to the oculist to have my eyes tested, but they had a box of spectacles which people had given them and they tried them out until they found some which weren't too bad. These ones were too big and they kept falling off so we kept them on with sticking plaster behind my ears, and at least I could see the blackboard now.

The third good thing was that there was a case of old books in the matron's room. Until I'd got my specs I couldn't really read much except the large-print books for small kids, and there weren't enough of those, anything like. Now I could read real books, though I still had to get my nose pretty well up against the paper. The books were the sort people give away when they're clearing out, mostly not for kids at all—old *Pears' Cyclopedia*s, or *Travels in the Holy Land,* or *My Life in Merchant Banking*—even those I'd read. But others were stories about things like explorers in the jungle, or young ladies who didn't want to marry the person their parents had chosen for them and ran away and got a job as a kitchen maid and fell in love with the under-gardener who her parents wouldn't approve of at all, only his father's really a lord who's not going to approve of him marrying a kitchen maid, and he's got his own reasons for not letting on who he really is, but they both find out in the end so they can get married after all. I used to read it all as if it was dead true. I even read H. G. Wells's *The Time Machine* as if it was true.

I was nine when the war started. This was the Second World War, against Hitler's Germany. I didn't understand anything about it. Nothing much changed for a bit, and then everything did. First, the people my grandmother worked for decided to go to America till the war was over, so she had to get a new job. While she was doing this my father's ship was sunk and he was drowned. Then the women who ran the orphanage said London was going to be bombed and we'd all got to move out, only they couldn't find anywhere for us to stay together. I remember one called Mrs. Wimbush going round actually wringing her hands and telling everyone she couldn't think what was going to become of us.

What became of me was that my grandmother got a job cooking for a rich woman in a big house somewhere out in the country called Theston Manor. My grandmother went for an interview and explained about me, and this woman—Miss van Deering, her name was—said I could come too provided I kept out of her way. I think she might have had her own reasons. Because of the bombing they were sending all the kids out of London—thousands and thousands of them. Evacuees, they called them, and they were going round telling anyone out in the country who'd got a bit of spare room that they'd got to have some. There was certainly plenty of spare room at Theston

Manor, but Miss van Deering didn't want any evacuees there if she could help it. She was the sort who likes everything just so, and a pack of London kids wouldn't have been that. Maybe she thought that having one kid there already would mean she didn't have to have any more. If so, it worked, or something did. The people looking for places left her alone.

2. Miss van Deering

I was at Theston Manor for the rest of the war and a bit after, until I was sixteen, and if you'd asked me afterward I'd have told you that in all that time I'd met Miss van Deering just the once. Really met, I mean, to talk to, alone. I saw her in church on Sundays because she passed quite close on her way out. We sat at the back and she had her own pew, third on the right in front, and of course we used to wait for the gentry and the people who wanted to think they were gentry to leave first. As she passed us she used to nod and give a tight little smile to show she'd spotted we were there. She was a small woman, plump but neat, with silver hair and a soft round face. I used to think that she was like one of those cats you see, sitting in the sun with its paws drawn in under it, looking as if it's got the world exactly the way it wants and you'd better not mess around with it.

The time I met her happened like this. It would have

been early in the summer holidays and I must have been coming up twelve. When the weather was OK I was supposed to help Mr. Frostle in the garden, if you could call it helping, because I was pretty useless at anything he gave me to do. Tuppence an hour I was paid, and I wasn't really worth that, but it meant I finished up with three shillings at the end of the week. Then I had all the long afternoons to fill up. Theston village wasn't that far off, where I went to school, and there were other kids amusing themselves down there, but I wasn't the sort to make friends, so I was on my own.

Now I'd better try and give you some idea of what the Manor was like. It was the sort of place you see in ads for Bentleys and Jaguars and such. There were twenty-eight bedrooms, not counting the attics where me and my grandmother slept. Heaven knows how many windows there must have been, and the wardens were very strict about the blackout, even right out in the country like that. And quite right too. A couple of villages away some people had been coming out of a dance one night and they'd left the door open too long and a German bomber who'd lost his way must have spotted it and dropped his bombs to get rid of them, and three houses got hit.

A lot of the rooms at the Manor they just took the electric bulbs out of and locked the doors, but the passages and such they had to do something about, and there wasn't anyone to go round taking the blackout down every morning and putting it up again in the evening, so it just got left up except in three or four rooms and a few other places.

So there was this huge old house, all so dark that even on sunny days you had to switch the lights on to get around it. Not that the lights were that good, what there were of them. The electrics had been put in way back, before the First War, and they ran off their own generator, which the fuel was rationed for and the ration wasn't enough, nothing like. So they'd taken out a lot of the bulbs in the passages too, and the rest were about ten-watt, and you had to remember to turn them off as soon as you'd gone by or you were in dead trouble.

And, my, was it cold in winter! But that's not part of the story, which I'd better get on with.

One of the rooms which was kept locked because it hadn't got any blackout was the servants' hall. This was where the maids and footmen and such used to have their meals and sit around when they weren't wanted. There'd been nine of them living in the house in peacetime, Kitty told me, just to look after Miss van Deering, not counting the ones who came in by the day from the cottages and the village. They'd all gone off to war work now. The servants' hall was along a corridor from the kitchen, at the back of the house and down from the main ground floor. I'd gone in there once to help my grandmother carry something she needed, and while she was rooting around looking for what she wanted she opened a cupboard and I saw it was full of books. I didn't dare ask, for fear of being told no (that was the sort of kid I was), but I spotted where she put the key after she'd locked up, and as soon as she was into her after-dinner nap (that's what people call

24

lunch now) I sneaked back for a look. They were just what I wanted, the same as I used to read at the orphanage, romances about gentry pretending to be servants and such, as well as a lot of old thrillers. So after that as soon as dinner was over I used to tell my grandmother I was going for a walk, which she was all in favor of as she couldn't bear to have me hanging around in the kitchen lounging and scratching, as she put it, and she had the idea that fresh air was good for me. "Never did your father any harm, out on the ocean briny," she used to say, knowing quite well he'd spent most of his time in a hot little galley frying stuff up for the crew. I'd put on my boots and my waterproofs if it was wet and start off on my walk, but as soon as I was out of sight I'd slip into one of the sheds and read. There were acres and acres of garden, mostly gone wild, with apple stores and an icehouse and log sheds and a coach house and potting sheds and stables and kennels and tool rooms and so on. I found a place up some stone stairs above the stables where there was a pile of musty hay and a window and nobody ever came. Winter I'd read till it got too dark to see. Summer I'd work out how many pages I'd get through before I'd got to go in and do my homework and mark the place and stop when I got there.

"Well, *you* ought to have a bit of an appetite," my grandmother used to say when I got in. Luckily, reading gave me just as much of an appetite as walking would have done, for my grandmother's food, at any rate. She was a really good cook. She couldn't bear to cook food which wasn't interesting to eat. Day after day we'd have meals better than any I've tasted since, and all out of the scraps of stuff she could get hold of in wartime. Apart from that I don't know that I can give you much idea of her. Like I've said, she was short and fat and had this bad hip. I don't know that she was fond of me, but she looked after me and did her best for me because that was right, but I don't remember that I ever had a hug from her or anything like that. She liked things to be very definite, so she knew where she was. Later on, when I took to reading to her, she used to bother about why anybody should go to the trouble of making stories up, and whether there wasn't something not really right about listening to what amounted to a pack of lies.

I must have found the books in the servants' hall the autumn before the time I met Miss van Deering, and by then I'd read most of them twice over. That morning it was sheeting with rain, and while we were finishing up breakfast Kitty came in for her usual cup of tea and said since there wasn't any point in my going out to help Mr. Frostle I might as well come and give her a hand in the library. Kitty was an old woman who'd worked in the house more than fifty years. She'd been an under-housemaid to start with, living in, but then she'd married the groom, Benjie Prior, and gone to live with him in one of the cottages. Now she just came in to clean the bits Miss van Deering used, her bedroom and so on, and a little room right above the kitchen, called the office, which was her day room. Doing the library was something else.

Getting on three years I'd been living at Theston, but I'd

never been up on the main floor, where the library was, and all the other big rooms. In the old days, when there'd been all those servants, the gentry liked to pretend they weren't there except when they needed them, so the servants had their own steep wooden stairs running up at the back of the house, with doors through to all the floors, so they could get in and out to do their work when the gentry weren't around. To get up to our bedrooms in the attics we used the back stairs as far as the second floor. Someone had decided it wasn't worth doing the blackout any further, so they'd shut the stairs off from then on, and we had to slip through and on up some other stairs to the third floor, which the gentry had used for guests who didn't matter that much, and for their own kids. Then one more lot of stairs took us on to the attics. (This is all going to come in later.)

Well, Kitty took me up from the kitchen into this long dark passage on the first floor, switching the dim lights on and off as she went by. Then she took a key from a shelf and unlocked a great big door and switched the light on until she'd drawn the curtains and opened the heavy wooden shutters behind them. The furniture was covered with dust sheets and all the shelves had newspapers on them, folded to cover the tops of the books and hang down the spines. It was still really summer outside, but it looked like winter in the room with the wet gray light falling on the snowy dust sheets. There were three tall windows with old blotchy mirrors between them. Otherwise it was bookshelves all the way round, from the floor almost to

the ceiling, except for the door and a huge fireplace opposite the windows. Each stack of shelves had a letter at the
top. We were doing stack C.

There was a special stepladder, made of shiny wood with
brass fittings, so you could reach the top shelves. Kitty
didn't like the ladder, which was why she needed me to
help. I climbed up to the shelf she showed me and passed
the newspapers down to her, carefully, so they could be
used again. Then the books, one at a time. They were all
bound in leather and felt heavier, more solid, than the
books I was used to, and they had their names on the back
in gold lettering.

When we'd got the whole shelf down Kitty gave me a
cloth and some special oil and showed me how to oil the
covers so the leather didn't crack, while she looked
through them one by one for woodworm and damp and
checked that the little leather labels with the gold letters
on weren't coming unglued. Then we put them all back in
the same order they were in to start with. It took us the
whole morning to do just two shelves. It sounds boring,
but it wasn't. I really enjoyed it, handling those lovely old
books and looking after them the way they needed. And I
did it right, too, not the way I worked for Mr. Frostle.
Kitty didn't have to tell me off once.

The first shelf, there were two volumes of something
and three volumes of something else and six of something
else, all different shapes and sizes. The second shelf started
like that, but then it settled down and they were all the
same. Of course I was reading the titles as I took them

down, and halfway along I came to *Ivanhoe,* three volumes of it. I nearly fell off the ladder. I'd read it at the orphanage, but I'd never found out how it ended because the last fifty pages were missing. I didn't bother asking Kitty if I could read it because I knew she'd say no. These were gentry books, not for the likes of her and me. I tried sneaking the third volume off to one side, under a dust sheet, but Kitty spotted it and I had to pretend it had just got in there somehow.

We stopped for dinner, and then my grandmother took me in to Worcester with Benjie in the pony trap to do the shopping, so it must have been a Thursday. She and me had our tea in the kitchen at six. Then she would finish cooking Miss van Deering's supper and put it in the food lift and I'd work the rope, which took it rumbling up to a room called the office, which Miss van Deering was using as her living room while the war was on. There was no way you could have kept a room like the library warm in winter.

After tea I'd wash the dishes and pots and we'd play crib, which was an old-fashioned card game for two. I didn't enjoy it that much, but my grandmother did. Then she'd send me up to bed at nine o'clock while she stayed down to listen to the evening news on the wireless. To know how the war was getting on, she told me, but it was really so she could have her nightcap, which was the redcurrant wine she used to brew, gin and stuff being difficult to get hold of. I think she didn't want me to know that was what she was up to, but of course I did.

I didn't like going off so early, because I wasn't allowed to read in bed, except for a few months in the summer when it was light enough because of the double summer time we had to help the war effort. They'd never bothered to put any electrics into the attics, so I'd collect my candle off the shelf at the bottom of the attic stairs and light it and use it to go to bed by, but my grandmother was dead scared of the house catching fire and us being trapped up there—quite right about that she was, of course, though it didn't bother me at the time—so she wasn't having me reading in bed, not at any price. Candles were hard to come by, wartime, anyway.

That night I never got right undressed. I took my shoes off and folded my trousers and sweater on the chair and got the rest out of a drawer and put them on top so my grandmother would see them all there when she looked in on her way to bed. Then I got into bed in my shirt and underpants and socks, and pulled the blankets right up and blew out my candle and waited for her. It was still just about light—I'd only needed my candle because of the blackout making everything so dark. Soon as I heard her come limping up the stairs I shut my eyes and pretended I was asleep. She put her head round the door and gave a sniff to check I hadn't only just blown my candle out— leaves a smell, that does—and went out. I heard her pottering about and then muttering her prayers and then the creak of her bedsprings, but I didn't move till she was truly snoring. Then, soon as the walls were shaking with the sound of it I got up and found my sweater and trousers by feel and put them on and crept down in the dark with my candle, picking up the matches as I passed the shelf at the bottom. I didn't know my way from the bottom of the next lot of stairs so I stopped and lit my candle and instead of turning right to get onto the back stairs I turned left along a little bit of corridor and then right again and out onto the main stairs.

By now my heart was really hammering. I was scared stiff of what I was doing but I knew I had to go through with it. Even finding myself out on the main stairs and seeing what they looked like didn't make me turn back. I was creeping along this short bit of corridor with my candle and then I found myself out in this great big cavern of a place, full of shadows and darknesses, all moving around as the candle flame shook in the draft. Two floors up through the middle of the house the stair-hall ran, with a white marble floor and a black star in the middle of it and the stairs, marble too, climbing up round three sides, with a kind of gallery above all round leading off into other corridors. In peacetime there was a glass dome over it to let the light in, but they'd run beams across and fastened the blackout stuff to it, just above my head where I was standing on the balcony, black, of course, and sagging a bit, saying to me—I don't know how—that I wasn't supposed to be there.

I went on, all the same, creeping down the stair and along the passage where I'd been with Kitty, till I came to the library door. I found the key and unlocked it and shut it behind me before I switched on the light. Dazzling bright it seemed, after my candle, far more than what I wanted, but I had to have something because my eyes weren't really good enough for reading by candle more than a little bit, and besides I'd be in real trouble if I used my candle up faster than my grandmother did hers.

I looked under the dust sheets. One of them was a big desk with a desk lamp on it. There was a socket in the floor so I plugged it in and tried it, and it worked. What's more, the hole in the middle of the desk for the writer's knees made a kind of cave where I could wriggle in, so I put the lamp down in there and went and got Volume III of *Ivanhoe*. We'd left the steps out ready for next time, so that was easy. Then I turned off the main light and crawled into my cave and pulled the dust sheet down over the opening and started to read. In a minute or two I wasn't thinking of anything except the unknown knight's assault on the castle of Front de Boeuf.

I never heard Miss van Deering come in. The first I knew was when the dust sheet was lifted aside and there was this face, all weird shadows in the light of my lamp, staring in at me from the mouth of my cave. I just gaped. My specs fell off—that lot of sticking plaster had been getting old. She didn't say anything, just crouched there, staring. I don't know how long it was before she said, in a strange, gasping voice, "I hope your hands are clean." Then she stood back and let me crawl out.

I was usually far too unadventurous to get into this sort of trouble, but when it did happen I always clammed up. "Dumb insolence," somebody said once, but it wasn't like that. My mind stuck and my tongue wouldn't work, which was what happened now. All I could do was show her my hands, which weren't too bad after the washing up.

"What are you reading?" she said in a more ordinary voice, but still gasping a bit.

I'd hung on to *Ivanhoe,* so I gave it to her. She looked at the spine. Her eyebrows went up.

"You are aware that there are two earlier volumes?" she said.

I nodded.

"You have read them? You have been coming in here like this for some time?" she said. She still didn't seem to be accusing me of anything. She just sounded surprised.

I shook my head. She waited.

"It was at the orphanage," I blurted. "Only the end was gone. I just wanted . . ."

I stuck.

"I see," she said at last. "So you have almost finished?"

I took the book and tried to show her, but I'd been holding my specs on with one hand and I needed two to turn the pages. In the end I managed somehow. There were only about ten pages to go.

"Very well," she said. "You may finish now. When you have done so please put everything back as you found it and then come and knock on the office door, and I will close up and check the lights. I'm afraid I must ask you not to come in here again. Some of these books are valuable. That one you are reading comes from a complete set of the first edition of the Waverley novels in the original bindings, which are rarer than you might think, as few people collected them all and those who did often had them rebound.''

I had no idea what she was talking about, so I just nodded.

''In any case,'' she went on, ''I think few of the books in here are likely to interest you, but at the further end of the West Passage on the second floor you will find some books which may be more to your taste. You may read those if you wish, provided you take only one at a time, and look after it, and put it back before you take another. I will tell your grandmother that you have my permission to do so. I will not, incidentally, tell her that I have found you here.''

I was still struck dumb and couldn't even say thank you, so I nodded again and stood there, staring. She stared back, ooh, for a long while, and then she said in the same gasping sort of voice she'd used at the beginning, ''I'm not much of a reader, myself, you know.''

Then she jerked herself round and left. I did as she told me and went to bed.

So that was the one time I met Miss van Deering properly, to talk to. Next evening my grandmother said to me, ''Miss van Deering says there's some books upstairs you can read, if you've a fancy to, and you'd better have new specs to read them with. She's given me the money. Funny old thing, some ways.''

The only other thing I noticed different was that coming out of church Miss van Deering didn't look at us and give her little smile anymore. She just walked straight past, as if we weren't anything to do with her.

3. Mr. Glister

On Thursdays, like I've said, Benjie Prior would harness up a willful dark pony called Starlight and take my grandmother into Worcester in the trap, to get the rations and anything else she could find worth cooking. School holidays I'd go along too, to help fetch and carry my grandmother said, but really it was because Thursday being market day the pubs were open all afternoon, and Benjie and my grandmother wanted me to keep an eye on Starlight while they went into the Royal Oak for a glass or two. That meant I could go to the oculist next Thursday, to have it sorted out about my specs, and he said I'd got to have two pairs, one for distance and one for reading. There wasn't enough money for that, so my grandmother paid for the other pair and I had to start paying her back out of the three shillingses I got for helping Mr. Frostle.

Now the best thing about going with them into Worcester was that next door to the Royal Oak there was a secondhand bookshop with a rack of cheap books outside, nothing over sixpence, like Woolworths used to be. That's what I'd been spending my three shillingses on. I used to hitch Starlight to a lamppost and stand out there, under the awning if it was raining, and read until Benjie and my grandmother were about due out, and then I'd slip into the shop, still keeping half an eye on Starlight, and buy something, more to pay for my reading than because I really wanted it. Paying for the specs I couldn't do that anymore, and I didn't think it was right, reading and reading and then not buying anything, so I just hung around, but the very first Thursday I tried that the fellow who owned the shop spotted me and came out and asked, joking, if I'd given up on the reading. A bit embarrassed, I told him about the specs, but he just laughed and said it was better for business if he had someone out on the pavement who looked interested in his books.

Most days after that he'd pop out for a chat, not about anything much, the weather or the war and so on. His name was Mr. Glister.

I left school when I was fourteen, which a lot of us did those days, and my grandmother said I had to do something by way of a job. She'd teach me to cook, she said, but I wasn't interested, any more than I was in starting with Mr. Frostle as a full-time garden boy. For once, I knew exactly what I wanted to do, and next Thursday I went into Mr. Glister's and asked if I could help him in his shop. I didn't think he'd say yes, because I'd hardly ever seen anyone else going in there so I didn't think there could be any money in it, but I thought he might give me an idea where to start. He said yes, straight off, and he'd pay me a pound a week, and one pound ten when I'd learnt the ropes. You could have knocked my grandmother down with a feather, she said when I told her.

I was in my seventh heaven. I used to bicycle the five miles into Worcester six days a week, rain or shine, and out again in the evenings. Wednesdays was early closing and I could have gone home dinnertime, but I mostly stayed on reading until Mr. Glister told me to clear out because he wanted to shut up. He lived over the shop.

I couldn't make him out for a long while. I mean, here he was, with several rooms crammed with old books and nothing much to do with his time, but he hardly ever read a word. He wasn't interested in books the way I was, what was in them, how exciting the story was, that kind of thing. Books weren't voices to him, the way they were to me, speaking to me in my head while I read them. To Mr. Glister books were *things*. How old were they? What kind of shape were they in? Were they by anyone famous? That sort of thing. I'd been right about not much trade coming in through the door. He couldn't have afforded my pound a week on the money he got that way. No, he made his living from the books he kept up in his office.

I remember one of the times he went off for the day to a sale and left me to mind the shop. Middle of the afternoon he telephoned, saying I'd got to shut up early and meet him at the station with the barrow, because he'd bought three cases of books. I helped unpack them. He was absolutely purring with glee.

"You see if you can spot what I've found," he said.

He never bought just the one book at a sale, in fact the

more interested he was in something the more books he'd buy which he wasn't that interested in, so no one would spot there was something tucked in among them that was really worth having. That's where most of the stuff in the shop came from. This time a lot of them looked really nice, with shiny leather covers and their titles in gold on the spines. Three of them were volumes of *Rob Roy* by Walter Scott, the same fellow who wrote *Ivanhoe.*

"I don't know if that's the first edition," I said. "But anyway it's not the original binding."

His little gold specs almost jumped off his nose.

"What do you know about original bindings?" he said.

I told him, and his eyes really glistened at the thought of a complete set of the Waverley novels, first edition, in the original bindings.

"Out of my league," he said. "Out of my league. Not but what I haven't done pretty nicely today, thank you. Carry on. Five bob to you if you spot it."

In the end I chose a big volume of sermons because it looked really old and really boring, so I knew nobody would want it for what was in it.

"Not bad," he said. "It's a second edition, but Donne was a very popular preacher so there were a lot of them printed, and quite a few around still. Still, we might get a few quid for it. I thought you were there for a moment."

He picked up another one I'd thought about because it looked boring too. It was poems by three people called Bell with silly first names, in just a green cloth binding.

"Ever heard of the Brontës?" he said. "Charlotte, Emily, and Anne?"

"I'm reading *Jane Eyre* to my grandmother, evenings," I said.

"Are you now? Are you now?" he said. "Well, this is their first published work. They called themselves Acton, Currer, and Ellis Bell so that people wouldn't know if they were men or women, but it didn't do very well, even so. I doubt if there's more than a few dozen in existence today. The auctioneers ought to have spotted it and sent it up to London, but that's wartime for you."

"How much will you get for it?" I asked.

"Oh, I'm not selling it," he said. "I want to have it around. . . . Maybe when the market improves."

Three years I stayed with Mr. Glister, and he taught me a lot about that side of books. But then the war was over and my grandmother wanted to move back to London—she'd never been properly happy in the country. She was getting on a bit, and she had her bad hip, so it wasn't easy finding the kind of job she was after, but she wasn't just a good ordinary cook. She knew how to do all sorts of fancy dishes, so she managed it in the end, with a rich family who'd got a house in Chelsea and another in Ascot. They played polo and such, and entertained a lot, and they'd ways of finding food despite the rationing which was still on. There was nowhere for me to live at their Chelsea house, and no reason why they should have me either. I could have stayed on in Worcester, but my grandmother and me were all the family each other had got, so I went to London too.

I'd saved a bit from what Mr. Glister had been paying me and I found myself a dingy little room in a back street off the poor end of the Kings Road, where pretty well every other shop was a junkshop or a bookshop, and those days a lot of the people who ran them didn't have much idea what was what. (Nowadays they're mostly sharp as needles.) So I went happily rummaging up and down, looking for stuff other people might have missed, and finding it too. Other days I'd take a bus into the West End and poke around there, sorting out which shops specialized in which kind of books, travel, it might be, or India, or military history or whatever, so I'd know where to take things to, to see what I could get for them. I made mistakes, of course, but there weren't many weeks I didn't make enough, buying and selling, to pay for my rent and my food.

There was one shop, on the corner of the street where my room was, where the owner hadn't a clue. Her name was Lucy Traill. Her husband had known about books but then he'd died and she'd carried on, but she wasn't interested, not my way, not Mr. Glister's way. If someone came in with books to sell she'd guess at a price and mark them up a bit and shove them on her shelves any old how and hope. What she didn't like was regulars, like me, coming in and poking around and buying something because we thought she wasn't asking enough for it. She may have been dumb about books but she was bright enough about people.

"And how much do you expect to be selling that lot for?" she asked me one day when I showed her what I'd picked out.

Inside the trade all's fair, and we pull the wool over each other's eyes as much as we think we can get away with, but somehow I didn't think Lucy counted, so I told her.

"That one's just to read," I said. "I might make a few bob on that. And three pounds on that, maybe."

"Three pounds!" she said.

"If I'm lucky," I told her. "I saw one in the Tottenham Court Road they were asking twelve for, and not in such good shape either. They do a line in African explorers."

"And you expect me to let you have it for three shillings!" she said. "You know what that is? That's stealing!"

"No, it's not," I said. "It's trade. I don't say it's fair trade, but it's trade."

"It's stealing," she said again.

"Tell you what," I said. "You let me have it for three bob, I'll see what I can get for it, and we'll split the difference."

In the end I only got three pounds ten shillings, so I gave her half that and she gave me my three bob back, and she was happy. After that I'd look in most days and she wouldn't put anything new on her shelves until I'd had a look at it and told her what to ask. If it was something good, which didn't happen that often, I'd sell it elsewhere for her and we'd take half each, as before. Getting on a year this went on, and then out of the blue she told me she was giving up and going to live with her sister in Wales, and I could have the shop, stock and all, for £500 if I wanted it.

Of course I hadn't got £500, nothing like. My grandmother had a bit put by for her old age, but she was very close about it, and no wonder. Who else was going to look after her, she used to say, if she didn't look after herself. I wrote to Mr. Glister to ask for a loan, but he said he'd like to help but it was too much of a risk, trade being what it was, not without security. The only other person I knew who'd got any money was Miss van Deering, though I wasn't sure she'd even remember me, but I wrote to her anyway. What I got back was a letter from a lawyer.

> Dear Sir,
>
> I am instructed by Miss van Deering of Theston Manor to inform you that she is unable to advance you the loan you request, but that since you are starting in the book trade she is arranging to forward to you, as a gift, some volumes that may be of use to you.
>
> Yours faithfully, etc.

That was all. I hadn't been expecting anything, really, so I couldn't say I was disappointed, and I'd never say no to a parcel of books.

They arrived a week later. They were a complete set of the Waverley novels in the original bindings. First edition.

I sat staring at them in my grubby little room, turning the third volume of *Ivanhoe* over and over in my hands. They were beautiful. (I'd discovered by now what Mr. Glister had been on about, when he'd fallen in love with a drab old book nobody'd ever want to read.) I couldn't imagine why Miss van Deering had taken it into her head to give them to me. Perhaps she'd gone mad. I didn't care. All I knew for absolute certain was that I wasn't going to sell them, ever, though they'd have fetched the £500 I needed ten times over. (Yes, I've still got them, with the lawyer's letter tucked into Volume I of *Waverley,* to show they're mine.)

What I did in the end was take them down to Mr. Glister in Worcester and tell him he could have them as security for my loan, if that was all right with him. I had to take a taxi from the station, as I couldn't decently ask him to come and meet me with the barrow.

You should have seen his face when I showed him, and told him what I wanted.

"They're worth a good bit more than five hundred pounds," he said. "You think you can trust me?"

"Yes," I said.

"Maybe you can," he said, "but we'll get a lawyer in all the same."

Which we did, and we fixed I'd pay him £125 a year for five years (the £25 was for interest) and if at the end of five years I hadn't repaid the lot he could insist on me selling

43

the books to square up. And that's how I came to buy my shop, and the little flat over it, which is where I still live. I wrote to Miss van Deering to say thank you, but she didn't answer.

And that's who I am, and that's where this story's coming from. I've told you all this partly to keep things straight, but mainly so you can see, in spite of me liking to read a lot of romantic nonsense, I'm not the sort to make things up. You're going to need that.

4. Tom and Mercury

Now, you'll have gathered I'm not the sort to have much by way of friends, but the last few years I seem to have taken up with a couple of young men called Tom and Mercury. (Yes, Mercury. His real name's Mike, but only Tom's allowed to call him that.) They drop in and check that I'm all right, and I'm glad they're around. I'd never have picked them for friends, mind you, not to look at. Tom's all right, apart from doing his hair in a pigtail with a fancy ribbon. He wears a tie, and suspenders to keep his trousers up, which even I've stopped doing. But Mercury's wild—leathers, and not just black biker leathers, either—green and silver and purple, and draped with chains. And he wears a pearl in his nose and earrings down to his shoulders. But he's a sweet, gentle person, and I don't know anyone I'd sooner turn to if I was in trouble.

By way of a living they do up rooms for rich people. It's Tom who designs the rooms, while Mercury looks after the business, but they let the rich people think it's the other way round, so they feel they're getting something wild and interesting, like Mercury. Sometimes, if it's a fine day, they go off and look at old houses that are open to the public, see if they can pick up any ideas for their business, and like as not they'll drop by my shop and ask me if I want to come along too, which mostly I do. I shut up shop and we all three get into the front seat of Tom's old Mercedes and off we go, with me in the middle between them. We'll have the roof down and the heater turned right up and the stereo playing the sort of pop you heard when I was as young as them. It makes a change, so it's probably good for me, and it's very kind of them to think of it.

They make a game of it, not telling me where we're going, teasing me, but there's no malice in it. I get about England quite a bit, going to book sales, but with my eyes I've never learned to drive, so I use trains and taxis mostly, which means I don't recognize roads for the most part. It was like that the day I'm going to tell you about. We'd left London as if we'd been going to Oxford, I noticed, but after that Mercury started telling me about some crazy rich people they'd been doing a job for, and next time I bothered to look we could have been anywhere in England, almost. I didn't mind. Then, an hour or so later it must have been, we were all three singing along with a bit of music, driving on a middling kind of road up a long hill with a wood on one side and fields and a couple of cottages on the other, and I knew exactly where I was. It was like when you've napped off in your chair and you didn't mean to, and suddenly you jolt out of your dream and find where you are. Day after day, six days a week, for three years and over, I'd biked up this road on my way back from Mr. Glister's.

I gave myself a couple of moments to recover and then, teasing them back for once, as if it was the most ordinary thing in the world, I said, "I see we're going to Theston Manor. I didn't know it was open."

I can't ever tell what's going to amuse them. Usually it's something I don't see what's funny about at all, but this time they laughed like kids, they were that delighted. And then we were turning in at the drive and apart from the National Trust notice boards it was just the same, with its lodges either side looking as if somebody hadn't made up his mind whether he wanted pint-sized castles or public toilets. Tom and Mercury thought I must have read the name off one of the brown road signs you get around show places, and I'd been holding out on them to spring it on them when I did—no, I don't know why they thought that was funny—but when I told them I'd lived here most of the war they were delighted all over again and said I'd get to show them round, so I had to explain I didn't know my way round anything except some of the servants' part. For instance I'd never once, in all the time I'd been at Theston, gone through the front door where we went in now to pay for our tickets.

Doing these trips we'd split up, once we were in, because Tom and Mercury wanted to go through them room by room and bit by bit, with Tom making sketches of anything that caught their eye, such as curtain fastenings or the finger-plates on the doors. I'd wander around and see what there was to see, and take a look at any books I could get close enough to, though you weren't supposed to touch anything and most of it was the sort of stuff you can buy by the yard to look good on shelves. Then I'd find the tea room and read the couple of books I'd have brought with me, just for this. Eight or nine cups of tea I'd have drunk, very likely, by the time Tom and Mercury came to look for me.

I didn't suppose Theston would be much different, apart from the kitchen and maybe the library. Everything else was going to be as new to me as it would have been in any other house. I was right about that, and not just for that reason. It didn't feel like Theston Manor at all, because it was all so *light*. No blackout, and the sun shining in through the great tall windows, and chandeliers blazing away, and new electrics in all the dark corners.

I bought the guidebook and started on the grand downstairs rooms. They'd got them looking pretty well the way they would have been a hundred years ago, with a posh dinner laid out on a huge polished table in the dining room, and in what they called the saloon, which was all done up with white peacocks—Tom and Mercury were going to go mad about it, I guessed—newspapers on the tables with headlines about the siege of Mafeking, and the sort of books people might have been reading around then. They'd got *Love and Mr. Lewisham* by H. G. Wells—that's the fellow who wrote *The Time Machine*—which was the same year as Mafeking, only this was the third edition, which wasn't till the year after. Then there was the morning room, with tea laid out on a big brass tray, and cakes on little stands and so on, and then there was the library.

I wasn't expecting much. I'd only seen it those few times, remember, all under dust sheets and newspapers. They'd got it to rights now, of course, and very handsome it looked with the books up the three walls, apart from the fireplace, and the windows opposite with the tall mirrors between—they'd got the blotches out of them too, somehow. And the desk could have been the very one I'd been hiding under to read *Ivanhoe* when Miss van Deering had found me, but the reading lamp on it was different, an old brass one with a green shade. One side of the fireplace there was a big leather sofa, with a winged armchair to match on the other side. They could have been the same ones too, to judge by the white hummocks they'd made under their dust sheets.

Next to the armchair was a black oak stool. I didn't remember that at all—no reason why I should, they'd have shoved it under one of the other dust sheets—but . . . I don't know. I must have stood staring at it a good couple of minutes as if I expected it to tell me something, until I shook myself out of that and took a look at the books.

The Waverley novels were gone from stack C, of course,

but it was too high up for me to make out what they'd put up there instead. But some of the others were ones I could remember helping Kitty clean, and it was nice to see them still there, though I don't suppose anyone had actually read any of them from that day to this.

Then I went and stared at the stool a bit more—I couldn't help it—and pulled myself away and went to look at the rest of the house. The other rooms were just as grand. There was a ballroom, even. But they didn't mean anything special to me. They'd done the office, where Miss van Deering used to be during the day, to look like the kind of room you could have used to run the estate from, so there wasn't anything there that reminded me of her.

That was all the rooms on the ground floor, so I went on down to the kitchen. This was a good bit more different than what I remembered. For a start they'd taken out the Aga my grandmother had used to cook on, and put in a big old black range instead. And the room was fresh-painted and a lot cleaner, and they were making out someone was cooking for twenty and more in the house, and servants too, so they'd got the huge scrubbed deal table all covered with doings instead of the corner my grandmother had for just her and me and Miss van Deering. The kitchen didn't do anything for me, much, make me feel strange or sad or bothered I mean. It was just a place I'd spent a good deal of time in when I was a kid.

They'd turned the servants' hall into the tea room so they'd taken out the old bookcase. I was sorry about that. I think I could have told you the story in each and every one of those books, after all those years. I wasn't ready for tea yet, so I explored back the other way along the corridor past the kitchen and found they'd barred the old back stairs off with one of those ropes, so I went back to the kitchen and found the lady who was there to keep an eye on things and told her about me living in Theston during the war and how I'd gone up those stairs every night to go to bed and would it be all right if I did it now? She was really interested and took me along and unhooked the rope for me, so up I went, twisting to and fro on the steep wooden flights, seeing it all by daylight, which I'd never done before because of the blackout, till I got to the red baize door we'd used to get through for the last bit. It was still there.

Now the next part is slightly complicated, but I'll try and make it clear. The door was right bang on the stairs, where they twisted back to carry on up. You pushed it, and there was a little landing to give it room to open, and then three more stairs ahead of you and then a short corridor. If you went along there and turned right you came out onto the gallery above the main hall (which I told you about before) and if you turned left you got to some of the grand bedrooms, but my grandmother and me never used to do either of those, because the stairs to the next floor went up from an opening in the left side of this short corridor.

There was a light on the back stairs, with its switch that side of the door, and a light on these other stairs with its switch just up round the corner. The door was on a spring, so you couldn't leave it open, with the back stair light still on for you to see by while you went up the three steps and got the other light on before you went back and turned the first one off. You had to do it in the dark. Instead of banisters there was a bit of rope fastened to the wall by those last three steps.

Now, if you'd asked me about all this anytime between then and now I could have told you, because I remembered it perfectly well. I could have told you too that I'd never liked doing it, and how some nights my grandmother would find me still there when she was coming up to bed after the news, with the smell of her red-currant wine on her breath, and tell me I was a stupid great baby minding a bit of darkness. I don't know whether it was worse in summer, when there was just enough light coming from somewhere in spite of the blackout for you to make out this dark sort of cave in the left-hand wall where anything might be lurking, or in winter when it was pitch, pitch black and you simply knew it was there. I don't think I was more than ordinarily afraid of the dark. I think any kid might have felt much the same, climbing those stairs alone in that huge old empty house.

What I couldn't have told you was what it was *like*. I couldn't have told myself.

5. Adalina

It was the rope that did it. The moment I was through the door my left hand took hold of it without me looking or thinking. Then it was like what I was saying about driving along the road up the hill and realizing that we were coming to Theston, the same kind of shock, or jolt, only far, far stronger. This time I thought my heart was going to conk. The rope felt so exactly the same as it did fifty-plus years ago, very dry and soft, as if it had had flour sifted onto it, which it hadn't, of course. It didn't feel like real rope, the sort my father used to keep a bit of by his chair with a knot in the end and pretend he'd larrup me with it if I didn't behave. It felt cobwebby, loose, like a bit of something alive. And I used to stand there holding it, looking at the black cave in the wall along the corridor, nerving myself to let the door go and feel my way up the steps in the dark, and on along the wall, and round the corner to where the next switch was. And something else, I didn't know what.

So now I stood in the same place, remembering the old sick, stupid terror that had sometimes stuck me there until my grandmother had come up and found me, like I've said. There was no blackout now, and good strong daylight shining across the end of the passage from the dome over the main stairs, and more daylight coming down the staircase on the left, but none of that made any difference, any

52

more than it had made a difference to me right back then, knowing perfectly well that there couldn't be anything horrible waiting for me round the corner where the switch was.

I heard my lungs empty themselves right out in a great sigh. That was the sigh I used to give when I'd actually made it round the corner in the dark and found the switch, and the light came on, and of course there was nothing there. But once, once, I had sighed like that standing where I was standing now, at the bottom of the three steps, holding the red baize door open, with the light still on behind me. Because by that light I had seen that this time there *was* something there.

Not up round the corner—I couldn't have seen that. Opposite me, a pale, thin shape, hovering just where the other passage crossed over, with the dark cave opening between it and me. My heart belted against my rib cage and my mouth opened to yell, but nothing came out. I stood there, stuck, staring.

So did the thing. It had a mouth, and eyes, in a white face, with a white sort of dress below. And then my mind took hold and I made out it was only a girl.

That's when I'd sighed, the selfsame sigh I'd just given now, standing in the selfsame place. It had to be a girl Miss van Deering had staying, someone I hadn't been told about. (No, my grandmother hadn't cooked any extra supper, but I didn't think of that right away.) What's more, she was as scared as I was. It would be a bad place, that cave in the wall, whichever way round you came to it, specially if the house was strange to you. But at the same time it made it all right for me, having someone else there.

"It's OK," I said. "I'll do the light. You wait there."

I switched off the light behind me and let go of the door. That meant it was pitch dark so I couldn't see her anymore, but I still didn't mind. Using the rope and the wall, I felt my way up and round the corner and slid my hand about till I got to the switch. It was always a bit further than you thought. The light came on and she was still there, still sort of hovering.

"It's all right," I said. "Nothing nasty waiting. Come along."

She didn't seem to hear me so I went back and gave her my hand to hold. She took it and held it tight. Hers was small and skinny and colder than mine, but it was alive all right. I mean she wasn't some kind of ghost, in case that's what you're thinking. I'd never thought she was, after those first couple of moments.

Soon as she was on the stairs she put out her other hand and groped around the switch as if she couldn't see it and when she got it she tried to turn it on again, only the wrong way, side to side instead of up and down. And then she let go of my hand and hurried up the stairs. She took me by surprise so she was a bit ahead of me when I got to the top and she was already doing the switches. There were three of them on a sort of panel by the first door. The top one did the far end of the passage, the middle one did the place where the attic stairs went up, and the bottom one did the light on the stairs we'd just come up by. She did all three, side to side again, so the lights didn't change of course. She didn't seem to mind. She turned and said something to me, too quiet to hear but it looked like just thank you, and ran off down into the dark.

I switched the lights on to watch where she went to. She stopped halfway along to turn off the middle light, only it didn't go out, and then ran on almost to the end. That light didn't go out either when she switched it off. She paused, pulling herself together, put out her hand to open a door, and walked quietly through.

I was bothered by the business with the switches and the lights—not scared, exactly, but feeling there was something wrong, something that didn't make sense—and I didn't want to leave it like that so I kept the lights on and crept along to the end of the passage, which I wasn't supposed to, and listened at the door she'd gone through. I knew it was the right one because it had the switches by it, and anyway it was the last door that side and there weren't any others for some way back.

I couldn't hear anything, and when I switched the light off I could see there wasn't any light coming under the door, so with my heart starting to hammer again I slowly turned the handle and gave the door a push. It was locked, but when they did that they usually left the key somewhere handy, so I hunted around and found half a dozen keys in a china pot on a shelf back down the corridor. Most of the doors along here had numbers on them, like in a hotel, and the keys had labels to match, but the door I'd tried hadn't got a number and there was just this one key labeled "Nursery." I took that back and tried again. The lock made a sort of screech, but nobody called out or anything, so I carried on and opened the door a couple of inches. It was dark inside, and still no one said anything so I pushed it wide open, till I could see in by the light in the corridor.

There wasn't anyone there. What's more, there hadn't been, not for a long time. It was a large L-shaped room with two windows over on the far side, which had never been blacked out. It was pretty well empty with just a huge old cupboard and a couple of chests. The floor was bare boards. The reason there'd not been more doors this side of the corridor was that this room had three other rooms opening off it, one in the bit left by the L and the other two on the other side, which was the end of the house so they could have windows of their own. They hadn't been blacked out either, and there was still a last bit of daylight left, just enough to see by. With my heart still hammering away I crept in and looked around. One of the rooms was empty, and the second one had only an old bathtub hanging on the wall, the sort you have to fill out of jugs, but the one right in the corner had a child's bed in it and a big old dolls' house. The girl I'd seen wasn't anywhere. I even looked in the cupboard, which had shelves on one side and a lot of old clothes hangers on a rail on the other. The chests were full of old blankets.

By now I was really bothered and pretty scared, but I still didn't think the girl could have been any kind of ghost.

I'd held her living hand in mine, hadn't I? I'd felt how hard she'd gripped, still trembling a bit from being afraid of what might have been waiting for her on the stairs. I certainly wasn't afraid of *her*. But anyway I knew I'd be in trouble if my grandmother came up and found me poking around where I wasn't supposed to be, so I went back out and lit my candle and switched the lights out and went on up to bed.

It would have been school as usual next day, and I must have spent a bit of time working out what to do. My problem was getting to that place on the stairs at the right time, and the day before I must have been going to bed early—I don't remember why. Anyway, come teatime I told my grandmother I'd got a headache, and after I'd done the dishes I made out it was worse and I wanted to go to bed. It meant her missing her crib, but to make up she could start her nightcap early, not having me in the room.

Mind you, I'd nothing to go on to tell me the girl was going to show up again same time, there on the stairs. It was only the way she'd hurried up the stairs and then run along the corridor, made me think she might be afraid of being late for something, and even then it could have been just that one night, not regular. I'd got to give it a try, though. There wasn't anything else. So twenty past eight I was up at the red baize door waiting and hoping, and not too soon either, because it can't have been a couple of minutes before she came creeping round the corner and stopped. And she must have been expecting me too, because she came along and put her hand in mine before I'd finished finding the switch. And yes, it was a real hand again, small, and somehow bony and pudgy together, but not shivering like it had the night before.

We both had to do the light again, but she wasn't in a hurry this time and she hung on to my hand all the way up the stairs, so her arm was touching mine and it was as real as her hand. Maybe she was thinking about the same kind of thing because she gave me a squeeze as if she was making sure, and when I squeezed back she smiled. When I'd first seen her I'd thought she was some sort of ghost so I'd made her thin and spooky, but really she was a bit fat, and not what anyone would call pretty, with dark hair done into pigtails and a piggy sort of face.

"What's your name?" I asked her.

She looked puzzled and said something back, but so quiet I couldn't hear she was making any sound at all, but I knew she'd been asking me what I'd said. OK, I'd whispered, but not that soft, so I tried putting my mouth right against her ear before I said it again. This time she jumped and looked really surprised, and then reached up and put her mouth right against my ear.

"Adalina," she said. "It's horrid, isn't it?"

I jumped, like she had. It was weird, because I'd heard her all right, but not the usual way, in my ear—no, right inside my head somehow.

I pulled myself together. Really stupid, we must have looked, if anyone could have seen us, standing at the top of the stairs switching our heads to and fro to talk into each other's ears.

"It's not as bad as Cyril," I told her.

"I have to go," she said. "If I am late . . . You will be here tomorrow?"

"I'll try," I said.

We worked the top switches, both of us, and this time I went with her right along the corridor, waiting for her to turn the switches off again, though the lights stayed on even so. When we got to the nursery door she gave me a prim little smile and took hold of the handle and turned it and pushed, only the door didn't open.

Instead, her hand went through the door when she pushed, just sliding in, like a spoon going into thick soup, and then the whole of her slid through and was gone.

6. Miss Tarrant

I wasn't scared, like you'd have thought, seeing Adalina walk through the door like that, and I was sort of prepared for it by that business with the switches. I could see from that, without having to think about it, that things were happening for her that weren't happening for me, and the other way round, and the same with going into the nursery after her the night before, and finding it all shut up and empty. But it was weird all the same, seeing her slide out of sight like that. I tried the door handle, but the door was locked, which was how I'd left it the night before, and the door was an ordinary hard door I couldn't have slid into to save my life.

But like I say, I wasn't scared, because Adalina just wasn't scary. She was as ordinary as the door. I'd held her hand in mine and I knew she was real, and that was all there was to it. I didn't bother unlocking the door and going in after her, because I knew I wouldn't find anything different from the night before. Instead I went back along the corridor and lit my candle and switched off the lights and went up to my room and got into bed and blew out my candle and lay there in the dark, thinking about it.

You'll have worked out by now, I daresay, that we came from different times, Adalina and me. I hadn't, though I could see her dress was old-fashioned. But then you've probably read stories and seen stuff on TV about people from different times, and the only book I'd read like that was *The Time Machine* where it doesn't go into this business about not being able to change anything in any time except your own. Besides, in stories and things you don't have to believe it, it's just an idea you go along with for the sake of the story. But when it's happening to you you're trying to think about something you just aren't set up to believe in, and that's difficult for anybody, leave alone a kid of twelve who doesn't know much about anything.

In the end I decided there were two Theston Manors, just the same as each other, and in the same place, only two different lots of people lived there, and they couldn't see each other or hear each other, so they didn't know about each other and they couldn't change anything at all in the other one's Theston Manor. Only because both of us, Adalina and me, had been scared stiff by the same thing—what I called the cave—and at the same time in our two different Theston Manors, our fear had somehow sort of joined up and let us through to each other. But only as far as each other. We still couldn't change anything in the other one's Theston Manor. We couldn't even hear each other, talking the usual sort of way, because voices are sounds and sound travels by moving the air around—I'd read about this in a *Pears' Cyclopedia* back at the orphanage—and it was no use me stirring the air in my Theston Manor with my voice because it still didn't stir anything in hers. Mind you, I didn't get that far all at once, that second night, but that's how I was thinking by the time, four or five nights after, when she was really late.

I'll have to go back. You'll have spotted I had a problem. I couldn't go telling my grandmother night after night that I'd got a headache or she'd have decided I was sickening for something, and then she'd have started dosing me with Syrup of Figs, which was always the first thing she tried—she'd have given me Syrup of Figs if I'd broken my leg, most likely, just to be doing something till the doctor came. So around quarter past eight I made out I was getting sleepy. I don't suppose I was much of an actor, because she just looked at me, sharp, and said, "All right, off you go, you great baby. It's a heap better than coming up and finding you dithering on them stairs."

So that was all right, and I was there before Adalina again and we went up together holding hands like before, and when we got to the top she trotted off into the dark. But next night I'd done the dishes early enough for my grandmother to get out the cards for crib, so all I could do when it was getting toward time was start yawning and playing all wrong until she lost patience—she'd a short temper at the best of times—and gave me a clip over the ear and sent me off. I really raced up the back stairs and Adalina was there already waiting so we ran on up together and it seemed she was just about on time. I managed it that way for the next few nights, hurrying through the dishes so as to get a few hands of crib in, and then running off, but it meant I couldn't hang around on the stairs explaining to Adalina what the problem was or finding out about what was bothering her end, so I hadn't got any further with working things out by the night she was really late.

A good ten minutes I must have hung about waiting before she showed up. Interesting point, come to think about it. I was there all that time, where I'd stood night after night scaring myself silly with ideas about what might be waiting for me round the corner, but now I wasn't scared at all. I was just worried stiff about where Adalina had got to. After a bit I switched off the light on the back stairs and let go of the door and felt my way up and round and switched on the other light, no problem at all, and then I went on along round the corner where she used to show up from. This brought me out at the top of the main stairs, which I've already told you about, when I was sneaking down that evening to read *Ivanhoe*. I'd had my candle then, but they were even creepier now, with only a bit of light coming from round two corners behind me, where I'd left the top light on, a great hollow cavern of a place I couldn't see much more of than just where I was standing and the bit of blackout sagging above my head, so I didn't see Adalina coming until she'd pretty well reached the top.

Really like a ghost she looked now, coming up those last couple of steps so slow, so dragging in her long pale dress, and not a sound from her hard boots on the marble, or not that I could hear in my world. She was crying.

"What's up?" I said in her ear.

"I'm going to kill myself," she said. "I'm going to jump out of the linen room window."

"What for?" I said. I knew where the linen room was, if it was the same one my grandmother and me went to get fresh sheets from when it was time for changing our old ones. I'd had a look out of the window, too. Being at the back of the house it was three storeys down to the paving of the back yard.

"She'll put me in the cupboard and I'll go mad, like Mamma did," said Adalina. "Mamma killed herself, you know. She drank laudanum, but I haven't got any."

"Well, you're not jumping out of any window," I said. "I'm stronger than what you are, and I'll stop you."

"She'll put me in the cupboard and I'll go mad," she said.

"No you won't, because I'm coming with you," I said.

63

"She won't let you," she said. "And she'll tell Father about you."

"She won't know I'm there," I said. "She can't see me. You're the only one who can see me."

She stared at me, and I realized she hadn't worked it out far as I had.

"You're . . . you're . . . ," she began, but she couldn't bring herself to say it.

"I'm as real as you are," I said. "Real to you, like you are to me. Look, is that door open or shut?"

"Shut, of course," she said. "You can't go in there. That's Father's bathroom."

"Just watch," I said.

I opened the door and walked in. It was a bathroom, like she'd said, but bigger than my room in the attics and with a bath you could have washed a horse in, and shiny brass taps and fittings. I came out again and shut the door behind me. She was still staring, but just amazed, not scared.

"And you're not going mad neither," I said, "not unless both of us are. I tell you, she won't see me any more than I'll see her. She'll never know I'm there, holding your hand. Come on, give it a go now."

She let me take her hand and lead her on round the corner and up the stairs. She was in a sort of daze and I had to put her fingers on the switches so she could turn the lights on and off in her world. I stopped outside the door I'd seen her go through.

"I'll go first," I said in her ear. "Then you'll know she can't see me. You're coming, though, aren't you? You're not going to chicken out on me, Adalina. And you've got to remember not to look at me direct, in case she spots something's up. Right?''

She nodded and I opened the door and went in. I left it open with the light still on outside, so I could check she wasn't going sneaking off to the linen room. This room— the nursery—wasn't any different to how I'd seen it before, just the cupboard and the couple of chests and the bare boards. Like I said, there wasn't any blackout up, and no bulb in the fitting, so I left the door open and the light on in the passage, for me to see what was happening. I didn't think anyone would spot it from outside, because the windows were at the back of the house with just woods and fields beyond.

You've got to remember that as far as Adalina was concerned I'd just walked through a closed door, like I'd done with the bathroom down below, and now she couldn't see me anymore. I watched her sort of brace herself and then she took a deep breath and put out her hand and took hold of a handle that wasn't there in my world and pushed open a door I'd only just opened and walked in. She was pretty good, just one quick peek at me to check, and then looking up and over my shoulder at something else.

Someone else, it had to be, someone who was telling her off, from the way her face crumpled and her mouth puckered and she started to cry. I ran over and put my arm round her shoulders but before I could get hold of her properly she was snatched away by something I couldn't see and rushed across the room to the cupboard and held there for a moment and then shoved through the door, through the actual solid wood, so I couldn't see her any-more. I don't know why this was so shocking this time, seeing I'd watched her doing the same sort of trick, sliding through the nursery door a few nights back. Maybe it was how it was done, real violently, the way nobody's got any call to behave to a kid, and there wasn't a thing I could do about it, though it all happened so sudden I don't suppose I'd have tried anyway. I just stood there gaping, and then I came to my senses and went and opened the cupboard door.

She was lying huddled into the bottom of the cupboard under the coat hangers, with her mouth a bit open and her eyes staring up. She didn't look at me, either. Then I remembered that the door wasn't open for her and she'd still be in the pitch dark so I knelt down beside her and took hold of her hand and gave it a squeeze. She jerked and screwed herself away, but then she got it that I was still around doing what I could and she squeezed back to show she understood. And she stopped doing that crazy stare and went normal.

Next I shuffled myself round on my knees till I could reach my head in and put my mouth against her ear and ask her what was going on. But when I switched over so she could tell me she just said, "Wait. She's still there."

It was uncomfortable kneeling like that so I twisted myself round, not letting go of her hand, and tried to get her to make room for me by sitting up a bit, but she turned her head away and from how she pushed up with her other arm I realized there'd got to be something stopping her, clothes on the hangers maybe, so all I could do was settle on the floor in front of the cupboard and hang on to her hand.

After a bit of that I got worried about the light still being on and no blackout so I let go of her and went and switched it off and felt my way back to her. I couldn't see anything at first, and then only where the windows were, and it was a bit creepy sitting there knowing there wasn't just Adalina in the room but this other person, the one Adalina called "she," who'd slung her in the cupboard. Then I thought it had got to be the same for her—I was there and she couldn't see me—and I wondered if there wasn't somehow I could give her the creeps like she was giving me, and I was still thinking about this when I felt Adalina moving around and then running her other hand up my arm until it had to stop where the door was in her world.

That shook her, and no wonder, finding it was just my arm poking through the wood. She tried to let go of my hand, but I hung on and gave her a squeeze and twisted myself into the cupboard and felt around with my other hand until I found her head and got my mouth against her ear.

"It's all right," I said. "I'm here. What's going on?"

"She's gone," she said, when we'd sorted ourselves out the other way round.

"How long for?" I said.

"I don't know," she said. "Ages. It's so she can flirt with Mr. Silvey."

"Look, I don't understand much about any of this," I said. "Far as I can make out, we're in two different places, only they've both got this house in them, but I can't see or hear anything in your place except you, and it's the same for you."

"I don't understand," she said.

"Nor do I," I said. "All I can tell you is this cupboard is in both places, only I've got the door open and you've got it shut, which is why you can't get out and I can. And when I switch on the lights in my place they don't come on for you till you've switched them on too. And you saw me walk through the door into your dad's bathroom, didn't you? I could do that because I'd opened it in my place."

"It doesn't make sense," she said.

"It's a bit easier when you're used to thinking about it," I said. "But you've got to understand I don't know anything about your place except what you tell me. I don't know who Mr. Silvey is, or this woman who shut you in here. Why'd she want to go and do a thing like that?"

"So that she can go and flirt with Mr. Silvey. He's Father's secretary. She wants to marry him so she can stop being a governess. At quarter to six I go downstairs to read to Father, so that he can see how I am progressing with my reading, and then I must be back in the nursery at half past six for my bath, and if I'm late Miss Tarrant is furious because of wanting to be off to see Mr. Silvey. So

Father lets me go at twenty-five past six. It's all right in the summer, when it's still light, but when it starts getting dark . . . there's that bad place on the top stair . . ."

I took my head away so she had to stop.

"I call it the cave," I said. "There's something waiting round the corner."

"I call it the black hole," she said. "I know there isn't anything there, really, but I still can't do it. Some nights I can, but some nights it's too horrible. When it started Miss Tarrant just slippered me and sent me to bed without my supper, but one night it was very bad and I couldn't and I couldn't and she came to look for me. That's how she found out about the black hole. After that she shut me in here to teach me not to be afraid of the dark."

"That's wicked," I said. "You ought to tell your dad."

"You mean Father?" she said. "Oh no, I couldn't. I couldn't."

I didn't tell her that was stupid, because I remembered my dad asking me how I was getting on at the school at Southampton, when I was having that bad time with the bullies, and I'd told him fine. Kids are like that, I suppose.

"It wasn't because of the cave tonight," I said. "You were late already, coming up the stairs. I'd been waiting ages."

"I'm sorry," she said. "He gave me a new book to read from. *Kings and Queens of England*. It was dreadful. I'm bad at reading, you see. And writing. I'm eleven, and everyone else who's eleven can read and write beautifully, but I can't. The words keep jumbling themselves while I'm looking at them. I'm good at other things. I can do sums like a boy, and I can talk French—better than Miss Tarrant, if you want to know—and I can play the piano of course, and I know lots and lots of poetry by heart, so they can tell I'm not stupid, but I still can't read and write as I should. Now Father is trying to help me. It was all right with the old book because Miss Tarrant used to go through it with me before so I could get it right, though she made me promise not to tell Father . . .''

I had to stop her because I'd heard the clock along the corridor strike the half past, which meant my grandmother would be on her way up to bed any moment.

"I've got to go for a little," I told her. "I'll be back as soon as I can. You'll be OK. Remember I'll be only just upstairs in the attics."

"You mustn't say OK," she said. "That's horrid American. Give me a hug."

That shook me. I don't suppose I'd hugged anyone since my mum ran off, but it was all right, apart from remembering not to pull her through the door which wasn't there for me. She hugged me like she was never going to let go, and then I felt my way out of the nursery and shut the door and turned on the lights so I could find my candle and carry on up to the attics.

Like I've said, I knew my grandmother would be looking in to check I'd folded my clothes and I hadn't been using a candle to read by. This time I got right undressed and put on my pajamas and lay in bed trying to think what to do for Adalina and how I could get her to tell her dad about this Miss Tarrant shutting her in the cupboard. One thing came to me. The *Kings and Queens of England* book her dad had given her to read from, that was on the shelves at the end of the West Passage, where Miss van Deering had said I could take books from to read. Not that I'd had it out, beyond taking a quick look at it and seeing it looked pretty boring, apart from the pictures. But maybe I could take it tomorrow and then somehow get hold of Adalina before she went to read to her dad and run through it with her, like Miss Tarrant had been doing with the other book . . . only she wouldn't be able to see it, not unless she got hold of it in her world . . . and anyway I'd have to get away out of the kitchen somehow all that time earlier, when we wouldn't have more than just sat down to our tea . . .

That's when it came to me, something you might have thought I'd have been puzzling about sooner, how it was half past eight I'd run into Adalina when she'd told me it was half past six she was hurrying to be back upstairs by. It was because of double summer time of course. The clocks were going to be changing in a couple of weeks, and Mrs. Corcoran in school had told us all about how it came in in the First War, to help us beat the Germans, like we were going to do again now, and how we'd stuck to single summer time after and only made it double for this war. But Adalina didn't have single summer time even, which was why there was that two hours' difference, so she must be from some time before 1914.

And then—it must have been thinking about school and

Mrs. Corcoran—I saw what I'd got to do for Adalina. When I say "saw," I mean I just started to see, because at that point my grandmother came creaking upstairs and I saw the light of her candle under the door so I shut my eyes and made out I was asleep while she poked her head round the door to check on me. As soon as she'd locked the door of her room—she always did that, I don't know why—I stole out of bed and found my sweater and trousers by feeling around and put them on over my pajamas, and my socks but not my shoes, and then waited and waited until I heard her snoring. Then I sneaked out down the stairs, not using any lights of course, just feeling my way, and what's more I wasn't scared at all, spite of the dark and the creakings, because all I was thinking about was Adalina not going crazy, shut into her cupboard without me.

How did I know she'd be there? I didn't, of course. It could've been just like first time I'd seen her go into the nursery, when I'd followed her through the door pretty well at once and she wasn't there because as soon as I'd lost sight of her the way through between her time and mine had closed up and I couldn't get through to her, not until we'd met on the stairs again next evening. It ought to have been like that again now, oughtn't it?

Yes, you'd have thought so, but it didn't cross my mind it would happen like that. She'd got out of sight once before, when I'd been switching off the light on the back stair, and I hadn't lost her then, though it can't have been more than a few seconds that time, and now it was getting on three quarters of an hour. All I can think is that the way through had somehow got used to staying open for us, meeting evening after evening the way we'd been doing, and then being together all that time while she was lying in the cupboard. Or maybe it was just me knowing she'd be there that made it happen. Anyway, she was there.

It turned out she was asleep. I suppose I could have left her and gone back to bed, but seeing I'd got dressed and come down to be with her I sat down with my back against the hinges and felt about and found her hand and made myself as comfortable as I could, which wasn't very. I was dead tired, but sitting there kept me awake and I passed the time thinking out the bits and pieces of what I was going to do next day. And I was glad I'd hung on, because a couple of times Adalina started to shudder and moan in her sleep until I reached in and grabbed her round the shoulders and held her fast till she calmed down.

I'd left the door open so I could hear the clock striking along the corridor and it must have been getting on twelve, my time, when Miss Tarrant came back. I didn't see her or hear her, of course, but all of a sudden something snatched Adalina out of the bottom of the cupboard and I'd only just time to let go of her hand before she went floating away. For all I know Miss Tarrant put her foot right through me to get at her. I wouldn't have felt it if she did.

The moon must have come up by now because there was a bit more light from the windows and I could just about make out how she was carried across the room and dumped on something that wasn't there and made to sit up and her clothes were stripped off of her and her nightdress put on. It was too dark for me to be sure how that was happening, but it looked as if the clothes were somehow going into nowhere as soon as they were clear of her and the nightdress sort of appeared as soon as it was over her head. She wasn't helping much, she was still that sleepy, and whoever was doing it shoved and jerked her around like a floppy doll, and then she was sent staggering off to the room with the bathtub on the wall and when she came back she knelt by the bed which wasn't there and said her prayers, and then lay down on it and curled herself up with her knees under her chin. I put my hand in hers and gave it a goodnight squeeze and she knew it was me because she squeezed back, and then I went groping up to bed.

7. The Man in the Chair

My grandmother and me had our tea six o'clock, like I've said, and neither of us was a quick eater, me being let read at meals and my grandmother liking to give each and every mouthful a thoroughgoing chew while she thought it over. Then there was Miss van Deering's supper to go up in the lift at seven-thirty, sharp, and then I'd the dishes to do before we could settle down to our crib. Now, Adalina had to be down in the library quarter to six, her time, which was quarter to eight ours, so I'd got to have a reason for being done a bit before then, and what's more, for clearing out of the kitchen.

Next day was school. I was near the end of my exercise book so while Mrs. Corcoran was writing on the blackboard I tore out the last few pages, leaving just a couple of blank ones, and I made a real mess of those doing my exercises. Mrs. Corcoran gave me a new book and made me stay in during break to do the exercises again, which I'd known she'd do, and she put my old book in the box to be pulped for the war effort. That meant I had the classroom to myself during the break.

I got my old book out of the box and held it sideways and dribbled ink out of Mrs. Corcoran's inkwell between the pages and then put it in my desk and settled down to do the exercises in my new book, using my best writing so I wasn't near finished when break was over. I asked Mrs. Corcoran if I could take it home to finish and she said yes.

When I got home I showed my grandmother the books and told her I'd spilt a lot of ink over the one and I'd got to copy it all out in my spare time. She didn't know anything about school. Kids had written on slates in her day. I settled down at the kitchen table so she could see I was getting on with it, and how slow and careful I was writing, but she liked to have the wireless on while she was cooking so I told her it was putting me off and I'd better go and do my writing up in my room in the attics, and I'd listen for the clock on the landing and be down by six. She didn't say no to any of that, so I went up and finished the exercises from that morning, and then read for a bit and went down. I ate my tea faster than usual and did all the dishes that was ready to do and then I told her I was going back up to carry on with the exercises as long as it was still light, so she could listen to the wireless.

She didn't like it. She never liked change at the best of times, and besides it meant missing a bit of her crib.

"How long is this going on then?" she said.

I had forty pages to do, I told her, so if I did four each day that would make ten days. (No, I'd no idea what I was going to do beyond that, but by then the double summer time would be over so that story wouldn't wash anymore because it would be dark already.)

"Well, I'm going to give that Mrs. Corcoran a piece of my mind, next time I see her," she said. That bothered me, but there wasn't any getting out of it now. So I went up the back stairs and through the red baize door, but instead of going on up I carried on and round the corner past the main stairs into the West Passage, where the shelves were which Miss van Deering had told me I could take books to read from. *Kings and Queens of England* was there all right, standing out from the others with its bright blue cover and gold letters on the spine, and nothing like as dusty as most of them either. When I opened it, there it was, in neat slanty writing inside the front cover—"To Adalina on her eleventh birthday, from her father, 1st October 1897." So now I knew which year she was in.

I went back past the main stairs and hung about by the red baize door waiting for Adalina to show up. I wasn't exactly scared, but I was nervous and excited. I had the feeling I was making things happen, instead of things just happening to me the way they usually did, and what's more I was seeing that they happened the way I wanted. And I fell to wondering how many people might be going up and down those stairs in Adalina's time, and I couldn't see them and they couldn't see me. I wasn't scared by that, either.

She came creeping down the stairs at last, and I really mean creeping. I didn't see her till she got to the corner at the bottom, and then she didn't see me because she wasn't looking my way. She sort of drifted along in tiny slow steps with her body all hunched together and her head turned sideways like somebody was just going to hit her. I thought she'd jump when I touched her elbow but she just turned slowly round and stared, like she didn't remember who I was.

"I'm coming too," I said. "I've got *Kings and Queens.* I'm going to help you read it."

She shook her head in a dazed sort of way.

"It'll be all right," I said. "He won't see me nor hear me, no more than that Miss Tarrant did. I'll read along of you in your ear. Just tell me where you're starting."

I put my ear against her mouth and waited for her to tell me but she seemed sort of frozen, so I tried again.

"You've got to pull yourself together," I said. "Come on, Adalina. I've gone to a lot of trouble to give you a hand, but it's no use if you won't do your bit. Where've you got to in the book?"

I said it real urgent, not telling her the book was the

77

selfsame one her dad had given her, because I didn't want to muddle her up. I felt something kind of click inside her and she came a bit awake.

"I have to read him Queen Elizabeth again," she said.

"All right," I said. "If he tells you different you scratch your nose and I'll get myself so I can hear you, and you can ask him about it like you were making sure. And the other thing is I've got to get a shutter open so there's a bit of light to see by, so you try and chat with him for a bit before you start. Got it?"

She nodded, but not quite so dull and dismal. Mind you, I knew exactly what she'd been feeling, being in for it, and no escape, like going in through the school gate at South-ampton and knowing the bullies would be there, wait-ing . . .

I took her hand and we went down the stairs together and along the big corridor far as the library door. She knocked and waited, and turned the handle, except it didn't move, and walked through the solid wood. I opened the door and went in and shut it behind me.

It was pretty well dead dark inside with the shutters closed and the curtains drawn, so I had to switch on the light to open up, first pulling on the cord that worked the curtains, the way I'd seen Kitty doing, and then fiddling with the iron bar which held the shutters to. Its fastening was stiff and I thought I was going to have to try one of the others, but then I shifted it and swung the shutters open. It wasn't as light as I'd hoped outside but I thought I could just about see to read. A few more days and I'd be needing the electric, but for now I ran back to the door and switched it off.

By the time I was ready Adalina was standing by the chair under the dust sheet, very straight and prim, with her hands clasped behind her back. She was talking with someone, listening more than talking, just saying two or three words and trying to smile. I picked up the book from where I'd put it and leafed through for Queen Elizabeth. (She'd been the only one then, of course, but we'd got Princess Elizabeth nowadays, so it looked as if we were due to have a second one.) By the time I was ready Adalina was holding out her hand for something, and taking it, and sitting down on something that wasn't there, except it was, like a faint, faint shadow, and now she wasn't shifting the book around I could just about see the faint shadow of it too, where she was holding it with her head bowed down over it and her finger on the page. There was no way I could get my mouth against her ear and read from my book at the same time, so I sort of crouched behind and saw what the first few words said and then leaned forward and told her.

"The greatest of all our queens was the Virgin Queen Elizabeth."

Her finger began to move along the line I couldn't see, in little jerks as it came to each new word. I read the next bit, not giving her more than she'd remember in one go easy, and soon as her finger stopped I told her again, and that's how we went on. It probably didn't sound that bad at first, because that's how kids at school read who aren't

79

that good at it, especially if I stopped when a word was coming up she'd have had to puzzle out. But it was tiring just crouching there, and concentrating so hard, and craning to and fro to get at her ear, and what's more it was getting darker and darker and by the time we got to the Armada I was having trouble making the words out myself and I knew I couldn't go on much longer, but I'd have to, the way he was keeping her at it.

In the end all I could think of was to tell her to stop somehow.

"You've got to have a fit of coughing or something," I said. "Give me a chance to get the light turned on. I can't see no more."

I didn't think she'd manage it, not the way she'd been when we came downstairs, but she must have relaxed no end because she didn't make a bad go of it at all, coughing and sputtering while I raced to the door for the light and then back to the window to get the curtains drawn for the blackout. I didn't have time to bother with the shutters, so I just had to hope the curtains were enough, and Miss van Deering wouldn't be coming along the corridor and spotting the light round the door. By the time I got back to Adalina she was standing up and being given something to drink, and then she went back to her place and settled down and we carried on as before.

He kept her at it, too. Leafing ahead I could see we weren't going to get through Queen Elizabeth, nothing like, by half past six. I didn't have my own watch, of course, but there was a grandfather clock by the foot of the stairs, which had struck six not that long after we'd started, and the quarter when Sir Francis Drake was sailing out to meet the Armada, and I knew it must be pretty close on half past before he let her stop.

Adalina knew too. She jumped up and handed her book over and gave a quick pecking kiss to the bit of air over the chair and didn't quite run to the door, where she turned and did a neat little curtsey and shot off through the door. I wasn't that far behind her. I'd no time to deal with the shutters but I switched off the light as I went and closed the door and ran up the stairs behind her. We got her through the nursery door and she was standing there being lectured at by this Miss Tarrant I couldn't see when the clock along the passage struck the half past.

It must have been about the same her time too because she didn't get slung in the cupboard but went and sat on the bed and started undressing. Neat little embroidered slippers she was wearing this evening, and as she took them off they went shadowy in her hand and disappeared when she let go of them, and the same with her jacket when she slipped out of it and put it on the bed beside her. The bed was there too, very faint and shadowy, now she was sitting on it. I'd left the door open and the light I'd kept on in the passage shone across her, and this was the first time I'd seen anything like this happening where I could really see it, so I suppose I must have been staring a bit when she gave me a sort of glance and frown, and I came to and got it that she didn't want me standing there watching her undressing. I wasn't interested in that, the way some boys might have been, so I went back down to the library and did the shutters and checked that I hadn't left anything where it oughtn't to be. Then I went down to the kitchen, getting through onto the back stairs by a little door Kitty'd shown me under the main stair, which was disguised as a bookcase so the gentry wouldn't need to notice there were a pack of servants in the house along with them doing their dirty stuff for them. My grandmother had the wireless on in the kitchen, so she didn't hear me slip past and put *Kings and Queens* in among the books in the servants' hall before I went in.

"Reading in the dark, then?" she said sharply.

"I had to go to the toilet," I told her.

"Don't tell me you're bunged up," she said, good as reaching for the Syrup of Figs already.

"No, I'm all right," I said quickly.

"Good boys go after breakfast," she said.

"Shall I get the cards?" I said.

"Time for a couple of hands, I suppose, provided Your Lordship's willing," she said.

8. The Man in the Chair Again

Next evening went much the same, only I left the light on in the library and didn't bother with the shutters, and Adalina was nothing like that upset and nervous, and I could see she was talking a bit easier to her dad before she started reading, and she was doing that easier too, and sometimes carrying on beyond the bit I'd read to her, which I could tell from where her finger'd got to on the line. We finished Queen Elizabeth that go and he talked to her a bit more and let her off in plenty of time to get up to the nursery. My grandmother was sharpish with me again when I came back down, but I was used to that.

Next day Adalina had off, because it was Sunday, she'd told me, and her dad would be doing something else. And besides, Miss Tarrant had her day out and she'd be in Worcester meeting with Mr. Silvey on the sly. It was only Friday, my time, so I told my grandmother I'd do some more copying Saturday and Sunday and we'd have a good long time for crib that evening. Even so I went off and read for a bit on the toilet, so as to keep her thinking that's where I went that time of the evening.

Saturday, which was Monday in Adalina's time, went all right, and Sunday too, but Monday evening—you've got to remember that when I wasn't actually speaking the words into Adalina's ear, and provided there wasn't a wind to rattle the windows, the library was dead silent, silent as an empty church—I fancied I heard someone coming along the passage outside and stopping at the library door. I froze. A couple of evenings before I'd tried leaving the light on and shutting the door with me outside, to see how much light came through, and it wasn't much but all the same you couldn't really miss it. If there was anyone out there now it could only be Miss van Deering. Like I say, I froze, and I didn't come to till Adalina jogged me with her

83

elbow to carry on, which I did, and if there was anyone there they must have moved on while I was still telling her what came next. Anyway no one came in, so I supposed I must have been fancying it.

Adalina asked me about it going up the stairs.

"I thought somebody was coming in," I told her. "I'm not supposed to be there, and I'd be in dead trouble if they found me."

She didn't say anything, but I could see that really bothered her. She didn't want me getting into trouble but she knew she couldn't do without me. I ought to have told her then I didn't know how long I'd be able to carry on this way, because I'd told my grandmother it was just the ten days I'd need to finish the copying I was supposed to be doing, but I hadn't the heart.

It was two evenings later it happened. I'd done the dishes and told my grandmother I was going up to get on with the copying and I'd be down in a bit for crib, and I slipped along to the servants' hall to pick up *Kings and Queens*. She'd given me one of her looks as I left, but that wasn't anything unusual, so I just wasn't ready when she whipped out and grabbed me just as I was sneaking past the kitchen door. She must have been ready and waiting for me, just inside. She snatched the book out of my hand and took hold of me by the ear and ran me back into the kitchen. Like I've said, she'd a short temper and I was used to her blowing up, but I'd never seen her that furious.

"Well, who's a wicked little liar?" she said. "Making

out he's got copying to do, and sneaking off to read his book instead of playing crib with his old grandmother who's always done her best for him? And a thief with it, stealing candles to read by. You know what happens to thieves? Prison is what happens to them. And don't come that with me . . .''

I couldn't have said anything even if she'd given me the chance, but I'd been shaking my head to tell her I hadn't been stealing candles.

''. . . Don't come that with me. Ran into Mrs. Corcoran in the post office, didn't I, and told her I'd a bone to pick with you about all this copying she'd set you to do, and it was the first she'd heard of it, she said . . .''

She went on at me like that for an ungrateful liar I don't know how long, but in the end she packed me straight off to bed. Not thinking about it, and still not saying anything because I couldn't, I held out my hands begging her to give me back *Kings and Queens,* but she snatched it away and put it on the shelf with her cooking books.

''Not on your life,'' she said. ''And what's more no more books for you, not another page, until I give you the say-so. Now be gone with you!''

Adalina was waiting for me just up beyond the red baize door. It was never any problem, not for either of us, coming down past that bit, because we were coming out of the cave and we could see there wasn't anything there. These last few days she'd not been creeping and staring either. Almost perky she'd been too, about going down and reading to her dad, like it was something she was looking forward to, and not getting jumpy again unless it looked like she might be getting back up to the nursery late.

She smiled her pursy little smile at me and put her hand in mine to carry on down to the library. We hadn't been bothering with hellos and such because of the nuisance of switching our heads to and fro to hear what the other one was saying, so she looked puzzled when I didn't smile back and then put my mouth against her ear.

"I haven't got *Kings and Queens,*" I told her. "She found out what was up and took it off of me."

She got it at once. Maybe she was the kind that keeps telling themselves, soon as things are going right for them, it means something nasty's going to happen just because of that. Her eyes went wide and her mouth fell open and she did her hunching thing and just stood there, stupid, shaking her head.

"You can do it," I told. "You really can. You've been reading pretty good, getting ahead of me sometimes. Look, why don't you tell him you've got a headache? Or about Miss Tarrant. You've got to tell him about Miss Tarrant one day, and you might as well get it over. Ah, come on, Adalina!"

It wasn't any good. She just stood there shaking her head and digging herself deeper and deeper into the hole she was in until there was no way she could climb back out of it, not ever. (I'd been there too, remember, back in Southampton.) In the end all I could do was grab hold of her hand and pretty well pull her down to the library.

I had to put her hand on the door handle, but then she pulled herself together and knocked and waited and went through. I followed her and switched on the light, not that it was going to be any use, me seeing what happened, and then I went and stood beside her with my hand on her shoulder, so she'd know I was there, but careful not to let her dad spot there was anything different. She was doing her best, smiling—just—and not crying—just—and you'd have thought anybody would have seen there was something wrong, something bothering her badly. Maybe he asked, because at one place she shook her head and said a few words and tossed her pigtails back and tried to smile a bit more.

Then she took the book and it became shadowy in her hands, and sat on the stool and made that come shadowy too and began trying to read. It was awful. I could see her stammering, and making a word out, and trying again, and getting it wrong again, with her finger hardly moving along the page at all. Then she'd reach out and hand the book over and take it back—he'd been telling her the word she was stuck at, I guessed—and struggle along a bit more.

On and on it went like that. I wanted to go away, pretend it wasn't happening. Not that it was as bad for me as it was for her, anything like, but I got close to screaming at there being nothing I could do to help, nothing at all. She never seemed to notice I'd got my hand on her shoulder. You'd not have known it to look at her, but when she got badly stuck her whole body set up juddering, like a lorry that's standing in the road, not moving along but with its engine running. I tried stroking her when that started but it wasn't any use. The clocks outside struck six, and getting on an hour later, it felt like, they struck the quarter, and he didn't let her go and he didn't let her go and she had to sit there hunched and juddering and trying to read and trying not to cry, on and on, till the clocks struck the half past.

Maybe he heard it too, because now she passed the book across and stood up and waited, listening and nodding her head and trying to smile and fidgeting with one of her pigtails. I went over to the door and waited till she came walking slowly across with her head up, proud, and turned and did her curtsey and walked through, never even looking at me.

I switched off the light and slipped out, and she was already running along to the main stair, not stopping for me, though she must have known it was no use and she'd be shut in the cupboard for sure. She went skimming up the main stair with me after and I only caught her up just as she was reaching the top. I tried to take her hand, tell her I was coming with her to the nursery, though what sort of trouble I'd be in with my grandmother if I didn't show up in the kitchen soon I don't know, but she spun round and said something I couldn't hear, with her face all set white and hard like a statue, and before she'd finished speaking she put out both hands and gave me a shove in the chest. I wasn't ready for it, and it sent me tumbling back down the stairs. I could have hurt myself really bad on that marble, but I must have been lucky how I fell, half against the rail, which I managed to grab hold of and stopped myself falling any further.

Soon as I'd got myself together I went tearing after her. She was almost up the top stairs when I reached the bottom of them, but I went up them two at a time, and left at the top, the other way from the nursery, switching on the lights when I came to them. That slowed me, and she was out of sight by the time I got to the next corner, but I knew where she was heading and went belting on round the next corner to the linen room. There wasn't any bulb in there, but there wasn't any blackout either, and I could see her against the window trying to get it open. She didn't hear me coming, of course, and the first she knew was when I grabbed her round the shoulders and dragged her clear. She tried to pull away but I hung on and put my mouth against her ear and said, "No you don't. Not yet."

She went on trying to pull away and get my mouth off her ear but I managed to get hold of one of her pigtails and held her head still and said, gasping after all that running, "Listen. I've thought of something. I don't know if it'll work but it's worth a try. Please, Adalina, give it a go. Please. But we've got to be quick. Now, at once. Oh, come on! You owe it me, you really do. I've stuck by you when I didn't need to, because I could see you were in trouble, and now I've gone and got myself in real bad trouble for you, and you owe it me. Yes, you do, and it's no use making out you don't, because you know it's so. You owe it me."

She'd been all rigid and juddering when I'd got to her,

and she didn't go soft now, not exactly, but she eased a bit and the juddering stopped and when I let go of her pigtail she put her mouth to my ear and whispered, "All right. But next time . . ."

"Next time you can do whatever you've a fancy to," I told her, "because I don't expect I'm going to be allowed to be here no more."

So we went out into the passage where I could see her, and I gave her a smile to show her it was all going to come out all right, though I knew in my heart it was a desperate long shot, and at least it would get her away from that window. She couldn't go jumping out of there, not if she was shut in a cupboard. She didn't smile back, but she let me hang on to her hand and take her back round to the nursery.

I was planning to stop outside and tell her I wasn't coming in, not just now, but I'd be back in a minute and I'd stay with her all night if I had to, but before I'd got a chance she was grabbed out of nowhere and hauled away through the door, and I could see from her mouth before she vanished she was screaming.

I didn't bother going in after. I didn't know how long I'd got so I pelted back down the main stairs and never mind the racket, and along the passage and in through the library door, and turned on the light and shut it behind me. I ran across to the chair she'd been reading to and tried to sit in it, only I couldn't because there was something hard and lumpy on the seat, so I looked under the dust sheet and there was the stool I'd just seen only the shadow of when she was sitting on it to read. I pulled it out and sat in the chair, on top of the dust sheet.

I gave myself a moment to get my breath back, and then I pulled myself up tall as I could and said, "Go to the nursery. Go to the nursery now."

I said it out loud, not shouting or anything, but slowly and carefully, as if everything in the world depended on it. If he wasn't still sitting there after he'd let Adalina go it wouldn't be any use—that's why I'd been in such a tear— and even if he was I'd no way of knowing if he could hear me, but my idea was if I could say the words right inside him, right inside his head, maybe that's how he'd hear them, the way Adalina and me could hear each other. In one of the books I'd read there'd been a bloke who'd heard his twin brother calling to him like that, and had gone and rescued him. I wasn't sure if that kind of thing could truly happen, or if it was just an idea the writer had made up, but all I can tell you is I had this feeling, very strong, it was what I was supposed to do, so I did it.

I'd been meaning to give it three goes, but before I'd drawn breath to try again I felt—I'm not sure how I can describe this, but it was like the bit of air I was sitting in had given a sort of kick. Or you know when you're coming downstairs and there's one more step than you'd thought there was going to be, and *before* your foot bangs into the floor you get this kind of jolt inside you? Like that, but without me moving at all. No, that's not it, either. But I did feel something, very sudden and strong, so I was pretty sure I'd gone and done it.

I didn't bother saying my words again. I just ran back up to the nursery to see if anything happened. It was pretty well dark by now of course, so I left the door open with the light on in the passage.

It was the same bare empty room with the cupboard and the couple of chests. I opened the cupboard door and there was Adalina lying shuddering under the coat hangers, staring up at nothing. I knelt down and took her hand and was leaning in to get at her ear with my mouth when suddenly she screwed herself almost into a ball and cringed even further into the corner with her eyes wider still and staring out past me. She couldn't see me of course because it was pitch dark in the cupboard for her, and she couldn't see out either, but it was like there was some kind of monster in the room now, snuffling round after her blood.

When I managed to get my mouth against her ear to ask her what was going on all she did was lie there making herself as small as she could. In the end I did the only thing I could think of. She was wearing hard little leather boots, the sort that lace up crisscross on hooks running up in front of your ankle, so I grabbed her leg and banged her foot hard against the door. It was the door in her time, of course, so I couldn't see it and I couldn't hear the racket it made, but I knew when it hit because it stopped, sharp, where the door would have been.

I did that two or three times with Adalina trying to fight me off, which would only have added to the racket, and then she jerked her leg free and I was getting ready to grab it again when she cringed back with her arm over her face and then she sailed right out of the cupboard and up into the air. Whoever it was must have reached right through me to get hold of her. Her boot banged against the side of my head as she went past and knocked my specs off.

I scrabbled around and found them and looked to see what was up. She was floating in the air, lying a bit forward with her head turned sideways and her knees a bit up and her arms spread out and round. I got it at once. Someone was holding her on their arm and she'd got her head on their shoulder and her arms round their neck. I moved where I could see her face and she was crying, great heaving sobs that shook her through and through, not like the other crying I'd seen her do, when she was trying her best not to. She was letting it happen now, crying her heart out because she was allowed to because she was all right at last. (You'll say this is silly, telling you that a twelve-year-old kid who didn't know much about anything would have spotted something like that, but you're wrong. Anybody could have seen it.)

After a bit she started floating to and fro because whoever it was was carrying her around comforting her, and when they crossed the light from the door I could just about see the shadow of him, or maybe I couldn't. And then they floated off out of the room and along the passage and all the way down to the library, where he must have sat back down in his chair to judge by the way she settled. And now I could see the shadow of him, for sure, but very faint and misty so that I couldn't have told you anything about him except he wasn't as big as I'd expected. And maybe he had a beard.

She'd got her head against his chest and she was still sobbing, but quieter now. I'd have liked to have just squeezed her hand or something, by way of saying good-bye, but I didn't want to come between them, so I turned out the light and went back up to the attics so I could be sure of being in bed before my grandmother came up to check on me.

Just to tidy up. In school the next day Mrs. Corcoran asked me what my grandmother had been on about in the post office. I mumbled and muddled until she got it into her head that I'd used the bit of copying I'd had to do as an excuse to get some reading in as well, instead of playing crib with my grandmother. After that I'd let on there was more copying I'd got to do so I could get off the crib most evenings and read my book instead. Mrs. Corcoran said I was a bad boy, lying like that, but I could see she wasn't that cross because she liked having a kid in her class who really wanted to read proper books. A couple of days later she gave me a note for my grandmother, who read it and put it away in her pocket, and next evening she fetched *Kings and Queens* off the shelf and gave it to me and said Mrs. Corcoran had told her something about a misunder-standing, but even so it wasn't all right because she still didn't think I'd been straight with her, but maybe it wasn't as bad as she'd thought so I could go back to reading, and if I was tired of playing crib with her then maybe some evenings I could read to her instead. (That was how I came to read *Jane Eyre* to her, like I told Mr. Glister.)

That was all right with me, but it meant that I wasn't likely to be going up past the bad patch on the stairs same time as Adalina might be, and anyway I didn't think Miss Tarrant would be staying on, so things would be different her time too. I didn't look around for her either, being pretty sure I wasn't going to see her again.

I put *Kings and Queens* back on the shelves in the West Passage, but next time I looked I found someone had moved a lot of the books around and it wasn't there anymore.

9. Me, Cyril Batson

Now, if you don't mind, we'll go back to me today, and me standing by the red baize door on the stairs at Theston, remembering about Adalina. And maybe you'll want to know why I didn't put all that in where it belongs in the story, after the bit about Miss van Deering finding me in the library, and before all the stuff about Mr. Glister and getting my own bookshop and so on. So I'll finish up with some explanations.

I'm not going to tell you I'd completely forgotten about Adalina all those years, the way you read about people completely forgetting horrible things that happened to them when they were kids, because they couldn't bear to live with themselves remembering. No, it would be truer to say I'd just stopped thinking about it, and if you stop thinking about something every now and then, then it begins to fade, if you know what I mean, and goes all misty and faint until maybe you lose it completely, until something happens that brings it into your mind, just a bit of it maybe, and you somehow can't get hold of the rest of it, or else you can tease it out from that one bit until you can see it all clear and think about it. That's what happened to me, going back to Theston. I'll come to that in a minute.

In some ways helping Adalina is the most important thing that ever happened to me. I did something all by myself with no one to help, and I got it right. It must have given me a lot of confidence I hadn't had before. For instance, do you imagine without it I'd have had the nerve to go and ask Mr. Glister for a job, all on my own? And since then I've made what I wanted of myself. People look at me and think *Poor lonely old man, no wife, no kids, no friends, just a grubby old bookshop and his cat to show for his sixty-five years.* They're dead wrong. OK, I'm getting on, but I'm not poor and I'm not lonely. If I could have my life over again with all my wishes coming true, this is how I'd have it, and one of the things I like about Tom and Mercury is that they can see this. Anyway, that's why the business with Adalina is important.

But against that, it was a very uncomfortable thing for a kid to deal with, after, all on his own. I didn't know what to make of it, and there wasn't anyone I could talk to about it. Certainly not my grandmother. She'd have called me a wicked liar, making up stories. And there wasn't anyone to talk to at school. So I suppose I felt I couldn't get on with my life if I was always thinking about it, and waiting for Adalina to show up, and knowing she wouldn't.

Bit by bit I put it away. I don't mean I forgot it, wiped it clean out, but I turned it from being something that had really happened to me into one of the stories I used to tell myself in which I had all sorts of adventures. I used to tell myself lots of stories, the way kids do, with me as the hero, but all the other ones came out of the books I'd been reading, and in them I knew about swordfighting and se-cret codes and driving fast cars and stuff. This one didn't come out of a book, and it had me doing just things a kid like me could have done. And then I read a lot more books and told myself a lot more stories and sort of buried it.

Suppose you'd asked me, anytime up till I went back to Theston with Tom and Mercury, about this girl from a different time, I'd have said it was just a story I used to tell myself, and I wouldn't have been lying. That's what I'd have believed. What's more I'd have been pretty hazy about it. I wouldn't have remembered it nearly as well as I can remember some of the stories in the books in the servants' hall.

You remember, for instance, how just after I'd come to Theston with Tom and Mercury, I stared and stared at that stool in the library? Now I'd seen that stool, solid, just the once, when I'd pulled it out from under the dust sheet so I could sit in the chair and speak inside Adalina's father's head, and even then I'd barely glanced at it. And I'd seen it too as a kind of shadow when Adalina was sitting on it to read aloud to her father. But I didn't make the connection, not with either time. All the same, something in me made me stare at it.

And then, why was I so keen to go up the back stairs that I returned to the kitchen to ask if I could? That's not like me. If something says "Private" I stay out of it. But I did ask, because something in me told me I had to go up that way, right up to the red baize door, and open it, and see what I found.

And I did, and that's where it all came back to me.

No, that's not right. Like I've said, I didn't get it all back in one go, all in its right order, like I've put it down here. In fact I'd just remembered seeing Adalina that first time on the other side of what I called the cave, when I heard some tourists coming chattering down from the top floor, so I went on up past them and had a look at the nursery.

They'd got it done up with a lot of stuff that could have been there in Adalina's time, toys, and a brass fender round the fireplace, and her dolls' house painted and tidied, and so on. The cupboard was there, with Adalina's sort of clothes in it, but they'd moved her bed into one of the little rooms. It was all very nice, but it didn't say anything special to me.

I went down and looked at the books at the end of the West Passage, and some of them were the same ones, but not *Kings and Queens* (I'm going to look out for a copy of that, now). Then I went down to the servants' hall and got myself a cup of tea and had a look at the guidebook, which I'd bought at the door.

It was really interesting, because they'd got a set of photographs taken of the house just about the right time, which was how they'd managed to get all the rooms looking right. The one of the library even showed the stool Adalina used when she was reading to her dad, standing beside his chair. And it said that the house had one of the earliest lot of electric lights put in in England, and the system had lasted almost as far as the First World War, so the lights we'd had when I was a kid must have been the second lot, and that was why Adalina moved the switches sideways to turn the lights on. I'd remembered her doing that before I read about it in the guidebook, by the way, in case you're thinking perhaps I've made the whole thing up without realizing. I should have said I'd been remembering bits and pieces like that all the time I'd been poking around upstairs, and they were still coming back, any old order, while I was sitting there drinking my tea.

There was one thing in the guidebook that shook me, though I don't suppose it's going to surprise you much. They'd got a history of the house and who'd lived there. Miss van Deering's grandfather had made a pile of money from chemical dyes, and he'd bought it in 1856, and her father had carried on with the business but he'd been a book collector too, and he'd had two sons but they'd both been killed in the First World War, so it had been his daughter who inherited, and she'd left it to the National Trust when she'd died. Not until 1978, that had been. The guidebook gave her full name. Adalina van Deering.

Like I say, you'll have got this long ago, I shouldn't wonder. I never did, not till I saw it in the guidebook. You may think it's obvious, but I tell you it wasn't. Apart from looks, they couldn't have been more different, Adalina and Miss van Deering. Adalina was troubled and unhappy and uncertain and not at all comfortable with herself, but Miss van Deering was just the opposite, like a cat in the sun, like I've said, apart from the moment when she found me reading *Ivanhoe* in the library and was so put out.

That was when she recognized me, I should think. It might have been something to do with the way the light fell on my face from the reading lamp under the desk, being like the light she was seeing me by when she met me on the stairs that first time. But I was wearing the wrong specs, so she told my grandmother to get me some new ones and gave her the money. And she told me I could borrow the books at the end of the West Passage and she made sure *Kings and Queens* was there for me to find. But that would have been after she'd got over the shock of finding me and realizing I was the boy who'd done her a good turn all those years back. Up till then, I think, she'd done what I did, like putting it away in a drawer and pretty well forgetting it was there. I'm good as certain she hadn't been waiting all that time for me to show up, or she wouldn't have gone on like she did, for instance giving us a smile in church before it all happened and looking the other way after. So it was a shock all right, having it come back and hit her in the library that night, and that's why she'd spoken like that, gasping, and only just able to get her words out.

She wasn't much of a reader, she said. Dyslexia, we'd call that now.

So why hadn't she said anything to me after, never even thanked me? Why had she tried not to notice me, looked the other way? Maybe you think it was mean of her, but I don't blame her. Think of it from her point of view: You've had this really bad time when you were a kid with your governess putting you in a cupboard when you're scared of the dark, and being shut in. Claustrophobia, it's called. And maybe you think you're going mad like your mother did, and imagining things, imagining this boy who comes out of nowhere to help you, only he can't be real, because only you can see him, and he can walk through doors, and so on. But provided you can carry on imagining he's there, things aren't so bad, because somehow you can imagine him reading in your ear the book you can't read for yourself, and you can imagine him holding your hand when you're shut in the cupboard, and you can even imagine him stopping you jumping out of the linen room window the night things got so awful that your dad cottoned on there was something bad going on in the nursery, and came up and found out. And after that you didn't need the boy anymore, so you stopped imagining him.

So it's a hell of a shock when forty years and more later he shows up for real, and you know he's real because he's your cook's grandson and you aren't imagining *her*. So he must have been real all along, but that isn't what you want. It isn't how you've got your world sorted out now, so comfortable. You've got to go along with it, though, and see that he's got the right specs, and put *Kings and Queens* on the shelf for him. But as soon as it's all over you want to go back to where you were before and turn him back into something you just imagined. So you don't say anything to him, in case he takes advantage of it and you've got to have more and more to do with him so he stays real and won't go away. You don't even look at him if you can help it.

I must say, I don't blame her.

All the same, I think she felt a bit ashamed of herself about that. Did you notice anything funny about the letter the lawyer sent me to tell me she was sending me the books? Apart from it being so sharp, I mean, when the books themselves were so downright generous? It was what he called her. "Miss van Deering of Theston Manor." Not her first name. That isn't the way lawyers go on. I've seen a few letters from lawyers, and they always tell you the first name to show they're talking about Mr. Cyril Batson and not some other Mr. Batson. I think she'd actually told him not to let on her name was Adalina, in case I made the connection, which she must have guessed I hadn't or I'd have said something, surely.

So that's that, and I've almost done. I had a few more cups of tea in the servants' hall while I thought it all out, and then I wandered around a bit more checking this and that. One interesting thing was a little room they'd set aside for the history of the house, and there was a photograph of Adalina and her dad, only she was grown up now and she was pushing him round the garden in a wheelchair. You could see the likeness both ways, back to the Adalina I'd known, and forward to Miss van Deering. She'd have been twenty-something then, but already she had that look of having her world the way she wanted it. Oh yes, and he did have a beard.

I was back in the servants' hall by the time Tom and Mercury came for me. They realized somehow that I didn't feel like talking, so they left me alone and let me sit on the outside when we drove home. That's another thing they're good at. I don't know if I'm going to tell them the story, though. Not that they'd laugh at me, but for the moment all I feel like is getting it all down here so it can't go away, and then putting it in a drawer and, maybe me, maybe somebody else finding it again one day.

CHECKERS

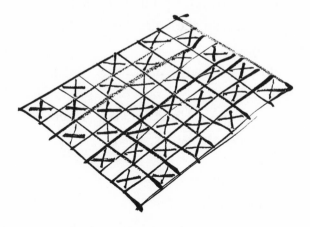

At last the car stopped. Its doors opened and jarred shut. Voices spoke briefly. Huddled in the stifling dark of the boot, Dave waited. He heard the sound of something being dragged, the creak of hinges, a quiet thud. A little later the click of a key in the boot lock, and the lid was raised.

He began to sit up but a hand grabbed him by the throat and jammed him back. The figure that leaned over him in the dimness had no face. The head was a bag with eye and mouth slits. The place smelt of musty hay, or straw. He tried to speak, to protest, but the hand, hard as timber, tightened on his throat. There was a sharp pain beneath his earlobe.

"No speak," said a level voice. "No noise."

A hand came into view between him and the masked face, holding a stubby knife.

"Understand?" said the voice.

"Yes," Dave whispered.

The hand relaxed its grip but did not let go.

"Your name?" said the voice.

"Dave Doggony."

"Your father rich man? American?"

"I suppose so. Yes."

"Man at Principessa Hotel no your father?"

"No. That's my stepfather, Chris."

"He rich man?"

"No. Not specially."

"Your father address?"

Dave gave it, spelling it out while another man wrote it down.

"OK," said the voice. "We wait. Four hour."

The hand loosed its grip and rose to close the boot lid.

"Please," whispered Dave. "I need a pee. Er . . . *gabinetti*."

He was jerked to a sitting position and a bag was thrust over his head and a drawstring tightened round his neck. He was lifted clear of the boot, set on his feet and pushed a few paces and held still.

"OK," said the voice.

He unzipped his fly and peed. They turned him, pushed him back to the car, and lifted him into the boot. They removed the bag and closed the boot lid, leaving a slit for the air to come through. After that all he dared do was lie and wait. When one position became too uncomfortable to bear he moved as carefully as he was able to, trying to make no noise. He felt sick with fear, unable to feel or think. At the slightest sound—the scrape of a match as one of the men lit a cigarette—his heart raced and sweat broke out all over him, so that his clothes were soaked. At other times, in spite of the heat, he was shivering uncontrollably. Apart from his little gold cross on the chain round his neck they had taken everything from him, including his watch. Time meant nothing.

At long last he heard the door of the place being dragged open, and then closed. There was a plopping sound and a new smell, animal manure, fresh, a horse or something. More time passed. The lid was opened. The bag was thrust over his head. He was lifted, taken to pee again, brought back and lifted not into the boot but laid stomach down across the back of the horse, where his wrists and ankles were lashed to the girth strap or something, so that the leather cut into his forearms. When they led the animal out he realized that it was now dark, but they left the bag on his head all the same.

For a short while they were on some sort of level road, but then they turned and started up what seemed to be a steep and winding track, so uneven in places that the animal stumbled. The jolting and the pressure on his stomach made him long to vomit. The blood drummed in his temples and roared in his ears. The cords cut agonizingly into his wrists. More than once he passed out. The track leveled and dipped and rose and dipped again, and at last reached a place where they had to climb steeply over rough ground, and the animal kept balking and had to be driven on with curses and blows, while bushes scraped against Dave's thighs and shoulders. Then, after a brief level place, they stopped and he was untied and lifted down, so stiff and pierced with cramp that when they set him on his feet he could not stand.

They gave him no chance to recover but dragged him up a slope as steep as the roof of a house, and laid him on his back and dragged him under some bushes. They turned him over, pulled his arms over someone's shoulders, and carried him down steep steps. His elbows scraped against stone and his dangling feet thumped onto the treads behind him.

They set him down and held him while he straightened himself out, then removed his hood. A flashlight shone, blinding for a few seconds until in the circle of light he made out some kind of stone wall, a pile of straw, and what looked like a few coarse blankets. A shove sent him to his knees. The light went out. Metal scraped on stone. He heard the rattle and click of a lock, and they were gone. He crawled forward and found the straw, felt around for the blankets, feebly spread one out, lay on it, and pulled the others over him.

He turned on his side and wept.

He was woken by the sound of a sigh.

"Who's there?" he whispered, his heart pounding, but there was only silence and the earth-smelling dark. He lay aching in all his joints but rigid with the nightmare and the knowledge that it was real and not a dream. The sigh could only have come from his own lips, but he couldn't rid himself of the feeling that there was someone else close by. Even when he had nerved himself to move and was lying fully awake and enduring the shock and terror of what had happened, this feeling persisted, persisted through the same useless thoughts and memories running and rerunning through his mind until he dropped for a short while back into sleep.

It happened again and again, he did not know how often. And then he woke in daylight.

At first he was afraid to stir, afraid even to do more than peep through almost closed eyelids. He was sure that someone was in this place, watching. The light was dim. It must be only just dawn, he thought. When nobody stirred or spoke he opened his eyes fully and looked at what he could see without moving his head. There was an arched roof above him and a wall beside him. Both were rough masonry. The light came through five round holes, each about the size of a Coke can, near the top of the wall opposite where he lay. Moving his head now, he saw that he was in a square cell about ten feet across. There was a door in the wall to the left of the light holes and a green enamel bucket in a corner to their right. From outside came the shrill whir of cicadas. That was all.

After a while he rose and peed into the bucket, assuming that that was what it was for. He was so stiff and weak and sore and sick that he needed to support himself with his shoulder against the wall while he did so. Then, without any hope at all, he went and looked at the door. It was a single sheet of rusty iron, with no handles or fastenings his side. It seemed shut fast.

On his way back to the pile of straw he noticed that in the corner beyond it was a opening. He went and looked, and found it was a niche like a narrow passage, several feet deep, ending in a solid blank wall. He had no idea what it was for, so he went back to the straw, lay down, and pulled the blankets over himself, since there was nothing else to do.

Not long after this he heard the sound of footsteps on the stairs. There had been three men last night, he thought. Two of them had worn sneakers, or something like that, but the third had worn boots, or shoes, of hard leather, which clicked or scraped when he walked on stone. Heart pounding, throat dry, Dave sat up and faced the door, waiting. The footsteps stopped outside. The voice that had spoken last night called out.

"You hear me?"

"Yes," he croaked, not loud enough, for the man called again.

"Yes," he managed to answer more strongly.

"Lie on bed. Look at wall. Shut eyes."

He did as he was told. Iron grated on stone. They came in, put the bag over his head, and lifted him to his feet. They led him a few paces, took his arms by the wrists, raised them above his head, and placed them against the stone of a wall.

"Stand so. Wait," said the voice.

He heard the grate of the door being pulled to.

"Take cover from head," said the voice. "Go lie on bed."

Again Dave did as he was told.

"Stand," said the voice. "Go to wall, same place. Cover on head. Hands on wall, like we show. Understand?"

"Yes," he called, and at once obeyed.

They kept him waiting in darkness for some while before the door opened.

"Good," said the voice. "You good boy. Now I bring food. You stay so. I call, take cover from head, eat. You ask question, you speak, no food. Understand?"

"Yes."

"So. Alway when I call, do same. Go to wall, cover head, stand so. Understand?"

"Yes."

"Good."

The footsteps moved about, the door grated, the voice called. Dave took the bag off his head and saw that they had left him a blue enamel mug, a plastic bottle filled with water, and a brown pottery bowl containing bread, a bit of cold sausage, a hunk of soft white cheese, and a couple of apricots. He carried them to the bed, sat down, and drank a little of the water. He'd thought he was too sick and scared to be hungry, but when he began to nibble a corner of the bread he realized that he had eaten nothing since breakfast yesterday.

As he ate he tried to think. He was pretty sure he'd

been kidnapped for ransom. They'd checked on his name. They'd asked about Dad. He'd read about kidnaps. They took weeks, months, to sort out. And Dad . . . Yes, months. He was going to be in here for months. He was going to go mad. Mad with boredom, mad with loneliness, mad with fear. Of course he'd been scared sometimes in his life, but he'd never been through-and-through afraid before, not like this. It wasn't just that he was afraid of what might happen to him. That wasn't the main thing. The main thing was that he was afraid of the men, particularly the one with the voice. When he was in the cell, when he spoke, Dave—all of him, mind and body and soul—vibrated like a tuning fork to the note of fear. Just thinking about it now made the note begin, pure fear.

Close by him somebody sighed.

His heart clenched.

"Who's there?" he croaked.

Nobody, of course. Outside the cell the cicadas shrilled in the sunlight. He could see small patches of sunlight on the far left-hand sides of the five holes. He watched them dwindle and go as the sun moved up and round, and forced his mind to work it out. The sun rose in the east, so that side must be west, so the airholes faced roughly north. And it had been full day when he had woken, not dawn. It was never going to get any lighter than this in here . . .

And there was nobody with him in the cell. And he was beginning to go mad already.

Though his stomach still told him he was hungry, he had stopped eating because his throat wouldn't swallow. By the time the sunlight had gone from the holes he had made himself think about something else—the trick Chris had once taught him for getting to sleep by imagining you're going out of your front door and taking the first right and then the first left and then the first right and so on and seeing how far you can get. This worked well enough to let him get most of the way through his breakfast before he heard the man's shoes on the stairs. Immediately he rose, stood facing the wall in the place he'd been shown, pulled the bag over his head, and raised his hands against the stonework.

The man called, and he answered, croaking, that he was ready. The man came in. He said nothing, but Dave heard him moving slowly all round the cell. At last the door closed and he called out to Dave that he could now move. He had left the water and mug but taken the bowl and the rest of the food. He had covered the bucket with a piece of sacking and left a heap of newspaper, torn into quarters, beside it. He seemed to have done nothing else. Dave decided he must have been checking the cell for signs of some attempt to escape, such as scraping at the mortar between the stones.

After that there was the day to get through, somehow. The first of many, many days. Dave started by exploring the cell more thoroughly than he had done earlier. It felt really old, but the bit round the door and up by the airholes had a different sort of cement. Dave guessed that it was part of an old castle or something up in the hills, which had fallen down centuries ago and got pretty well buried in the hillside, and then somebody had found this room still there and had put the door and the holes in. It wasn't these men. They just knew about it. Their fathers or their grandfathers or someone had used it before them. Several times, probably.

He'd thought the floor was just earth, but scraping with a sneaker, he found flagstones beneath the dirt. He tried stamping on them, but none of them sounded hollow. It struck him that the niche in the corner might once have been a passage somewhere, now walled off. The light didn't shine directly into it, so that the end wall was too dark to see. He groped his way in and felt around, but it seemed to be made of the same kind of masonry as the rest of the cell, and seemed just as solid when he thumped it.

There was only one other slight oddity. Opposite the door, close by where the man made him stand, there was a stone set into the wall at about knee level which was different from the rest. It was larger, over two feet long and about nine inches high, and smooth. It probably didn't mean anything, Dave decided. It was just a bit of some other building, a Roman temple or something, which they'd found and shoved in here because it fitted.

Anyway, there was no chance of escape. Dave found that a bit of a relief, as he knew he wouldn't have had the nerve. For the time being his only plan was to do exactly what the men wanted, to show them he wasn't going to be any trouble, and just hope they'd ease up on him a bit. That was all that mattered, getting to a setup where he wasn't sick with fear every time they showed up. He lay down on the bed and stared at the ceiling. Time passed. Somebody sighed.

"You think you've got troubles?" he said.

The silence waited. Of course nobody had sighed. He was imagining it. Or else he'd sighed himself, without realizing. But talking was something to do. It passed the time.

"OK, I'll tell you about it," he said. "My troubles are that I'm being held for ransom by some local thugs who've cottoned on that my dad is loaded. How've they done that? Dad's in America, and I was out here on an ordinary package holiday and we weren't throwing money around. But I've got this stupid name. There's not many Doggonys in the phone book, but you've heard of Doggony Ribs—or maybe you haven't, out here in the sticks. Doggony Ribs—Doggone Delicious. There's one here on the island, right by the harbor. My great-granddad switched from Dolgoni when he emigrated. I've got dual nationality, but we haven't bothered to get me a U.K. passport so I'm here on an American passport in the name of Dave Doggony. You with me so far?"

It was a relief to talk, to piece his jumbled thoughts and fears together into some kind of order and make sense of them. Usually when he'd tried anything like this—rehearsing a presentation he was going to do in class, for example—he couldn't keep it up, lost confidence, let his voice trail away. But here, somehow, it was no effort to pretend that he was actually talking to somebody else, the imaginary sigher, who was friendly and interested and attentive.

"That's point number one," he went on. "Point number two is that my mum likes to talk, and she likes to practice her Italian. Put her down in a bus and before she's gone a couple of stops she'll be telling the passenger next to her her whole life history. Not that I actually heard her telling one of the waiters how she used to be married to this all-American millionaire and splitting up with him when I was a baby, but I wouldn't put it past her. Pretty thick of her in a place like this, and maybe Chris should have stopped her, but maybe he wasn't there, and anyway you never think it's going to happen to you, not in this day and age.

"So it doesn't look so bad, you think? All I've got to do is sit tight and wait for Dad to come up with the ransom. Trouble number two is that Dad's not going to come up with the ransom. Not until he's tried everything else he can think of. Let me tell you about my dad. I don't see that much of him. He lives in America, pretty well all over America. He's got six homes, last I heard. I live with my mum and Chris and their kids in England in a town called Basingstoke. That's where I go to school. Dad didn't take much interest in me when I was small. He didn't know how to handle little kids, and the wives he had then didn't want to know, so he'd look in when he was over in England for the polo and he'd send me crazy expensive Christmas presents and that was it. But soon as I was old enough for him to do things with he began to take notice. These days I go and visit him a couple of times a year, and that's good fun. I wouldn't want to live that way, but it's fine for a bit at a time. I fly over first class to Chicago and on to Butte, and Dad's plane is waiting for me there and takes me on to his ranch, which is right under the Rockies. Winter we do a bit of skiing. Summer—he's got terrific horses—we ride out, just the two of us, and camp somewhere and build a fire and barbecue steaks and do man-type things together like shooting rattlesnakes and tracking bears and filming them, only if the weather turns nasty he can whistle up a helicopter to bring a couple of the ranch hands out to ride the horses back while we fly home in comfort.

"So why isn't he going to come up with a ransom, if he's like that with me? Because nobody gets to put one over on Dad. Nobody takes him for a ride or shakes him down. No way. He's a funny guy. You'd think if he loved me . . . Well, maybe he does, or maybe he just likes having a son. Apart from me he's got just a couple of daughters. A real American guy has got to have a son. It's part of the deal. I'm not saying he won't mind if I get hurt, but he'll mind a lot more if he just knuckles under. He'd sooner shell out five million dollars hiring a private army to get me out of here than he would pay a couple of million to buy me free. At any rate you can be pretty sure he's going to dig his heels in, and these men aren't going to like it. They're pros. They know what they're doing. No need to tell you that, I suppose."

He took himself by surprise. He hadn't been aware of the thought coming into his mind before he spoke the words. He twisted onto his elbow and looked round the

117

empty cell. Perhaps madness was like this, telling you things you didn't know you knew, giving you reasons as if you'd thought of them long ago. This place had been built to hold prisoners. He wasn't the first. If he was going to have an imaginary sigher it would have to be some kind of ghost, so it would be someone who'd never got out. Nobody had come up with the ransom. It made sense. Of course madness makes sense, if you're the one being mad.

"Look," he said, still comforted by the sound of his own voice, "no offense, but I don't believe in ghosts. I never have. Actually I don't believe in any of that sort of stuff, not just UFOs and poltergeists and all that. I'm supposed to be a Catholic. Mum promised Dad when they were splitting up she'd bring me up a Catholic, so I go to Mass a couple of times a year but that's about all. It's not my scene, and I'm giving it up soon as I can without causing a lot of grief between Mum and Dad. Sorry about this . . . Look, I'd better have a name for you. Mind if I call you Giovanni? Sorry about this, Giovanni, but it means I don't believe in you either. I'm imagining you, but I'm making a pretty good job of it because I'm going a bit crazy. Hell, I've got to have someone in here with me, otherwise I'll be going all-out crazy. Hope you don't mind."

He lay for a while and thought about it. The silence waited. He realized that for the first time since the ambush at the picnic there was something between him and the naked fear of what was happening to him. The fear was still there, still the main thing in his life, but it no longer clutched him round and enclosed and smothered him. He had moved a little apart from it. He could breathe. He'd done it by inventing Giovanni and talking to him in an ordinary voice, not just pretending he was there but actually persuading himself he was. Because, honestly, he *felt* there. That was the madness. The trick was going to be to stay just mad enough to keep him there, and not go any further over the edge.

"Like to hear a bit more about my dad, Giovanni? If I get going on him, I can keep it up for hours. Look, most of what I'm going to tell you will make you think I'm against him, and I just go along with him because he's loaded and he gives me a good time, but it's not like that. For some reason, I actually like the guy. He thinks the rest of the world is out to get the United States, and everyone in the United States is out to get Dick Doggony—that's his name, Richard Doggony II—but there's something about him, a kind of bounce and go you don't get from most people . . ."

Dave talked on to the patient silence until his voice ran out. Listening to the cicadas, smelling the faint herby dry smell that came through the airholes, he guessed that the sun must be almost overhead, beating down onto the parched hillside. He got up and walked to and fro, corner to corner across the cell until the need came on him to use the bucket. He wiped himself with pieces of newspaper and covered the bucket with the sacking, then returned to pacing the cell until he had made another hundred crossings. Next he scuffled the straw into a steeper mound so that he could sit rather than lie. There was no movement or sound in the cell, other than those he made himself, but that did not prevent him from continuing to believe that Giovanni was there, watching.

"OK, we've got to have something to do," he said. "Tell you what. Ever played tic-tac-toe? Noughts-and-crosses we call it in England, but I played it with my dad first time he took me camping, so I call it tic-tac-toe, like the Americans. It's a pretty stupid game, actually, because if you start you can always win, so after that we took checkers along, but I wonder if there isn't something you could do to gear it up a bit. Suppose you tried on a bigger board, for instance . . ."

He rose and scuffed at the dirt with his sneakers to loosen it. Something tinkled faintly. Feeling around, he found a rusty nail, with its head bent over.

"Just the job," he said, and went on scuffing the dirt until he had loosened a good patch. He gathered it into a pile, smoothed it flat, and drew three parallel lines with the nail, crossing them with another three.

"Right," he said. "That gives us one square extra each way. When I tried this with Dad we couldn't make it work, because it's too easy to get three in a row and you can always stop the other guy getting four. But suppose we blank out a couple of squares . . ."

Systematically he tried different variations. Some worked better than others, but in the end they all seemed to fail one way or the other. Either whoever started was almost bound to win, or the game couldn't be won at all.

Still he kept at it, chatting to Giovanni about what he was doing, easing the slow minutes by. He was smoothing the dirt out for yet another try when he realized that the silence was no longer listening. Giovanni had left. A few moments later he heard a shoe click on stone. Fear closed round him. Rapidly he scuffed out the tic-tac-toe diagram, put the nail in his pocket, went to the wall, and was ready when the man called. Again he said nothing at all, but from a light clanking and his movements across the cell Dave realized that he had brought another bucket and was taking the used one away. Like mucking out a stable, he thought. A cow byre. Yes, that's spot on. All I am to them is an animal they're going to make money out of. They'll keep me alive as long as it suits them, but that's all. But I'm not going to be their animal. I'm going to be me. I'm going to stay human, and Giovanni's going to help me. I mustn't let them know about Giovanni. He's mine.

The man had left more food, the same as that morning. Dave ate as quickly as he could. He was hungry and wanted to finish before it was taken away, but this time the man didn't come back. Giovanni didn't seem to show up either, but Dave wasn't sure. Perhaps just eating was enough to make him feel himself, human. Nobody else can eat for you. He didn't need Giovanni.

He didn't feel like returning to tic-tac-toe, so he spread some of the squares of torn paper out on the floor and tried piecing them together. Most of it seemed to be stuff about Italian football, but he found a *Peanuts* strip. That hurt.

Before long the light began to fade, so Dave rearranged the bed while he could still see, took off his sneakers and socks and jeans, and lay down in his T-shirt and underpants. He wasn't sure that he was going to sleep but he closed his eyes.

"OK, Giovanni," he whispered. "Thanks for showing up. Bedtime now. Sleep well. And no sighing, please."

It turned out that after yesterday he was still tired enough to sleep fairly well, but when he finally woke fear and worry rushed in on him. He dressed and lay down again, gazing at the ceiling and trying to concentrate on how he was going to get through the day. He'd had enough of tic-tac-toe. Checkers was a much better game. The board was easy. The problem was how to make the checkers. Twelve of each kind.

He was still thinking about this when the men came, more than just the one, because he heard a low voice speaking somewhere on the hillside close by. Then shoes on the stairs, as usual. He rose and went to the wall. This time the man walked straight over to him and fastened the drawstring round his neck.

"Come," said the voice.

With his heart thudding, Dave allowed himself to be led to the door. On hands and knees he felt his way up the stairs and onto the sharp slope of the hill.

"Stop down," said the voice behind him, so he halted, but the voice said, "On. *Avanti*," and a hand gave him a shove in the buttocks. Feeling his way, he crawled forward under bushes until he was lifted to his feet by the men waiting there. Dad's paid up, he thought, but he didn't believe it and didn't bother to hope. They're going to kill me, he thought, but he didn't believe that either. It was too soon.

They took him a short distance and made him sit on a lump of rock. He heard them moving about close by. Again there seemed to be three of them. The sun warmed deliciously on his shoulders. Something—a newspaper—was put into his grasp and his hands were positioned to hold it across his chest.

"Shut eyes," said the voice.

He did so and the bag was untied and removed from his head.

"Open eyes," said the voice. "Stay."

The glare of sunlight blinded him and made him blink and screw his eyes up. When he could begin to see he made out that a man was standing in front of him and looking at him through the viewfinder of a camera. The man was wearing a hood with eye and mouth slits, a blue denim shirt buttoned at the wrists, blue jeans, and dirty sneakers. Behind him rose a steep hillside covered with wiry scrub. There must have been a hundred hillsides like that on the island.

The man took several pictures with the camera. It was an instant one, and Dave looked steadfastly at it while the man waited for each picture to develop. From the movements behind him he guessed that the other two men were holding up some kind of sheet as a backdrop, so that all that would show was Dave sitting on a boulder and holding that day's newspaper.

When they had finished they put the bag on his head and took him back to the cell. Apart from the voice instructing him when to crawl under the bushes and stand again and feel his way down the stairs, they said nothing to him at all. They left him food and water and a fresh bucket, and did not come back till the evening.

He went back to the bed and lay there, shuddering. He was their animal. If they'd wanted to shoot him instead of photographing him they'd have done it just as efficiently, and with just as little feeling. If they decided to cut off bits of him to send to Dad to put pressure on him, it would mean no more to them than docking a puppy's tail. Every time they came, day after day after day, he was going to be smothered by the same numbing, shriveling dread.

He must count the days. He must do it so that they didn't know he was doing it. An animal can't count. It would be something else human. Marks in the dirt, like the tic-tac-toe board? They would see them and scuff them out and take his food away to punish him for trying to be human. Scratches on the wall, which only he could see? Yes.

He rose, picked up the bowl of food, and knelt by the shaped stone in the wall opposite the door. Chewing while he worked, with the rusty nail he scratched three short vertical lines, starting in the top left-hand corner. Three days. Standing back to see how they looked, he discovered that they were much more noticeable from a distance than they had seemed from close up, so he rubbed dirt into them until they had almost vanished.

How many days in a row? Using his forefinger, he started to count off the imaginary days. Halfway across the stone he discovered they were already there, seven of them, more slanting than his and more widely spaced. Moving to a different angle, he began to see more, all very faint, but once he'd found them unmistakable, almost three full lines . . .

At his elbow somebody sighed.

He spun, but there was no one there. He was certain the sigh had not come from his own lips. It must have been in his mind.

He swallowed, his heart pounding, and took hold of himself.

''Hi,'' he said. ''These yours? This how long you were in here? Let's see . . .''

He counted the second row—forty-eight days. Ninety-six, and call it another forty. Four months, plus. Jesus!

''Don't let's think about it,'' he said. ''Listen, I had an idea in the night. Ever played checkers? It's draughts in England, but I call it checkers because Dad's the only one I ever play it with. I thought we might give it a go. OK?''

It took him a good long while to set up, but long whiles were what he needed, so he didn't lose patience. He began by scuffing around in the dirt for chips of stone and mortar, and feeling along the walls for bits he could ease out without making the man think he was doing anything to try and escape. He found about twenty, but some of them weren't much good so he picked out the best twelve. Next he chose straws from the bed, moistened them with water from the bottle to make them less brittle, and wound them one by one round his finger and tucked the loose ends several times through to hold the circle in shape. Some broke and some wouldn't stay put, but he carried on until he had a dozen little hoops of straw.

Finally he smoothed the area which he had used for tic-tac-toe, measured the distances with the nail, and carefully drew out the sixty-four squares of a checkerboard. To tell the black squares from the white he put a cross into alternate squares. All the while he chattered to Giovanni about what he was doing.

"Not bad," he said as he started to lay the pieces out. "I'm using the black squares instead of the white because it won't matter so much if I smudge them. Right. Toss for start?"

He balanced one of the spare chips on his thumb.

"Flat side up, you start, bump side, I do."

He flipped the chip.

"You start," he said. "That means you have the straws. Dad says this is the best move. OK?"

He made the first few moves of one of the openings Dad had taught him.

"Right, now you've got a couple of options . . ."

He played on, trying to put one lot of plans out of his mind while he looked at the possibilities for the other. Nothing spoke in his mind to tell him what Giovanni wanted. He hadn't expected it to. Checkers wasn't like feelings or imaginings. It was something you did with the logical bit of your mind, and madness wasn't logical. Well, maybe it had its own kind of logic, but it wasn't the sort that would work on a checkerboard. The only difference that Giovanni made was that if he'd simply been playing himself, left hand against right, sometimes he'd have taken moves back to try something else. That didn't seem right with Giovanni. The game ended in a draw.

Next he forced himself to do some exercises, press-ups and full knee bends and toe touching and stuff, setting himself targets and not giving up till he'd reached them.

"Got to tell you, this is not my scene," he muttered. "Kids at school would have hysterics if they saw me. But look at it this way. It's going to be pretty good hell stuck in here week after week—no offense, Giovanni—but at least if I keep in reasonable shape it won't be quite such hell as if I'm feeling grotty, not having any exercise day after day. Right? Anyway, that'll do. Let's not get fanatical about it. Like another game of checkers?"

They played again, and then Dave talked for a bit, about Mum and Chris and the kids, and after that they had another game, and so the day wore on. Around what he guessed was the middle of the afternoon Dave said, "Let's try speed checkers for a change. Real lightning. Five seconds a move. Toss? OK, I start."

He dashed through the opening moves and scrambled on. With almost no time to think, Dave found himself making the moves pretty well on impulse, his hand hovering over the pieces and snatching the one beneath it as his lips reached the count of five. It was close until near the end, when he was reaching for one of Giovanni's pieces, changed his mind and moved another and then, after his next move, found he'd left Giovanni with the chance to take three pieces in a turn. Absurdly that put him on his mettle, just as if he'd been playing a real opponent. Still keeping to the count, he fought back, thinking about his own moves and barely glancing at the board from Giovanni's point of view before he moved for him, but it was no use. He was creamed. What was more, he minded.

Minded, that is, for the moment or two it took him to realize how absurd it was. He laughed aloud.

"Watch it," he said. "I take after my dad some ways, and he's not a good loser. Anytime he loses it's a plot against him. With the FBI in it too. . . . You know, I should have got back. I was doing your moves any old how . . . wasn't I? Wasn't I, Giovanni?"

He tidied the board up, set the pieces out, and tried again, but this time the random moves he made for Giovanni really were random and Dave won without effort.

"OK," he said. "So I was trying too hard not to try. It's going to be some trick, this, Giovanni, making nonsense moves without thinking about the nonsense. Let's give it a rest now, shall we, and try again tomorrow? I don't want the goons finding this stuff when they come."

He picked up the pieces, folded them into a couple of the sheets of torn newspaper, and hid them under the straw. It struck him that the men might at some point search him, so he took the nail out of his pocket and inserted it between two of the flagstones until the bent head was level with the floor. He smoothed out the board and drew a couple of tic-tac-toe games in, because it was obvious he'd been up to something there. Doing these things to deceive them made him feel good. Whether he played checkers or not didn't matter a bit to them, probably, but it mattered to him not just because it was a way of getting through the endless days, but because it was one little bit of his life they weren't in control of, because they didn't know about it.

Eleven days followed, all on much the same pattern, apart from Dave's not being taken out again to be photographed. He began to long for a change of clothes. At home Mum was always getting at him to change more often, but he couldn't be bothered. Now a clean shirt would have been paradise. On the evening of the fourth day the man who took the bucket away and brought the food wasn't the one with the voice. *"Domani domenica,"* he told Dave. Apparently he didn't speak any English at all, and Dave had no idea what he'd been talking about until the next day's food didn't come for what must have been several hours later than usual. It was a double ration, and the man who brought it changed the buckets at that point. It took Dave quite a while to realize that this must be Sunday. That's what the man had been telling him the night before. Yes, the picnic had been on a Saturday. So kidnappers went to Mass on Sundays, like almost everyone else on the island. Perhaps that was why they had left him his gold cross.

Slowly over these days the way they played checkers changed, as Dave learnt to attend to what Giovanni wanted, not pushing him for an answer or rushing in with his own ideas, but waiting, listening, the way the silence which was Giovanni listened. At first he could only do it with speed games, and then not all the time, but after a while he developed a system of reaching for each piece in turn, keeping arm and hand relaxed, not expecting anything, and he'd find he was picking up a piece and moving it almost without noticing what he was doing. It didn't always work, because his Dave-mind couldn't help interfering sometimes—or if not actually interfering at least watching what was happening and thinking about it—and that spoilt things. But when it did work they had some interesting games, because Giovanni seemed to think of moves which Dave mightn't have. They were well matched and often had close finishes, winning, losing, or drawing about equally.

When they weren't playing Dave thought about it quite a bit, and talked to Giovanni about it sometimes.

"It's really interesting," he said. "Most of the time, as far as I'm concerned, you're pretty well as real as I am, and you're different from me—somebody else. But if I had to bet my life on it—if the goons came in and pointed a gun at me and said, 'We're going to shoot you unless you tell us whether Giovanni's real or not, and you've got to get it right'——then I'd have to say I've made you up. I'm hallucinating you. You're a trick of my mind. Those lines on the stone, for instance——I don't think I'm hallucinating them. They're there all right, but somebody else made them, and I just worked them into my Giovanni hallucination.

"But if you're a trick of my mind, you're some trick. You realize I can play a game of checkers against myself with part of my mind thinking for me, and knowing all about it, and another part of my mind thinking just as hard for you and I just don't know that's happening? Weird."

On the fourteenth morning of his captivity Dave woke with violent diarrhea. It was before dawn but he just got to the bucket in time, groping across the cell in the dark. Almost before he had finished he was on his knees vomiting into the reeking mess. He cleaned himself up as best he could and crawled back to the bed, where he lay sweating and shivering. He needed to get up twice more before he heard the voice call from the door. The hood was ready with the clothes by his bed. He groped for it, dragged it on, and turned his face to the wall.

The man must have realized what was up from the stench. Dave heard him pause inside the door. He came and crouched by the bed.

"Senti male?" said the voice. "Sick?"

Dave groaned. A hand slid under the hood and felt his forehead, then tried his pulse.

"OK. No food. Drink plenty water," said the voice.

131

The man left, taking the bucket. When he brought it back some while later he placed it by the bed and left again without a word.

By evening Dave was delirious. From then on it was sometimes night and sometimes day but mostly dreams. There were people in the room sometimes. Somebody, a woman, he thought, washed him carefully in tepid water. Another time somebody took his temperature and pulse and laid him on his back, and hands that knew what they were doing felt inquiringly over his stomach. In his dream the hands belonged to someone who was deadly afraid. Later there was medicine, bitter and shriveling in the mouth but causing a comfortable glow once swallowed. After that, sleep. And through the nights and days and wakings and sleepings, in dreams, in the times when he was aware of the shrill of the cicadas and almost knew where he was and why, a feathery cool touch on his forehead, a something in his hand too vague to be another hand, but patiently holding his, hour after endless, restless hour.

On the morning after they had given him the medicine he woke and saw Giovanni standing by his bed.

Dave knew at once it was him. He was a dark-haired boy with a rather square face and a deep dimple in his chin. He had eyebrows with an upward tuft at the outer ends, soft brown eyes, and a large mouth with smile marks at the corners. He looked very sure of himself, almost grown up, though Dave guessed he was probably about fifteen. He was wearing a white shirt, open at the collar, a brown cardigan, slacks—not jeans—and absurd pale brown suede shoes with laces and pointy toes. It was as if he'd been dressed for a play set about forty years back, Dave reckoned. Something like that.

In spite of his being so obviously there, so obviously himself, Dave could see he wasn't solid. Not that he was transparent or misty or anything like that. He was more like a really good 3-D TV image might be—you could tell that if you put your hand out it would go right through it. Even if he'd been feeling less feeble Dave wouldn't have wanted to try that. It wouldn't have felt right—it would have been an intrusion.

None of this surprised him. He hadn't expected it, but somehow he was ready for it to happen.

"Hi," he said. "Good to see you."

Giovanni smiled and said something but Dave heard nothing, or if he did it was only the faintest whisper of a whisper. When Giovanni sat down the straw beneath him did not stir, but when he patted the back of Dave's hand Dave felt the faint touch and recognized it from his delirium. He didn't feel like talking. He felt emptied, wasted away, barely real—just like Giovanni, in fact. He wondered how many days he'd been ill—three or four, he thought, but there was no way of telling.

After a while Giovanni cocked his head, said something, and rose. He smiled down at Dave, raised a hand, and walked away into the niche in the corner, out of sight. A couple of minutes later Dave heard the man's shoes on the stairs. He felt too feeble to rise and he couldn't see what they'd done with the hood, so he rolled over to face the wall and covered his face with his hands. The man didn't call out, but simply unlocked the door and came in. The footsteps came to the bed. After a pause Dave felt the rough hand on his forehead.

"You hearing me?" said the voice.

"Yes. I think I'm a bit better . . ."

"OK. No talk. Shut eyes."

Dave heard slight movements and the chink of metal on glass.

"OK. Now sit. *Medicina,*" said the voice.

An arm slid under his shoulders and helped him to raise himself onto his elbows. A spoon nudged at his lips. He sucked carefully at the bitter stuff, and barely prevented himself from coughing it out, but as it trickled down toward his stomach the glow of warmth began to spread through him. He sighed and lay back. That's good stuff, he thought, whatever it is. He wondered if it had opium in it, or something. He wasn't into drugs, though he'd tried pot a couple of times. This wasn't the same, but the effect was sort of like. Perhaps that was why he could see Giovanni now. Opium was supposed to make you see funny things.

"OK," said the voice. "I bring little food. Drink plenty water."

He left. Dave lay where he was, feeling weak and stupid but strangely happy. Things weren't really any better. He was still being held for ransom by these ruthless bastards, and he was still certain that Dad wasn't going to play ball and he'd be stuck in this hole for months and probably never get out alive, but it didn't matter. He realized that even when the man had been in the room with him he hadn't been afraid. It would have been too much effort. He was wondering vaguely about this when he fell asleep.

He was woken by the feet on the stair, but he still didn't have the energy to be afraid. The man didn't come in at once. Instead there were noises of metal on metal, followed by a low, vague roaring which it took Dave a couple of minutes to recognize as the sound of a camping stove. It stopped, the lock rattled, and the voice called, "Shut eyes."

Dave did so. The man came in, told him to sit, and tied a blindfold round his head. Dave could already smell the meaty steam of some kind of broth. The man supported his shoulders and with no apparent impatience held a mug to his lips while he slowly sipped. The soup was pretty good, with herbs and garlic in it. It was probably what the man was having for his own lunch. Dave finished and lay back.

"Thank you," he said without thinking. The man didn't answer.

He slept again, and when he woke Giovanni was there, sitting patiently by the bed.

"Hi," said Dave. "How does it feel to be an opium dream?"

Giovanni smiled but said nothing.

"I'm pretty feeble," said Dave. "Not up to checkers, anyway. Sorry about that."

Giovanni shook his head and made a forget-it gesture with his hands.

"I hope there's more of that soup," said Dave. "One thing about these goons—they're not slobs. They do the job right. I wonder if I couldn't persuade them to give up kidnapping and open a restaurant, and we'd get Dad to put up the capital. He wouldn't mind . . . Hey! You mean you can hear me?"

Giovanni nodded.

"And you understand English?"

Giovanni gave a little shrug, tilted his head, and fluttered his right hand, palm down. *A little bit.* He could talk with his hands better than some English people can talk with their mouths.

"I can't hear you, you know."

A different shrug. A different gesture. *Doesn't matter.*

"The question is, are you going to stay around when they stop giving me the medicine. I suppose I could go on being ill, but the runs are going to be tricky to fake."

Sorry, you've lost me.

"Forget it, I was just talking."

And even that much talk had been an effort. He closed his eyes and lay still, enjoying the feel of his own body slowly righting itself, of the goodness in the soup starting to seep its way through his digestion toward his bloodstream.

Giovanni stayed with him all afternoon while he dozed and woke and chatted for a minute or two at random and lay silent until he dropped off to sleep again. Finally he woke and found Giovanni gone, and a minute later heard the footsteps, followed by the roaring of the stove. This time, though, the man fed him a new kind of medicine, a sweet yucky cream, and left him with two soft-boiled eggs and some bread and a bottle of some sort of commercial drink, fizzy and sweet. Peering at the tiny print on the label, barely legible in the dim light, Dave worked out that it must be something like Gatorade, with glucose in it. They were looking after their sick animal pretty well, he thought. They'd got the vet in, and now they were following instructions, so it had better be worth their while. He peeled the eggs, put them in the bowl, and mopped them up with the bread, enjoying every mouthful. Giovanni did not return, and in an hour or so it was dark. He slept all night as peacefully as if he had been in his own bed.

Next morning Dave was already dressed by the time he heard the footsteps, so he rose and stood facing the wall and wearing the hood as he had done before his illness. He had debated whether to do this or to go on being an invalid, and had decided that he would rather choose himself to do it than wait to be told to. The man didn't call out, and grunted to himself when he came in and saw Dave standing there, but this gave Dave no satisfaction because by then the old dread had descended. The man removed the hood and blindfolded him so as to feed him more of the new medicine. When he'd gone Dave found that as well as breakfast—bread and cold chicken—he'd left a plastic bag with clean clothes, used but fresh-smelling and about the right size.

Dave changed, folding the old clothes into the bag, and ate his breakfast. Next, falling back without thought into the old routine, he prized his nail from the crack and knelt by the calendar stone to record a fresh day. He'd decided to leave a gap for his illness, but as he started to scratch the first mark he was aware of Giovanni standing by his shoulder, though he had neither heard nor seen him come. He looked up.

"Hi," he said. "How many days is it, do you know? I lost count."

Giovanni held his hand up with fingers and thumb spread.

"Thanks," said Dave, and carefully scratched the five marks in, and then dimmed them with dirt. After the first two, which had overlapped with what he thought of as Giovanni's old calendar, he had allowed his line to dip so that it ran along the gap between Giovanni's first and second lines, matching the one above it day for day. It was part of the whole business of keeping himself human, deciding on the right way to do the few small things he could do of his own will, and then doing them right. That was how Giovanni had kept himself human too. It was important not to cover up his older record, so that both of them would still be there to find long after Dave, too, was gone.

When he had finished he went back and lightly touched

in Giovanni's first nineteen marks, just enough so that they shouldn't be lost.

"OK?" he said.

Giovanni smiled and raised a thumb.

"Right," said Dave. "I don't know whether I'm up to checkers, but shall we give it a go? I sort of remember someone mucking around with the straw when I was ill. Let's hope they didn't find them."

In fact the checkers were where he had left them, under the bedding close in against the wall, but by the time he had drawn the board and laid them out he was exhausted and had to lie down. Giovanni settled cross-legged by the bed and waited patiently. It didn't seem to make any difference to him whether he sat on the hard flagstones or the straw. Of course if your body's not really there, Dave thought, it probably can't feel things. It doesn't ache or get cramp or pins and needles from staying too long in one position. But to look at, Giovanni seemed just as "there" as he had yesterday—still somehow not quite solid, but opaque and definite. The change of medicine didn't seem to have made any difference. That was something.

"OK," he said after a while, "let's give it a go."

He scooped a couple of armfuls of straw nearer the board, spread one of the blankets onto it, and lay down on his side, propping himself on his elbow. Giovanni settled opposite him.

"This is great," said Dave. "You can just point to me what you want. You start."

They played a slow game. Dave needed to rest a couple of times more but he kept his end up and they finished in a draw. His next rest drifted into a doze, and when he woke he realized that several hours must have passed. What's more, he was now actually hungry. He didn't feel like another game, so he simply lay and talked, or else just lay, barely thinking.

"Another thing about my dad," he said at one point, "he's got a pretty good voice. He says he wanted to be a professional singer—folk, like Pete Seeger or someone—but his dad made him go into Doggony Ribs instead. I don't think that's true. I think it's just one of the things he tells himself. He just loves being rich, you see, and having his own airplane and stuff, but that doesn't mean he can't sing really nicely. He's got a banjo he takes camping, and he likes to sit on a rock by the fire and sing when we've finished eating. Songs like 'El Paso' and 'Ghost Riders in the Sky' and 'Tom Dooley.' I mean, how phoney can you get? Here's this fifty-year-old guy who makes his living selling junk food, and he's sitting out on a piece of prairie which he owns far as you can see, every direction, and he's got his over-the-top cowboy outfit and his forty-thousand-dollar horse and he's singing these corny old songs . . . and it's great! There's stars and night smells and stuff, and the fire dying, and maybe a moon getting up so you can see a bit of snow along the tops of the mountains, and you sing your heart out. Me too. I can't sing like Dad, but that doesn't matter—I can follow. And they're terrific to sing, whatever anyone says. You know 'Tom Dooley'?"

Giovanni shook his head.

"I don't suppose you would," said Dave. "It's very American. I'd never heard it till Dad sang it. The story's a bit hard to get, but I think it's about this guy called Tom Dooley who killed some woman and went on the run. And he was hiding out in Tennessee when another guy called Grayson tracked him down and brought him back to face trial. And now he's been tried and he's waiting to be executed. Right? It starts straight in on the chorus:

> "Hang down your head, Tom Dooley.
> Hang down your head and cry.
> Hang down your head, Tom Dooley.
> Poor boy, you're going to die.

"Give it a go?

> "Hang down your head . . .

"What's up?"

Giovanni wasn't singing. Or smiling. Instead he was looking at Dave, who was lying half propped on the straw. He shook his head and gave one of his small shrugs, not getting it, bothered.

"Oh, come on, Giovanni. It's only a song! It doesn't mean anything. Anyway, I'm not. Not yet. If your calendar's anything to go by—supposing it was yours—it'll be three months, minimum, before they decide to cut their losses and pack it in. Anything can happen in three months. And I'm not going to stop singing my favorite songs because of these bastards!

> *"Hang down your head, Tom Dooley.*
> *Hang down your head and cry . . ."*

He watched Giovanni's lips start to move, and they sang all four lines together.

> *"I met her on the mountain . . ."*

sang Dave, and at the end of the verse conducted Giovanni into the chorus again. He sang with more than enjoyment, with a kind of exhilaration, discovering as he did so that what he'd just said without thinking was in fact true. He was not going to stop singing his favorite songs because of these bastards. That was another thing they couldn't take away from him, even if he had to sing them under his breath.

This mood was still on him when, a little later, Giovanni got up and slipped off into his corner. Dave heard the sound of a hard shoe on the stair, so he knew it was the man with the voice, but as he stood by the wall with the hood over his head and his arms above his shoulders and listened to the man moving about, he realized that for the first time he wasn't being crushed and made stupid by fear. Not that he had any impulse to demonstrate this by rebelling in some small way. He would go on being the model prisoner, but because he chose to—it was the only sensible thing—and not because he was paralyzed into obedience by fear. Right to the end he never lost that certainty.

Day followed day and then week followed week, almost without variation, until Dave's marks reached the end of the calendar stone and he started a second line. He wasn't ill again, but he didn't really get better either. He stayed weak and tired, and slept off and on through the day, sometimes even going into a doze halfway through a game of checkers. Then he would wake and find Giovanni sitting waiting the other side of the board, and he'd apologize and Giovanni would make his forget-it gesture, as if he had all the time in the universe. Which he had, of course.

Occasionally Dave still reminded himself that Giovanni wasn't real, not even a real ghost—that he was Dave's own hallucination which he kept up to stop himself from going mad. But mostly he didn't think about it. Giovanni was there all right, and he was probably the ghost of someone who'd been held for ransom here by the goons' fathers, or grandfathers, even, until either he'd died of some illness or they'd killed him. It was sad, but it had happened so long ago that the sadness didn't seem to matter much anymore, even to Giovanni.

Being a ghost didn't make Giovanni seem much more different than being an Italian, but Dave couldn't quite forget it. Not being able to hear anything he said was one thing. Another was that he didn't like to be touched. Dave from the first had felt that it would have been a sort of bad manners to force his own solidity and reality onto Giovanni's vagueness, his hardly-thereness, by coming into contact with it, and after a while he noticed that Giovanni too was careful to keep his distance. Neither of them wanted to be reminded, more than they could help, of the immense difference between them, the difference between being alive and being dead.

Giovanni would show up while Dave was marking the calendar stone after breakfast, standing behind Dave's shoulder, watching. They'd exchange greetings and Dave would finish making the mark and rub a bit of dirt into it, and then he'd use the nail to draw out the checkerboard and fetch the pieces and they'd play a first game. They didn't play endlessly, starting another game as soon as they'd finished the first, but spaced them out, playing two or three in the morning and again in the afternoon. They took it seriously, thinking about their moves sometimes for several minutes at a time. And Dave thought they were getting better, learning about it from practice, though they still played about level.

Toward the end of the day they had a singsong, all Dad's songs Dave could remember, though he'd had to make up lines to fit the tunes for some of them. They always finished with "Tom Dooley." As far as Dave was concerned it was a sort of talisman. He could sing it because it wasn't about him. It meant he was going to live tomorrow, and the day after that, and the day after that . . . He kept his voice down, of course. The goons would punish him if they heard him making any kind of noise you could hear out on the hillside. But, singing quietly, he still gave it all he'd got.

One thing did change, but so gradually that for a long time Dave didn't realize it was happening. He started to hear Giovanni's voice, not the actual words, but the sound of the words, like the sound of a radio turned so low that you can only just hear that somebody's speaking, but not what they're saying. Because of the cicadas shrilling in the bushes outside it was never really silent in the cell. Dave was so used to them that he didn't normally notice them, but they were there and at first they drowned out the faint whisper of Giovanni's voice. Then either it grew slowly stronger or Dave learnt to listen through the noise of the cicadas, but still without noticing he started to hear it. Not that Giovanni spoke much—there wasn't any point—but once Dave had registered that it was happening he realized that he'd been taking it for granted for a long while.

It must have been a foul day outside. Inside the cell it was almost too dark to play checkers. It was cold, too. Dave wore one of the blankets over his clothes, keeping it on by clutching it round his neck. The man who had brought his food had squelched as he moved, and now Dave could hear the hiss of rain into the bushes outside. The wind threshed to and fro. The cicadas were silent.

Dave was staring at the board, concentrating on a chain of possible moves, when Giovanni spoke.

"Hey! I heard that!" said Dave.

Giovanni smiled and pointed at the airholes. His lips

moved. It seemed lighter outside and the rain seemed to have stopped and the wind for the moment had died away, almost into silence.

"Yeah, I know," said Dave. "It's going to turn out fine, after all, and a fat lot of good it'll do either of us. But listen, I heard you! Don't you get it? You said something loud enough for me to hear."

Giovanni looked surprised, frowned, and spoke slowly with a lot of lip movement. Dave caught the faint whisper—three syllables, and the upward lilt of a question.

"That time too," he said. "Not what you actually said, but I could hear you were talking. Let's try if I shut my eyes."

He did so and strained for the sound, but it was still too faint. They experimented, moving around, Giovanni speaking directly into Dave's ear, but by now the wind had risen again, and then the sun came out and the cicadas began, so they went back to checkers.

More days passed, and the gradual change continued, but now that Dave was aware of it he noticed each small improvement in his hearing—first the ability to pick up the whisper through the sound of the cicadas, then to make out the shape and tone of the remark, enough to hear whether Giovanni had been talking English or Italian, then a word here and there, and then, straining to listen, whole sentences, and they could have a proper conversation.

It was very tiring, concentrating so hard on the tiny sounds, but Dave seemed to be finding everything tiring.

He had spent almost fifty days now in the cell, and though he tried to take exercise—knee bends, toe touchings, sit-ups, walking a hundred times each way, corner to corner of the cell, morning and evening—it didn't seem to help much. It was an effort to get out of bed and stand against the wall when the man called to him first thing, it was an effort to concentrate right through a game of checkers, it was an effort to sing more than a couple of songs at the end of the day. And now it was an effort to talk and listen for more than ten minutes at a time.

"How come you talk English?" said Dave.

"My governess—Miss Wolf—English," said Giovanni.

"Governess!" said Dave.

"Only when I am little," explained Giovanni. "But she visit often the *palazzo* to speak English with my papa."

He laughed and gave a knowing little jerk of the head, so that Dave instantly understood that Miss Wolf wasn't one of those grim, gray, thin-lipped governesses you read about. *Hadn't been,* not *wasn't.* Giovanni was talking about forty years ago, or more, only Dave wasn't sure if he knew that. And he didn't feel like asking, nor about what had happened to Giovanni in the end, or anything like that. It was the sort of thing you didn't talk about.

"You live in a *palazzo*?" he said.

"*Si.* My papa has five, but two are empty, and one too small. My grandmother live in that one."

"Five *palazzos*! Dad's got six homes, but two of them are only apartments, and none of them's a *palazzo*. What's it like, living in a *palazzo*?"

Giovanni started to explain. One *palazzo* was in Rome, and another out in the hills somewhere, and they moved to and fro. There was something about the servants not wanting to come back after the war, but by then Dave was losing it again, so that though Giovanni's English seemed pretty good it was like listening to a foreign language Dave about half-knew. Bits made sense but the whole thing was fuzzy, and trying to work it out just made him tireder still.

"Sorry," he interrupted. "I'll have to pack it in for the moment. This is too like hard work."

So they talked off and on through the day, in dribs and drabs, between dozes and games of checkers and stretches of doing almost nothing, with Dave just lying on the straw like a dog in its basket, letting time drift past. In the evening, for a change, Giovanni taught Dave an Italian song, *"Aspetta Qualcuno?"* which seemed to be about a guy trying to pick up a girl and not getting anywhere. Not Dad's sort of song at all, but Giovanni hammed it up beautifully. He wouldn't have had much trouble picking the girl up, Dave thought.

Next morning Dave was settling down to scratch his forty-ninth mark onto the calendar stone when the men came back and took him out to be photographed. When he had crawled clear of the bushes and they told him to stand, he almost fell, and his legs seemed so uncertain that instead of simply guiding him the short distance to the photographing place, they had to support him with a hand under each arm.

Then there was some delay. As he sat on the rock, waiting, his skin crawled with the unfamiliar caress of sunlight. It seemed to be a still, clear day, but he could both feel and smell that it was no longer summer. Forty-nine days. Half of August gone, and all of September. It was early October now, so it wasn't surprising that the warmth of the morning was merely pleasant and the tang of last night's chill still lingered faintly in the air. Even so, the sunlight seemed to strike clean through him, as if he was hardly there at all, a ghost like Giovanni. Suppose Giovanni were out here on the hillside, in this brightness, would he be visible, even to Dave? Maybe if I go on getting fainter like this, Dave thought, next time they bring me out there won't be anything to photograph.

It was only a whimsy, a fancy that floated into his mind while he waited, but once there it changed. He was slowly becoming fainter. Giovanni was slowly becoming less faint. The two things went together. If they kept him long enough in the cell the time would come when Giovanni would be the solid one and he would be the ghost.

It was nonsense. It couldn't happen. Giovanni was just his own hallucination, nothing more . . . but once lodged in his mind the idea changed again, growing as it did so, becoming more hideous. These men were not kidnappers. They were friends of Giovanni's, brothers, yes, their brother Giovanni had died, years ago, but now they'd found this way of bringing him back to life by witchcraft. There was a lot of witchcraft on the island, Chris said. And all the stuff about ransoms and photographs was just a cover so that Dave didn't suss out what was happening, because it depended on him trusting Giovanni and thinking he was a friend . . .

And it was still nonsense, but it wouldn't go away. Dave barely noticed the rest of what happened out on the hillside. Even when at last they took off the hood and he had to endure the shock of brilliant daylight he simply blinked and waited for his eyes to get used to it and then stared at the camera until they had finished. They covered his head again and helped him back in under the bushes and down the stairs.

Though he felt utterly drained with the effort of the last half hour, Dave didn't go and collapse on the bed as soon as they released him, but removed his hood and stayed where he was, leaning against the wall, waiting till he was sure they were clear.

"Giovanni?"

From where he was standing Dave could see straight into the niche. Giovanni appeared out of the darkness at its further end. He looked at Dave, puzzled.

"Sorry about this," said Dave, "but there's something we've got to sort out. How come you seem to be getting stronger all the time while I seem to be getting weaker? Is it something you're doing to me?"

He'd half-expected Giovanni to give one of his shrugs and laugh it off, trying to get away with it by charm, but he didn't. He looked at Dave for a few seconds, unsmiling, and nodded.

"Sì," he whispered. "I do this."

"Jesus! I don't believe it!"

"You also do this, Dave."

"What do you mean?"

"You give. I take. You do not choose. I do not choose. It is happening. This place is doing this to us."

"OK . . . if you're right, what are we going to do about it? Let's sit down."

With immense relief Dave settled onto the straw. Perhaps he was simply too tired not to believe Giovanni—suspicion was too much effort. No, it wasn't just that. It was the way Giovanni had taken it. Not that either. It was Giovanni himself, everything about him, his whole nature. When he was there, Dave knew without having to think about it that it was nonsense not to trust him.

"I tell you," said Giovanni. "When you come—came—to this place you feel I am here. You speak to me. You make me . . . real for yourself, yes?"

"I suppose so. I needed someone."

"But you make me also real for myself. I am here—I and others also—a long time before you come. But I am not real. How can I tell you? I am an idea only. Or a memory. Not real. But when you talk to me, you begin to make me real. You give me this, talking to me. I do not take it without you give—giving—it to me. Understand?"

"Yes, I remember. Jesus, I needed you!"

"So. And now you are—were—ill. Very sick. I stayed with you. I am there because even more you need me, only to hold my hand. Someone to hold the hand, when you are so sick. And all of the time you are making me more real. I feel it . . . move, moving like water . . ."

His hands explained what he was trying to say.

"Flowing?" suggested Dave.

"Yes, flowing from you to me, so when you are well, now you can see me because you have given me this. I do not—no, I did not think then that when you give, I take. I did not see this, but it is so. When I am made more real, you must be not so real. I take *from* you. Understand?"

"Yeah, that's how it feels."

"So what must I do? I think perhaps if I do not touch you . . . When I am touching you, I feel the flowing, into me, through my hand . . ."

"Yeah, I've noticed you've been keeping clear. I thought it was because it felt a bit creepy to you being touched by . . . by someone like me . . ."

"No. No, it is good, this feeling. It is like standing in the sun when you are cold inside. Good."

"I didn't realize. But it's still going on, isn't it? The reason I can hear you isn't that I've got better at hearing. It's because your voice is stronger. Hell, what are we going to do? I don't want you to go away, but when the goons took me outside just now I could only just about stand."

"But I take so little, Dave, so very little . . . I show you. You put the checkers on the floor."

Dave groped down under the straw against the wall and

found the two envelopes of newspaper that he had made to contain the checkers.

"Two only," said Giovanni. "One stone, one straw. So. Now you lift the stone. Good. Now the straw. So. You do it easy—easily—yes?"

"Well, they don't weigh that much, not for me . . . I see what you're getting at, though."

"Now, I do it," said Giovanni.

He crouched over the two checkers and with his forefinger and thumb took hold of the end of the knot of straw that projected upward, but there wasn't enough for him to grip properly and it slipped from his grasp. To help him Dave tilted the checker onto its edge so that he could take hold of it using both thumbs and forefingers like two sets of pincers. He heaved. His hands quivered with the effort of maintaining their grip. The checker rose a couple of inches from the floor before once more he lost his grip and let it fall. By then he was gasping.

"OK, I get the point," said Dave. "Don't kill yourself trying the other one. Maybe it's because I've still not properly got over being sick, so I notice the little bit extra you're using. I ought to be able to spare that much, I'd have thought. We'll give it another couple of weeks, shall we, and see how we're doing. The goons must have noticed I wasn't up to much. Maybe they'll try and feed me up a bit now. I'll have a bit of a rest, and then I'll mark up the calendar, and then we'll try a game of checkers. OK?"

———

The day fell back into the usual pattern, games of checkers with rests between, and a few minutes' talk, and another rest, and another game, and time drifting by until something—perhaps mere habit, perhaps a heightened awareness of the tiny changes of sound and light from the airholes—told Dave that evening was coming on.

"All right," he said. "Time for the concert."

He settled cross-legged with an imaginary banjo across his knees. He felt stronger this evening, so they sang half a dozen of their favorites, "El Paso" and *"Aspetta Qualcuno?"* and "The Yellow Rose of Texas," and finished as always with "Tom Dooley." Giovanni rose as they were swinging through the final chorus:

> *"Hang down your head, Tom Dooley.*
> *Hang down your head and cry.*
> *Hang down your head, Tom Dooley.*
> *Poor boy, you're going to die."*

He nodded, walked to his corner, smiled his wide, easy smile, and raised a hand. His lips moved.

"Ciao," he was saying.

"Ciao," said Dave, and watched him disappear into the darkness of the niche.

He's a really good guy, thought Dave. I was just being stupid out on the hillside.

The man came as usual, bringing food and a fresh bucket. He didn't speak, and there was nothing different about his visit from most other evenings. The days were shorter now, and it was almost too dark to see by the time Dave had finished his supper and groped his way into bed. He was lying there, waiting to fall asleep, when doubt and distrust came sidling back into his mind. It was something to do with the man's visit, something about the way he had moved round the room, that seemed to tell Dave that he knew Giovanni was there, knew all about him, that even now, at this very moment, Giovanni was out with him somewhere on the hillside, telling him what had happened, telling him that Dave had somehow guessed about their plot but that he, Giovanni, had managed to persuade him it was nonsense.

And nonsense it was. Dave knew that perfectly well, but it was no use telling himself, or trying to drive the idea away by thinking of other things, doing sums in his head, mapping imaginary journeys or whatever. It was like a door whose catch won't hold. The moment you let go of it, it pops open, and the stuff you were trying to tidy away is there in the open. When at last he got to sleep it was only for an hour or two, and he woke with the same stupid suspicions already fizzing in his mind, so strong despite their stupidity that he thought he must be getting his fever back. In the end he slept deeply, and woke only just before he heard the man's footsteps on the stairs. By the time Giovanni appeared it all seemed so silly and childish that he was ashamed to mention it.

The next three days followed the same pattern—as long

as Giovanni was there, companionship and trust. But then, when he vanished into his niche, nights of loneliness and miserable betrayal.

The third night was peculiarly bad. The nonsense invaded his dreams. He was being pursued across empty moorland by men with guns, pretending to be hunters. Somebody shadowy beckoned him into a place of hiding and left him there, but then he saw through a crack in the rock his rescuer talking to the hunters. Later he was riding across the prairie looking for Dad to warn him that the wolves were loose. He saw the spark of the campfire and rode toward it, but his horse was gone and he was trying to run, and Dad was sitting singing by the fire in his cowboy outfit. He had someone with him. Dave crawled at last into the camp and Dad looked up and said, "Who the hell are you?" And Giovanni, sitting beside him, smiled at Dave and pretended not to know him . . .

He was woken in the middle of another nightmare by something light and chilly pressing against his cheek. He turned his head away but it followed.

A voice whispered "Wake, Dave. Quick! *Presto!*"

His eyelids dragged up. It was barely light. Somebody, Giovanni, was kneeling by the bed.

"Up! Quick!" came the urgent whisper.

Weakly Dave levered himself onto his elbows. Giovanni seized him by the arm as if trying to drag him to his feet, but Dave could barely feel the faint touch through his shirt. Groaning, he rose and stood.

Urgently Giovanni held out his hands for Dave's.

"Give! Give!" he whispered. "Quick!"

Unthinkingly Dave did as he was told. He seemed to have no will at all.

"What's up?" he muttered.

"No time," said Giovanni. "Give, Dave. Make me strong!"

"Hey . . . !"

"It is for you. Not me. It is no use for me. Only for you. Dave, give!"

"But why . . . ?"

"No. I cannot tell you. But listen, Dave. I give you back all you give—have given me. I will give all back!"

Dave looked at him. He remembered the night, and the night before and the night before that. Giovanni was gazing at him, urgent, earnest, and still everything that he had been to Dave through all those endless days. No, the nights were nonsense. He would trust the days. He had to.

"All right, if you say so," he said.

He closed his eyes, bowed his head, and relaxed.

The life flowed from him. He could feel it, a gentle steady movement, out and away through his arms and wrists, and a faint unusual warmth where his palms touched Giovanni's. Elsewhere he felt cold, colder than the early-morning air, a creeping chill that seemed to be rising into him from the floor, the chill of deep earth that has never been touched by the sun.

"Enough," said Giovanni in a much stronger voice. "Now, help me to dress in your clothes."

He let go of Dave's hands and stooped to pick up the

jeans which Dave had left folded as usual by the bed, but though he managed to heave the waistband a few inches from the floor the weight of the cloth dragged it from his grasp.

"No," he said. "You must help."

Dave too found the jeans strangely heavy as he arranged them so that Giovanni could step into the legs. Giovanni was still wearing his slacks, but their cloth seemed insubstantial, hardly there at all, compared to the hard denim. As Dave heaved the jeans up the slacks disappeared into them, became them. He fastened the waistband and zipped the fly. There was no belt—the goons had taken it. Next the sweater. As Giovanni took the weight of it he staggered and almost fell. Dave caught him and eased his arms into the sleeves.

"What about my shoes?" he said. "You'll have to take yours off."

"No. Wait. Too heavy. Help me. To the wall. Then shoes. And the hood also. Quick! They are coming!"

Dave drew Giovanni's arm round his shoulder and pretty well carried him across the cell. He weighed almost nothing, barely more than the clothes alone. Giovanni faced the wall and with a huge effort raised first one arm and then the other above his shoulders and placed them against the stonework.

"Now the shoes," he gasped.

Dave fetched them, knelt, placed them on either side of Giovanni's feet, leaned his shoulder against his thigh to help him balance, lifted a foot by the ankle, and with his other hand slid his own shoe under it and crammed the foot back down before Giovanni could fall. Again it was as if Giovanni's shoe didn't exist compared to the sneaker, and the foot, two or three sizes smaller than Dave's, slid in without effort. He crawled round and did the other shoe.

"They are here!" whispered Giovanni. "Quick, the hood! *Ciao*, Dave."

He turned his head and smiled, and Dave understood what was going to happen. I can't do this, he thought, but his lips said "*Ciao*, Giovanni," and he slid the hood down. Feet sounded on the stairs and he ran for the niche, but as he reached it he turned and hesitated. Giovanni had taken his right hand off the stonework, and slowly, effortfully, like someone moving under water, was crossing himself.

The voice called from beyond the door.

"I'm ready," he croaked, and scuttled to the darkest corner of the niche.

He crouched there, with his head in his hands and his eyes closed.

The lock rattled and the door grated on stone, but the man's footsteps made no sound on the thick dirt. Dave pressed the balls of his thumbs against his ears, but it was no use. Something struck him like a hammer on the back of the head. Then he was in darkness.

In the darkness he heard voices, sighs, curses, shouts of anger, sobs, groans, pleadings. He knew where they came from. There were others, Giovanni had said. He was not the first, nor Dave only the second, nothing like.

Then he was lying on stone, facedown, with a shaft of pure pain piercing his skull and a terrible empty sickness filling chest and stomach, but he knew where he was and why, and managed not to groan. He lay still. The headache throbbed and dwindled. Cautiously he lifted a hand to the back of his head and felt. Nothing, not even a bruise.

A heavy drumming racket passed close overhead, a helicopter. The sound faded and returned, rose to a roar and died. It had landed. Shouts. A shot, and another. Silently Dave worked himself onto hands and knees and inched toward the corner. Nobody there. The door closed. His sneakers, jeans, and sweater lay spread out beneath the calendar stone like the map of a sprawled body. The head was the hood. He walked over and picked it up. There were two neat round holes in it, on opposite sides, but no blood. Close to, it smelt singed.

He realized that this was why they had made him stand hooded against the wall from the very first day, so that if it ever came to this he would be just waiting there as usual, not suspecting anything, and the man would come in . . .

What bastards, he thought. What absolute bloody bastards.

He hesitated, picked the clothes up, and put them on. It felt strange, but it would have felt stranger not to. They were cold still, as if no one had worn them since last night.

160

So Giovanni was gone, not real anymore. Just a memory, an idea. What would have happened, Dave wondered, if I hadn't trusted him, if I hadn't let him persuade me, if it had been me standing by the wall when the man came in? Well, I'd be dead for a start, but Giovanni? He'd be gone too, an idea, a memory, because it had been me keeping him real . . . So you could say it didn't make any difference to him . . . All the same, he died for me. I let him die for me.

He stood there thinking about Giovanni until he heard, above the sound of the cicadas, voices moving around on the hillside, calling. He shouted back, but they were too far off, so he went and tried the door. There was no handle inside, and though he managed to work his fingertips in at the edge he couldn't budge it.

The voices came nearer. They were calling his name.

"Dave! Dave Doggony! You there, Dave?"

He shouted again. At first they didn't hear him, but then somebody passed close by. He knew the voice.

"Chris!" he yelled. "Here! It's me, Dave!"

"Dave! Hey! He's here! He's here! Dave, where are you?"

"Here. Under the ground. There's some stairs. You have to crawl in under the bushes. I think the door's locked."

"Right, we'll find it. Dick! Somebody tell . . . Dick! Here! This way!"

Voices gathering, shouts, questions, Chris telling them to be quiet. Dad's voice.

161

"Dave? You OK, fella? Tell me you're OK."

"I'm fine."

"Right, we'll soon have you out of there. How . . ."

But somebody had found the stairs and was rattling uselessly at the lock. There were shouts and orders in Italian. Dad's voice, now at the door.

"It's locked, Dave. Goddam massive padlock. They're fetching a saw. We'll soon have you out of there."

"I can wait. Is Mum there? Can somebody tell Mum?"

"Chris is calling her up right now."

A pause. People jostling. Dad's voice again.

"OK, Dave, it's the guy with the saw. No room for two down here, so I'm standing clear. But we did it, Dave! We did it! We won!"

The saw started to whine into steel. The racket filled the cell. Dave backed away, knelt, and scrabbled in the dirt beneath the calendar stone for his nail. He eased it out, moved on into the niche, and scuffed around with his shoes till he found a crack between two flagstones. He jabbed at the crack with the nail till he had made a short, deep slot, then lifted the gold chain from round his neck, undid the clasp, and slid the little cross free. Carefully he poked it down into the slot and smeared dirt back over to hide it.

I don't believe in any of this, he thought, but I bet Giovanni does.

He rose and stood with his head bowed.

"Holy Mother of God," he whispered. "I pray for the

162

soul of Giovanni. I don't know his name, but you do. Take care of him, please. Amen.''

There was a lull in the sawing, some problem, mutterings in Italian. Outside he heard Dad's voice again, bellowing to someone that they'd won. No, he thought, we didn't. It was Giovanni who'd won. He won it for us, because he'd lost it for himself, long, long ago.

THE LION TAMER'S DAUGHTER

Before all this happened I'd have told you there wasn't anything special about Melly, apart from her being a bit dopy sometimes, and maybe the business with the yellow dog, but that was a once-off.

I don't know that we'd have picked each other for friends if our mums hadn't been friends too. They'd got to know each other waiting for us outside junior school, and found we lived only a couple of streets apart, so they took turns collecting both of us. Then Melly's mum, Janice, got the chance of a full-time job and my mum, who just worked mornings, said she'd take care of Melly till Janice got home. That way we saw a lot of each other and got used to each other being around, a bit as if we'd been brother and sister, I suppose. We were both only children, and Melly's parents had split up.

We went on together from Ashley Junior to Ashley

High. Sometimes we were in the same classes, sometimes not. We each had our own lot of friends and we didn't hang about together at school, but we'd help each other out over anything we needed and Melly came home after school with me most days, long after it would have been all right for her to have her own key and go back to her own house.

My mum and dad were crazy about sailing, and ever since I could remember, Friday nights, they'd load me and the cats and themselves into the van and drive half the night to a little cottage we had at Penmaenan, in Wales, where they kept their boat. (We weren't rich people, mind you. The cottage was pretty primitive, and the boat was all they ever spent money on.) Sundays it was back in the van and all the way home to Coventry. Holidays were always sailing too, as much time off as they could get from their work.

It took them a while to get it that I wasn't that keen on sailing, even on fine days, and I loathed it when it was cold and wet. So some weekends they'd ask Melly along and she and I'd hang around at the cottage and Mrs. Pugh next door would keep an eye on us while they went out in the boat. Other times I'd stay back in Coventry at Melly's place. So all in all, you could say I knew her pretty well. But if you'd asked me to give you a list of my friends, I'd have started off telling you the three or four other boys I mostly hung around with, and then maybe I'd have said "and Melly, of course." Or maybe I'd have forgotten. Same with her, I should think.

We didn't have fights, that I remember. We were just easy with each other, and that's about it.

When I say Melly was sometimes a bit dopy, I don't mean she was stupid or silly. Most of the time she was ordinary, bright but not brilliant, better than plain but not pretty, with black hair and a bit of a foreign look, Italian or something. She was a chatterbox, and hung out with a gang of girls who were that way too, and when they got going it was like a flock of geese squawking away. You'd hear them coming round from the gym, fifty or sixty it sounded like, cackling and shrieking, but when they got to the corner you'd see it was just five or six of them, all talking at once and rolling their eyes and shrugging and waving their arms around. Body language, it's called.

But every now and then Melly would go dreamy and far away, and you'd pretty well have to pinch her to bring her back, and she'd still be sort of dazed as if she'd only just got out of bed, and grumpy too, which wasn't like her. It happened enough for one of the teachers to get the idea she might be on drugs. There were some kids at Ashley High who took drugs, but we knew who they were, and my lot didn't have much to do with them. Nor Melly either. She was too careful for that sort of thing.

The stuff with the yellow dog happened when we were a bit younger. One of Melly's crowd, Karen, had just had a birthday and she'd been given a puppy, and her mum had brought it along so she could walk it home. Melly and I and one or two others tagged along. Mum wasn't picking us up that day and we were supposed to go straight home, but Karen's wasn't far out of our way and the puppy was a beagle and dead cute.

We got to the edge of a big open place, playing fields and such, when this other dog came lolloping across. It was a large, bony thing, yellowy brown. It didn't seem to have an owner. It probably just wanted a sniff, the way dogs do, but Karen's mum got all anxious and started trying to shoo it off.

It didn't like that. It stopped in its tracks and looked at her. It put its head down and the fur on its shoulders stood straight up and it began stalking slowly toward us, growling in its throat as it came. All of a sudden it looked really scary.

Karen's mum started to back off, gabbling to Karen to pick the puppy up and telling the rest of us to get behind her. Then Melly walked past her and faced the dog.

"Beat it," she said. "Go on. Beat it."

The dog stopped and looked at her. It was still growling and the hair was still up on its shoulders, but you could see it was making up its stupid mind.

"Beat it," said Melly again, not yelling or anything, just talking like a tough teacher who knows you're going to do what he tells you, so you might as well. She was still walking slowly toward the dog.

It looked away, still growling, and then it swung round and lolloped off.

Karen's mum didn't say thank you. In fact she began rabbiting on at Melly about being stupid, and dogs like that are dangerous, but Melly smiled at her and said, "It's all right. My dad's a lion tamer."

That shut her up for a moment, so we said "See you" to Karen and the others and went off our way, but we could hear Karen's mum telling them about dangerous dogs for quite a distance.

"Is he really?" I asked her. "How come you never told me?"

"Yes, but Mum doesn't like me talking about him," she said. "If any of the others ask you, tell them I said that just to stop Karen's mum from going on at me."

A bit before I was fourteen, Dad died. He was sitting in his chair, talking about this rugby match we'd been watching on TV, when he stopped with his mouth wide open. For a moment he just stuck there, but before we could do anything his arms jerked up—you could see he couldn't help it, it was as if they were being yanked around from outside him—and then he was jerked to his feet with his face gone all sort of sideways and his tongue sticking out, and then he gave a couple of shudders and keeled over half across the chair. Mum was screaming. I got to the phone and rang for the ambulance.

The men did all the things you see on TV, but I knew it wasn't any use. He was dead already. There hadn't been any warning. He'd never had a heart attack before, not even a twinge. It just happened like that. Bang, you're dead.

Mum didn't know what to do. That's not just a way of

talking, it's what I mean. I'd never caught on before how much Dad mattered to her. He was what she was for. Take him away, and she wasn't for anything. (Except me, I suppose, but I'm not sure it wasn't because I was *his* son, mainly.) Sailing, for instance. I said they were both crazy about it, but the fact is she was crazy about it because he was. If he'd been crazy about gardening or something, she'd have been crazy about that too. It wasn't that he was selfish and made her go sailing—she really loved it because he'd shown her how to love it, and neither of them could understand why that didn't work with me.

Anyway, she wasn't going sailing without him, so she sold the boat and the cottage. And they'd lived in our house in Coventry ever since they were married, and she didn't want to be reminded of him every time she opened the door, so she sold that too. Her job was helping with the costumes for the Royal Shakespeare over at Stratford. Theater people all know each other and I think she must be pretty good because she got herself a new job almost at once, working for the Scottish Opera in Glasgow. So we left Coventry and went to live up there.

One other thing before I go on. My dad was a good careful guy who liked to do things right. He was pushing forty when he married Mum, and she was only nineteen, so he'd taken out proper insurance for her. Not that he'd expected to die that young—he was only fifty-five—but it meant that she had a bit of money to help us get by.

Glasgow wasn't that bad, in fact I found the change easier than Mum did. She'd got her work, but she didn't seem to want to go out or make friends or anything. Some of the kids at school tried to give me a hard time about being English and not Scottish, but nothing I couldn't handle, and I soon found a crowd to hang around with. Our new house was nice, not in the rough bits you hear about but out on the edge, a place called Bearsden, with little farms and steep hills and a golf course close behind. I hit it off with a boy called Ken who lived fairly near. He was nuts on bird-watching and summer was coming on, so we did a lot of that.

But it was amazing how much I missed Melly. There wasn't anything special about her I missed, it was having someone like that around, someone just there. I'd get home from school, evenings, and put the kettle on and without thinking I'd get two mugs out of the cupboard. . . . The one Melly used had an elephant on it. I put it right at the back of the shelf, but I still found myself looking for it.

This is going to sound silly, because we weren't in love or anything, Melly and me, let alone being married seventeen years, but missing her like that gave me a bit of an idea how my mum must be feeling. We wrote to each other sometimes, and we tried telephoning, but it wasn't the same. We didn't want to chat, we just wanted to have each other around. I'm guessing about her. She didn't say and neither did I. It's not the sort of thing you *can* say.

Scottish Opera doesn't stay in Glasgow all the time. They go on tours all around Britain, and abroad sometimes. The costumes are all made by then, but they have to take a couple of people from the wardrobe department along to do last-minute fixings. Mum doesn't usually do that, but that first year, just as they were starting off to do a fortnight in Edinburgh at the beginning of the tour, one of the people got hit by a van and had her leg broken, and the other one got stranded on holiday somewhere, so Mum agreed to do the Edinburgh fortnight. I stayed over at Ken's and stopped in at home every evening to feed the cats and check the post and the phone messages.

At the weekend Ken fed the cats for me while I went up to Edinburgh on the bus. She'd said to pick her up at the theater, but when I found her they'd got a crisis on, with a stand-in soprano who was a good bit shorter and fatter than the one the costumes were for. I said OK, I'd go out and bum around Edinburgh for a bit and be back at lunchtime. Someone said to go and look at the castle, which seemed a good idea, but I took a wrong turn and found myself moseying up Princes Street. If you don't know Edinburgh I'd better describe it. There's this sort of canyon running into the middle of the city. It's laid out as a park, with the castle along the top on one side and this famous street on the other, so that you can walk along looking out over the park at the battlements and stuff up on the skyline. There's steps and paths going down and up the other side. There's a lot of stuff for tourists, buskers with bagpipes, tartan souvenirs, that sort of thing, and classy shops the other side. It's worth seeing.

I walked along as far as the last lot of steps and started down them. They zigzagged to and fro. Turning one of the corners about halfway down, I saw a couple of girls coming up. One of them was Melly. She was chattering away like she used to, with all the body language going. I stopped dead in my tracks and stared. Then I saw her hair was all wrong and she was wearing a mass of makeup and smoking a fag, so I stared some more. I couldn't help it. She was staring back by now, but she'd have done that anyway, the way I was gawping at her. She said something to the other girl, who stayed where she was while the one I'd thought was Melly came stamping up the steps—she was wearing Doc Martens—straight at me. I was still thinking how to say sorry when she said in a low, furious voice, ''Hey! You were in that effing boat when I was chucking up!''

She didn't say ''effing,'' of course. Most of the kids I know swear a bit, some of them every third word, like breathing. Melly was one of the ones who'd sorted out it was cooler not to. Anyway, I knew exactly what this girl was talking about. It was one of the weekends Melly had come to Penmaenan and it had been pretty good sailing weather and Dad had talked her into giving it a go and she'd been as seasick as hell.

''That's right,'' I said. ''That was at Penmaenan.''

''That was in an effing dream!'' she said, still furious.

''It was real, Melly,'' I said.

''Melanie,'' she snapped. She did a double take and stopped being furious.

''How come you ken my name?'' she said.

Yes, *ken*. But she had a funny accent. Edinburgh people

talk different from other Scots, but this was something else.

"You're Melly—I mean Melanie—Perrault," I said.

"Perrault," she said, putting me right. It's a French name, because Melly's dad was French. This girl made it *sound* French.

"What's your name?" she said.

"Keith," I told her.

"What more do you ken?" she said.

(Really she said something like "What mair dae ye ken?" but I'm not going to try and write like that. I hate reading dialect, and I wouldn't get it right, and anyway that would make her sound much too Scots. She had this other accent—French, I guessed, from the way she'd said her name. What I'll do is use some of her words, like "ken" for "know" and "aye" for "yes." She sometimes said "wilna" and "dinna" instead of "won't" and "don't" and so on, but mostly she said them the English way, so I'll stick to that. I'm not going to try and do anything about her accent—it was too weird. What's more it shifted about. Sometimes it was much stronger than others, but it was always there a bit. While I'm at it, I'll leave out most of the swearing, but she didn't do that all the time either.)

So what else did I know? I didn't know where to begin.

"Your name's Melanie Perrault, and you live, you used to live, in Coventry, like I did, and you went to Ashley Junior with me and then Ashley High, and we'd walk home to my place after school because your mum—"

She grabbed my wrist so hard that her nails dug in. She'd been frowning and shaking her head about what I'd been telling her, but now she stared as if she was trying to look right into my head.

"Promise this isn't a put-on," she said.

"Promise," I said.

She thought.

"All right. When I'm at . . . your place, I get to have my own mug."

"That's right," I said. "The one with the elephant on it."

"And yours is a green one with white spots," she said.

"It got broke in the move," I said.

"What's my ma's name, then?"

"Janice."

"Janice," she said, trying it out. I guessed she'd known about the elephant but not about Janice. She was pale now under the makeup, and trembling. She took a long suck at her fag and threw it away.

"Wait there," she said, and went running down to the other girl. They talked for a bit. The body language was different. The other girl was obviously fascinated and wanted to join in, but Melanie wasn't having any. In the end the other girl came on up the steps, pretty sulky, staring at me as she went past. Melanie came up behind her, a bit calmer now.

"Probably thinks I've gone on the game," she said.

"Funny kind of place to start," I said.

She looked at me for the first time as if I was human,

and smiled. The way she did it was so like my Melly when I'd said something to amuse her, my heart almost stopped.

"Got any money?" she said.

"A few quid."

"Buy me a Coke?"

"OK."

She took me to a place up another lot of steps, in a sort of shopping mall, with booths and big windows looking out at the castle. Soon as we were sitting down she lit up again. The pack was empty so she threw it away.

"It's got to be there's two of us," she said. "Twins. When they split up they took one each and they never told us about the other one. What's she like, then?"

"Spitting image of you," I said. "Except she doesn't smoke and she doesn't do makeup, much."

"Right little pious snob, then? Bet she doesn't dress this way, neither."

I haven't said that as well as the Doc Martens she was wearing fishnet stockings with tears in them and a fake leather mini and a shiny red jacket and she'd got her hair short and chopped-about.

"She would, too, if Janice let her," I said. "Tell you what, a bit before we came north she was having one of her dopy fits and she was drawing in a dreamy kind of way and when she'd finished she showed me. 'That's me looking at myself in the mirror,' she said. It could've been you, now. Lipstick and all. The fag, even."

"Jesus!" she said. "Just after Christmas, this would be?"

"Around then. We came north in January."

"I bought this lot with my Christmas money, and I remember what a kick it was trying it on in the shop, and feeling effing great looking at myself in the mirror until this cow of a woman came and told me it was no smoking in there. She tell you about that?"

"No. But . . . she made a sort of sour face and tore the drawing up."

"Yeah. . . . You said dopy fits."

"When she sort of goes away for a bit."

"Me too. That's when I get these dreams. Not like night-dreams—they're something else—but . . . Jesus! She'll have been watching what I've been up to! Not just watching, neither—doing it along of me. Like me being sick in that effing boat!"

She looked a bit shaken by the thought, but then she laughed—Melly all over again.

"Well, she'll have learnt a thing or two," she said, "and maybe she wouldn't have learnt them in . . . Coventry? Right? I knew it had to be England, someplace. OK, then—tell me about my ma. Skinny, with red hair—right?"

"No, that's my mum. Janice has got dark hair and she's not so tall. She's not really fat, but she's a bit that way. She's sort of tidy. Nice clothes, but a bit boring, suits and things—but that's for her job. I don't remember I've ever seen her in jeans."

"That's my ma! I thought she was some kind of aunt. Go on, everything you can remember."

"You didn't even know her name, then?"

"Papa gets mad if I ask. Real mad . . . you know . . ."

I could guess. Well, I settled down and started telling her everything I could remember about Janice, which was quite a bit. Thinking about it, I wasn't surprised, if Melanie'd only seen them in these sort of dreams, that she might have thought my mum was really her mum. Mum's a feeling person. If someone's in trouble, she's right there with them in their trouble. Janice is more of a thinking person. If someone's in trouble she'll look things up in books and ring round and find what's the best way to get them out of their trouble, and then she'll put it onto her PC and print it all out for them with numbers at the start of each bit. They'd have made a great troubleshooting team, together.

I took a while telling her. Then she borrowed some money off me and went to buy herself more fags. Yeah, she was two years under age, if she was Melly's twin, but she knew her way round. While she was gone I checked the time and it was getting on half past twelve, when I'd told Mum I'd be back at the theater, so I was up at the bar paying the bill when Melanie came tearing back and shoved what I'd lent her into my hand.

"I've got to go," she said. "I'm in dead trouble already. How do I get to talk to you again?"

"I'm coming with you," I said. "What's up?"

"I work in the restaurant Saturdays, and I'm on at

twelve. He'll beat the eff out of me. Got enough for a cab?
Pay you back—honest.''

She was panting it out as we raced up the steps, and
there was a taxi just finished being paid off. I jumped out
and stopped him driving away. (It made me feel good,
valiant-knight-to-the-rescue stuff. Silly, sure, but it
happens.) She gave the address to the driver as we
got in.

''We've got to sort out about meeting up,'' I said.
''What's this about the restaurant? Can't I just come
there—''

''Chrissake, no. I told you about Papa.''

''The one who's going to take it out on you for being
late?''

''Right. Mind you, he won't let anyone else lay a finger
on me.''

''But Melly says her dad's a lion tamer.''

''He used to be, but something happened at the circus—I dinna ken what, he wouldn't say—and he packed it
in. Sold his lions and came to Edinburgh and got a job at
Annie's doing the bar. He married her after a bit. I do
waitress when I'm not in school. . . . Do something for
me?''

''Sure.''

And I meant it. No messing around whether it would
get me in trouble or clean me out. I'd have done what she
wanted as if she'd been Melly.

''You'll have to act up a bit,'' she said, and leaned

forward and asked the driver to stop. She got out and scuffed around in the gutter for a handful of dirt and rubbed it into the side of her face, using the wing mirror to see what she was doing. Then she dirtied her forearm and knee and took off her jacket and scuffed it along in the gutter and put it on and got back in. While she was doing this I found a scrap of paper and copied down our hotel number, which Mum had given me, and our number and address in Bearsden. She glanced at them and tucked them into the pocket of her jacket.

"Ta," she said. "Right. I've been knocked down by a bike and you've been looking after me. You're new in Edinburgh? OK, there's this steep little street, cobbles, in behind the station. Doesn't have a pavement. You're coming up and I'm coming down—it's a way I could've been taking back to Annie's—and there's this van just come up past you and a bike coming down, and the stupid sod on the bike thinks he can get between me and the van, and he can't. Got it? So you've picked me up and got a cab and brought me home because you're a good guy, right? Don't overdo that, mind. You better pay the cab off in case Papa comes rushing out to grill him about where he picked us up, but then you look like you were hoping to get your money back. Do that for me, Keith?"

"I'll give it a go, sure."

It wasn't that far. We stopped in another touristy kind of street, only this one was all gift shops and Scottish woolens in genuine little old houses. Melanie stayed in the cab while I paid the driver.

I helped her out of the cab and she put her arm around my shoulder and I put mine round her waist and she hobbled along beside me into an alley and there was the restaurant, Annie's Genuine French Bistro, next to a haggis bar. It didn't look too bad. I'd hardly got the door open when a square, tough-looking woman looked up and came striding toward us, but before she reached us a man came rushing out from behind the bar, shouting at Melanie in French. They both stopped when they saw the state Melanie had got herself in, and I started explaining to the woman about the accident I was supposed to have seen, while Melanie mumbled away to the man in French. The woman calmed down at once, but the man stayed very het up, but not in your standard comic-Frenchman way. He was short and skinny, but his head didn't look like a small man's head. I don't mean it was too big for his body, but it had this heavy, hungry look, with high cheekbones and deep-set eyes. I could see he was still furious, but in a frustrated kind of way, because the people he wanted to take it out on, the cyclist and the van driver, weren't there for him to get at.

"I don't think she's really hurt," I told the woman, because I knew Melanie wouldn't have any bruises to show. "She's just pretty shaken up. She wasn't making any sense at all at first, and then it took us a while to get to where we'd find a taxi . . ."

"The taxi's waiting to be paid, is he?"

"He's gone. I've paid him. It was three pounds fifty with the tip. I hope that's all right."

"Course it is," she said, and went off to the till.

I looked to see how Melanie was making out. The man had grabbed a chair and sat her down, but as soon as he saw me turn he drew himself up with his head held back like a soldier on parade.

"I give you most profound gratitude," he said.

He had a very strong foreign accent, but he spoke slowly and solemnly, so that I could pick up what he was saying.

"That's all right," I said, and took the chance to tell him too about Melanie not being hurt, just pretty shook up.

He nodded.

"You will accept luncheon?" he said. "On the house, naturally."

"I can't, I'm afraid," I said. "I'm supposed to be meeting my mother. I'm late already."

"Very good. In that event you will bring your mother to dinner this evening. I would wish to express my thanks to her also. Excuse me."

A customer was getting impatient at the bar. He strode off. The woman who'd gone for the cab fare was dealing with two new customers, so I'd a few seconds to talk to Melanie alone. I wanted to see her again, but I didn't want any dealings with her dad, if he was the sort to beat her up, and certainly not to take free meals off him. But when I told her she grinned Melly's quick wicked grin.

"That's worked out terrific," she said. "You've got to bring your mum round so I can see her. The food's pretty good, tell her."

"I don't think she can. There's two shows Saturday, and she'll be on for both of them. What are you doing tomorrow morning?"

"Mass, first off, and then nothing. But I've got to be back here twelve."

"Mass" shook me. Melly didn't go to church at all, and nor did we.

"Meet you for another Coke, then?" I said. "Same place, ten?"

"Great," she said. "If you get to bring your ma along here, tell her to keep her mouth shut, whatever."

She'd glanced past me, then muttered this last bit. Now the woman came back with the cab fare and I explained about having to go now, and how Melanie's dad had asked me to bring Mum that evening, but I wasn't sure if she could because of her job, and would she tell him. She was really nice about it and got me a card and told me to ring if we were coming and made me feel she really wanted us to. Then she took Melanie off and I went back to the theater.

I was over an hour late, but Mum isn't good at time and she hadn't missed me. In fact I found the opera crisis was still full on and she was kneeling by this woman with her mouth full of pins, fitting her dress, while the woman was belting out practice notes in a voice you could have heard up at the castle and not paying any attention to Mum at all. It was only half an hour to curtain up and there was still another costume to go, so I went off and got myself a sandwich and brooded about what had happened and got nowhere except that it was weird but it was terrific having Melly around.

OK, that sounds stupid. She wasn't Melly, she was Melanie, and it wasn't just smoking and swearing and going to Mass and talking French and stuff. She was someone else. Her whole life was different. There was no way she'd fit in with my life, the way Melly had, any more than I'd fit in with hers. She'd have been bored stiff and I'd probably have been scared stiff. But it wasn't any good telling myself that. Melly was who she was—a new, exciting sort of Melly.

Second time I got back to the theater the opera had begun and Mum and another woman were stitching away like fury getting the costumes sewn for the other two acts.

"I'm really sorry about this, darling," Mum said. "Especially when you've come all this way to see me. But it'll be done in a couple of hours and Alicia here is going to be a saint and take over for the evening, so you and I can go out and do something together."

"That's great," I said. "I've got us a free meal."

"That's nice, darling," she said, and then—oh—a good ten seconds later, "What do you mean, a free meal?"

"I met someone who works in a restaurant and got her out of a jam," I said. "It's all right, Mum—nothing crook about it. And she says the food's good. It's supposed to be French."

The woman at the restaurant sounded pleased when I called her, and I got the idea they were going to lay things on a bit for us, so when Mum said, "Is it the sort of place we dress up for?" I thought maybe yes. I hadn't brought much, but I got myself tidy, and Mum can be a very pretty woman when she bothers, which she did. It must have been about the first time since my dad died, and it was nice to be taking her out looking like that.

It wasn't too far from the hotel, so we walked. When we were just about getting there I said, "Now, listen, Mum. You're going to recognize someone. And you're going to work out who someone else is. It's going to be a bit of a shock, but you've got to act normal."

She stopped and faced me.

"Will you please tell me what this is about?" she said.

I hadn't told her anything, not even the story about the bike and the van, because that would have meant lying, and I wanted her to see Melanie for herself first. Besides, I was having fun. I grinned.

"It's all right," I said. "Promise. You'll see."

"Oh, God, you remind me of Mike sometimes," she said.

(Mike was my dad, of course.)

I was glad we'd dressed up, because they really laid out the red carpet for us. The woman was watching out for us and stopped what she was doing and came straight over. I'd guessed she must be Annie so I introduced her to Mum, and then Melanie's dad showed up and did his soldier trick and gave her a stiff little bow and said, "I am Gustave Perrault, Madame."

She knew what to do at once. She gave him her hand to

185

kiss and said she was enchanted to meet him and she was Patricia Robinson.

"Madame, I felicitate you upon your son," he said. "He is an English gentleman."

I could have sunk through the floor, but Mum smiled and said, "I'm glad you think so," as if she meant it.

Annie's wasn't much more than a tourist cafe, really, but they showed us to what was obviously their best table, in the window. They'd laid it out with candles and ranks of cutlery and extra glasses, and Melanie's dad—M. Perrault I'm going to start calling him—went to the bar and came back with a bottle of champagne, which he poured into three glasses and then looked at me and offered me some in mine. I looked at Mum and she said, "Well, since it's a special occasion," and he gave me half a glass.

The four of us were just starting to drink each other's health when Melanie showed up with a plate of little pastry things to nibble. Mum had her glass to her lips, pretty well brim full, but she didn't spill a drop.

Melanie shook Mum's hand and smiled her Melly smile and said, "Keith was really good to me this morning, Mrs. Robinson." She was so terrifically on her best behavior I wanted to giggle. M. Perrault poured about a thimbleful of champagne for her and we drank the healths and then M. Perrault said, "We have, with regret, the restaurant to conduct this evening, but Melanie will arrange that you have all you require."

Mum smiled and thanked them and they pushed off. As soon as their backs were turned Melanie let out a long sigh of relief and we both had to bite our lips to stop the giggles.

"Will somebody please tell me what's going on?" said Mum. "It really is the most amazing likeness. And your name's Melanie Perrault? You must be our Melly Perrault's first cousin."

"For God's sake be careful," I whispered. "We think they're twins, but she's not allowed to ask anything about her mother. Hold it. He's turning this way."

Mum didn't blink. She smiled across the room and raised her glass to M. Perrault.

"We better tell her what's supposed to have happened," said Melanie.

"Only it didn't really," I said, and we explained about the van and the bike and so on, making it seem as real as we could, and Mum reacted as if she was believing every word. In the middle of this M. Perrault came and said that they had chosen a meal for us, but we could have something else if we wanted, so of course we said we'd be happy with whatever they gave us. He seemed very struck with Mum, which made him even more stiff and gallant and difficult not to laugh at. Mum was wonderful with him, playing along with him and getting it just right, not overdoing it. In fact I thought she was rather enjoying that, but I also got the idea something was bothering her.

"Keith's alone in Edinburgh," she told him. "He hasn't got anyone his own age to talk to. Will it be all right if Melanie sits with us when she isn't busy? I'm afraid Saturday's a bad time for that."

"But of course," he said. "Already these arrangements are made. She has just the two other tables she must attend."

He poured her more champagne with a great flourish and went back to the bar. Melanie had to go to serve someone else. Mum waited for her to get out of earshot.

"Tell me something, Keith," she said. (She never calls me Keith unless it's serious.) "I gather this story about Melanie being knocked down by a bicycle isn't true."

"I'm afraid not," I said.

"But you told me all this was aboveboard. It seems to me we're getting a free meal—and they've gone to a lot of trouble over it—on false pretenses. I hope we aren't. I wouldn't like that at all."

This absolutely hadn't struck me, I'd been so swept along by the adventure. I couldn't think what to say.

"It wasn't like that, Mum. Honestly. Wait till I've . . . And anyway, he'd have beaten her up for being late. I mean beaten."

I hadn't said it on purpose, but it's one of the things she really minds about. Anyway, it did the trick.

"I'm sorry to hear it," she said. "I was finding him rather attractive."

"Mum!"

"Champagne is wonderful stuff, darling," she said, with a look that didn't let me guess whether she was teasing or not. Either way it would have been the first time since Dad died.

"Listen, Mum," I said. "You're not to go cold on him.

You've got to find things out. If he comes back, talk to him in French. Ask him how he got to Edinburgh, that sort of thing. Get as close as you can to when Melanie was born without letting him see that's what you're interested in. I'm not just being inquisitive. It's important. Listen. This is what really happened . . ."

I started to tell her about that morning, from me going down the steps and seeing what I thought was Melly coming up. Melanie came back and joined in two or three times, but she kept having to dash off and wait, so it was mostly me. I didn't finish till Melanie was clearing our main course away. Mum didn't say anything, so I asked her what she thought.

"I believe every word you've told me, darling," she said. "And I don't understand it at all. But let's wait till Melanie comes back."

It didn't work out like that. First, Melanie was too busy to talk, and then when we'd finished our sweet, M. Perrault came and asked Mum if she'd like brandy or liqueur. I've forgotten to say he'd given us red wine with the meal, which Mum said was pretty good, though I didn't like it much. When he came back he'd got a large glass of brandy for himself, and asked if he could join us. Mum said, *"Enchantée, Monsieur,"* and he was delighted and answered in French and she batted it back to him and they got going. She speaks pretty good French. She actually met my dad while she was au-pairing out there, so she didn't have any trouble keeping her end up. I speak a bit—better than most kids my age—but going that fast they lost me, so when Melanie came back we talked about the obvious things, mostly music. I knew she'd like Hole and P. J. Harvey, because Melly did. We didn't get any chance to talk without M. Perrault hearing, but when we were saying good-bye I looked at her and she gave a little nod to tell me the arrangement to meet next morning was still on.

We walked home. As soon as we were round the corner I said, "You see, they've got to be twins, haven't they?"

"I don't want to talk about it now," said Mum, "not after all that wine. I suppose you're seeing her tomorrow?"

"Ten o'clock," I said.

"Do you mind if I come too?" she said. "I'm sorry—I expect you want her for yourself, darling, but I've got things to tell her which I'd rather say directly to her. I can't stay long. I ought to be at the theater by half past ten. Is that all right?"

"Yes, of course," I said, though it wasn't.

The place where we'd had the Coke didn't open till twelve on Sundays, but Melanie was waiting on the terrace, leaning on the railing and looking at the view. She was wearing a black skirt and a white lacy blouse and a black cardigan and no makeup. Oh, yes, and white socks and little shoes like dancing slippers. Apart from her hair she was a real Miss Prim. She didn't look at all disappointed to see I'd got Mum with me.

"Hello, Mrs. Robinson," she said. "I'm like this because it wasn't worth going home after Mass."

"Melly calls me Trish," said Mum. "I can't stay long, but I've got something to tell you. Is there anywhere we can sit?"

We were lucky and found a bench in the sun.

"Is it OK if I smoke?" said Melly.

Mum made a face. She smokes a couple of fags a day but doesn't like to see kids doing it.

"I don't have to," said Melanie, and stopped getting her pack out. Mum touched her arm.

"I'm sorry," she said. "Please smoke if you want to. This may be hard going for you."

"Thanks," said Melanie, but she didn't light up.

"Last night I said to Keith that I believed every word of what you'd told me, both of you," said Mum. "So the first thing to say is that there's no way you and Melly can be twins, Melanie. I'll tell you why in a moment. I thought you might be cousins. Suppose your father had a brother, possibly a twin brother, they might both be lion tamers—circuses are very family affairs, I believe. Then these extraordinary . . . visions you and Melly seem to have of each other—I'm assuming she has them too, because she does have these absent fits—they might make a sort of sense. But last night I got your father to tell me a bit about himself and he was quite open about it. The main thing is that until four years ago he lived and worked in a traveling circus based at Arles, in the south of France . . ."

"That's right," said Melanie.

"Melly was born in a circus based in Arles," said Mum.

191

"Her birthday is the nineteenth of March. She was fourteen this year."

"Me too," said Melanie. "And you don't get two lion tamers in the one circus, no more than you get two circuses in the one town. And I'm dead sure Papa didn't have a brother, neither. Only this sister, Tante Sylvie, sold the tickets. She liked to talk. She'd have said."

"Then we'll rule that out," said Mum. "Now, about your not being twins. This is something Janice told me in confidence, but I think Melanie has a right to know."

"Shall I clear off for a bit?" I said.

Mum hesitated.

"I don't think Janice has told Melly," she said. "I don't know . . . It'll probably be simpler . . . Just don't talk about it to anyone. Is that all right with you, Melanie?"

"Course it is," she said.

"Well," said Mum. "I don't know if Keith told you that his father died last October."

"I think maybe I was at the funeral," said Melanie. "It was pissing down, and everyone had their brollies up and I cried like I was never going to stop."

"Oh, God . . . ," said Mum. "Sorry . . . I'll be all right in a moment . . . Can you spare me a cigarette?"

They both lit up and Mum took a puff or two and stubbed hers out and tried again.

"I suppose we'll get used to this," she said, "but there's something very uncomfortable about it . . .

Well, I had a bad time after Mike died. Keith will tell you. I really went to pieces. I spent a lot of time weeping on people's shoulders, and of course Janice was one of them. I gather Keith's told you about Janice, so you'll have got it that she's rather . . . well, uptight and controlled, and perhaps not very good at emotions.''

"Keith tell you I thought you had to be my ma?" said Melanie. "She wasn't my idea of a ma, the other one."

"She's been a very good friend to me, though," said Mum. "She's the sort who sticks at it. A stupid emotional female sobbing her heart out over the coffee biscuits isn't her scene at all, but she must have read up what to do, and talked to professionals, and somehow I think she got the idea that it might be a help if she told me about something dreadful in her own life. So one evening she took a deep breath and screwed herself up and told me about what happened when Melly was born. She was twenty, and she was on a cycling holiday in the south of France with a couple of girlfriends, and one evening they were riding along—late, because they'd had a puncture that wouldn't mend—when they came across this circus camped out in the middle of nowhere, so they asked if they could put up their tent alongside them. They got chatting, and one of Janice's friends decided she fancied one of the acrobats, so they spent the rest of their holiday zigzagging around so as to meet up with the circus as often as possible. By the end of it they'd made quite a few friends in the circus, and they went home thinking they'd had an amusing holiday and that was it.

"So Janice just wasn't ready for it when a couple of weeks later she got a formal proposal of marriage from the lion tamer. The extraordinary thing, she said, was that she didn't think twice about it. As soon as she got over her surprise she knew she was going to say yes. It wasn't that she'd secretly fallen in love with him, or anything. Several of the men had tried to get somewhere with her, and one of her English friends had slept around a bit, but the lion tamer had been formal and gallant and serious, and he didn't speak much English, either. But Janice had found him rather attractive in his odd way, and after last night I can see why. Besides, winter was settling in, and the relationship she'd had for a couple of years had come apart that summer, and she was hating her job, so she went back to Arles and married him.

"She must have been crazy, she told me. It didn't work out at all. She didn't understand circus life, and the other circus people treated her now as an outsider, and her husband was madly jealous if he saw her say even a couple of words to another man, and he had an appalling temper. He didn't actually beat her, but when he got into one of his rages he could be absolutely terrifying."

"That's right," said Melanie. "Fact, it's better when he gets to hitting you. Annie's got him sorted out, mind. She won't stand for any of that."

"On top of that, he was a Catholic," said Mum, "and he wouldn't have any truck with contraception. Janice did her best not to get pregnant, but of course it happened in the end. As soon as he knew she was carrying his child he

194

became very kind and considerate, and she thought it might be all right after all. And then the baby was born, a little girl, and he insisted on calling her Melanie, after his mother. He adored her. In fact, from what Janice told me, he was pretty well obsessed with her. He wanted to do everything for her himself. He even resented the fact that Janice could breast-feed her and he couldn't . . .''

"I'll buy that," said Melanie. "That's Papa."

"Yes, I got a bit of that impression last night," said Mum. "Anyway, for Janice life became even worse than it had been before. Her husband didn't just revert to being madly jealous. He had this great ogress of a sister, and they both had desperately primitive ideas about child-rearing, really dangerous and unhygienic, some of them, but if she stepped out of line in the smallest detail they'd scream at her that she was trying to kill his child, and it wasn't long before Janice began to suspect that the sister was working on him to take the baby away from her and give it to one of the circus women to look after.

"So she decided to leave him. She'd got a little necklace and a bracelet and some other things which she sold secretly, and bought a railway ticket, and just as the circus was getting going one evening she slipped away with the baby. It was a local train and it took her only about twenty miles back to Arles. There wasn't a train out until the morning and she knew he'd come after her, so she went and hid in a little hotel in a back street, but somehow he found out where she was, because in the middle of the night he came to her room with half a dozen other circus people. When she started to scream they put a gag in her mouth and tied her up and took the baby away, but two of them stayed with her all next day. After a bit they untied her and took the gag out, but they told her that if she made a noise they'd use it again. Apart from that they wouldn't say a word to her. They offered her food but she was too frantic to eat. They stayed with her all next night, but next morning her husband's sister came and gave the baby back. The other two left, but the sister gave her some money and said, 'If you try to find my brother again, your child will die. That is the truth. Now, go.' In case you're thinking it might have been some other baby they'd found somewhere, it wasn't. You know your child after the first half hour.''

''Anyway, they wouldn't look the same now,'' I said.

We sat and tried to think about it. Melanie stubbed out her fag and blew out a long smoky breath and stood up and stretched. As she did so the sleeve of her cardigan slid up, so that I saw, halfway up the forearm on the inside, a white scar like an inside-out ''N.'' I grabbed her by the wrist and showed Mum.

''I don't know how much more of this I can take,'' said Mum.

''What's up?'' said Melanie. ''Oh, that. Caught it on a nail one time we were loading the ponies. Papa was making me learn bareback.''

''Only Melly's is on her left arm, isn't it?'' said Mum. ''You're right-handed, aren't you, Melanie? I noticed when you were lighting your cigarette just now.''

"Right as right," said Melanie. "Melly's left, is she? Mirror images, then? Don't you get that with twins?"

"Not always, I think," said Mum. "And anyway, those scars . . . What's more, Melly caught her arm on a nail at some stables where she was having riding lessons. This is making me feel most peculiar."

"Did M. Perrault say anything to you about why he left the circus, Mum?" I asked. "I mean, if he was making Melanie learn bareback he must have been expecting to stay on."

"As a matter of fact he was rather odd about that," said Mum. "I remember Janice saying that one of her problems was that he adored his lions . . ."

"That's right," said Melanie. "He was nuts about them, and if one of them got ill . . . Always getting sick with something, lions."

"But he was very offhand about them last night," said Mum. "It seems there was some sort of disagreement in the circus, but I'd have thought he'd have taken his lions off to some other circus, rather than giving it all up and moving to Edinburgh. It's almost as if he wanted to get as far away as possible . . . Look, I've got to go. I think the first thing is for me to try and ring Janice. No, hell, she's at a conference this weekend. She'll be home this evening. I'll try and . . . No, I can't—it's *Giovanni* and that goes on forever. Maybe I can find a gap. Please, please, be careful, Melanie. It isn't just your father. There's something going on here . . . And you and Keith have got to work out a way of staying in touch."

She was standing up by now.

"I'm really concerned about this," she said. "You were right in a way, Melanie. I do think of Melly as almost my own daughter."

"Do I get in on that?" said Melly, not joking, or not much.

Mum looked really pleased, but a notch more and she might have been crying.

"If this crazy business is true, you're in already," she said. "I'll see you at the theater, darling. I might be clear by one."

"I'll be there," I said.

When Mum had gone we just sat there, not saying anything. I was thinking about Mum. It was a crazy business, like she'd said, but it had really done something for her. I hadn't seen her so alive, so interested, since my dad died. Suited me, anyway. If she actually wanted me to keep in touch with Melanie . . .

"He took me away from my own mother," said Melanie, quietly, to herself, to nobody, to the world. She looked down at her arm and stroked the scar with her fingertip. "And now we're being pushed around, I'm thinking. Yon's more than a wee coincidence, Keith. And it was more than a wee coincidence you happening down the stair just as I was happening up."

"Your dad's doing it somehow, you mean?" I said.

She shook her head.

"Not him, no—he wouldn't want it. Maybe like your ma was saying, he came to Edinburgh to get as far away as possible. And maybe now it's come after us . . . It'll be all about what he did when he took me away from my ma, when I was a wee bairn."

She was dead serious, but it didn't make any sense to me.

"It's got to be something to do with the circus," I said. "They were all in it together. I don't believe in magic and stuff. I always knew Father Christmas was just a story."

"This is no Father Christmas, Keith, but you'd best start believing in it."

"If you say so . . . Well, supposing I did believe, I'd still say it was something to do with the circus. Was the circus just animals and acrobats and clowns, or was there something else? Palmists, I suppose, and fortune-tellers and stuff. They're making out they do magic, sort of. You must have had some of that."

"Just Madame Raquel," she said. "Herbs and potions, she sold, and she'd a crystal ball she looked in, but that was only, like, advertising for the potions. Herself, she'd tell you that, though she made a hocus-pocus of it for the customers. Buy me another Coke, then?"

"If you like."

We wandered off and found a place where we settled down.

"Tell you what," I said. "We haven't got a holiday fixed for this year—Mum didn't have the heart. I could try and talk her into taking us out to Arles, see if I can find anything out."

"They'll never talk to you."

199

"What about you coming along too?"

"Don't be thick. And it's not just Papa—we get wall-to-wall tourists here, August. I'll be working my arse off in the restaurant."

"Suppose . . ."

"It'd give me the creeps, besides."

I looked at her because she'd said it in an odd way, more to herself than me.

"What do you mean?" I said.

"I dinna ken," she said. "Just sometimes I'm dreaming about it, and it's aye bad."

"That figures," I said. "Is this something new? Have you always had these dreams? When did they start? After you left, or before?"

"On the train it was, and very, very bad. It wasn't the whole dream then, only the flying. When it's the whole dream, I'm in the circus and I'm watching Papa feed the lions, and then a body comes—I don't see who it is, and he tells me he's going to feed his animal and I can watch if I've the fancy to, so I start off with him across this big open field, and there's one of the traveling cages way over on the other side. And then it comes into my mind that this fellow's planning to feed me to his animal, and he's a bit ahead of me and I turn and tiptoe away, and then I'm flying. I can see Papa far down below, waving to me, but I'm flying away, free as a bird. It's beautiful, Keith. But then I feel something following after me. It can't fly, but it's down there, following, calling for me, waiting until I am tired with flying. And then I'm getting heavy, and I ken that I can't fly much longer . . . and that's when I wake up. There's nobody I've told that to before, Keith. Nobody ever.''

''Melly has nightmares. I heard her having a bad one, once, at Penmaenan. That was about flying, I think. She didn't want to talk about it.''

''No, she wouldn't.''

''Was there anything in the circus you were particularly afraid of? Your dad's lions, for instance?''

''Not they. I was feared of Tante Sylvie, of course, but so were all the others. A great ogress, your ma called her, and that's about right. Even Papa was feared of her. And one of the clowns, Monsieur Albert, I dinna ken why, since I'd nothing to do with him. They said he was a great miser, and if you looked out in the wee small hours you'd see the light in his caravan, where he was sitting up late counting his gold. And Madame Zazu, who rode bareback. Most days she'd be fine, but then the devil would be in her . . . when I was a bairn I heard a body say, 'Keep away from Zazu, the devil's in her today,' and I went and looked and I could see it glaring out of her eyes . . .''

''Run herself short of smack or something?''

''Maybe. But I kenned aye that Papa wouldn't let a body touch me, and there was nothing to be feared of. Only him.''

We talked around and around until it was time for her to go back to Annie's. She'd told M. Perrault she was meeting me, so it was all right for me to go along with her. On the way I bought a bunch of flowers for Annie to say thank you for last night's dinner. I started to bother about what Melanie might be thinking of me. I'd got the feeling she liked talking to me, but I was pretty sure I'd be a lot younger, and a lot less streetwise, than the sort of boy she usually hung around with.

I glanced at her, trying to guess what she felt, but she wasn't noticing me at all. I could tell that at once. We were almost at Annie's by now, and she was walking along looking calm and sure and set. I'd seen exactly that look before once, on Melly, when she'd dealt with the yellow dog. The lion tamer's daughter.

Mum was almost through when I got to the theater, so she took me out to a not-bad vegetarian place for lunch. The business with Melly and Melanie had really got a grip on her. She'd obviously been thinking about it pretty well solidly since she'd left us.

"I've had a thought," she said. "It's almost too crazy to mention, but so's the whole business."

"Except that it's happening," I said. "It's all right, Mum. I won't stomp on you. I've been swapping crazy stuff with Melanie all morning."

(I'd better explain that Mum's more into believing weird stuff than I am. UFOs for instance. She thinks there are intelligent somethings visiting us from space. I think there aren't. Dad used to say, Yes there are, and they're conducting experiments to see just how gullible humans can be.)

"Well," she said. "Do you know what a doppelganger

is? We did a play about one four years ago at The Other Place. It was by one of those gloomy old Germans, very intense and poetical and utterly boring, I thought, but the point was that the hero had this double who seemed to be some kind of fiend, who stalked him, and if ever they came face to face the hero was going to die. I think the idea came from an old German fairy story . . . I know it sounds stupid as soon as I say it, but do you remember what Melly's aunt said when she gave the baby back? I'd assumed it was just a threat, that he'd kill Melly if Janice tried to get in touch with him, or the aunt would, or something, but if you think about the doppelganger story . . . I mean, I've never understood why the aunt brought the baby back, after M. Perrault had taken all that trouble to get hold of her. Janice's explanation is that he was under his sister's thumb, and the sister wanted Janice out of their lives, and she knew that as long as they'd got the baby Janice wouldn't stop trying to get her back, so the sister bullied him into giving the baby up."

"I'd go along with that. Melanie said everyone was frightened of her aunt, including M. Perrault."

"But then where did Melanie come from?"

"I don't know. And you're not going to tell me either of them's any kind of fiend. Or that Melly's the real Melly and Melanie's her doppelthingy. I'm not having that. They're both just as real as you or me."

"You don't have to shout, darling. I completely agree with you about that. If you'd brought Melanie home out of the blue one evening and she'd not been Melly's double and so on, then I don't say I wouldn't have been a bit alarmed for you, but as things are I feel just as concerned for her as I do for Melly. In fact, though I've met her just twice, I feel as if I've known her for most of her life. I want you to do something for me, darling. You're going to think it's stupid, but I have a very strong feeling it's important. It's the sort of feeling I've learnt to trust. Are you going to be talking to Melanie again soon?''

''She's ringing me at home tomorrow. After school. Is it all right if I ring off and call her back, so that it's on our bill?''

''Yes, of course. And when you're talking to her I want you to try to persuade her not to get in touch with Melly for the moment. Melly's staying with Christine''—that's a friend of Janice's and Mum's in Coventry—''but she'll be home this evening. I want you to ring her too . . .''

''I was going to, anyway, and tell her about Melanie.''

''Yes, of course. Then will you say the same to her, about not getting in touch? Try and get them to take it seriously, darling, even if you don't believe in it yourself.''

''Look, Mum. I take *you* seriously. I believe in you.''

That shook her. It shook me too. It's not the sort of thing you say.

''Do you want me to tell them about the doppelthingies?'' I said, to cover it up.

''Doppelgangers. Um . . . I think not . . . There's no point in frightening them . . .''

''It's all right. I'll just say you've got a bad feeling about it. They'd probably pay more attention to that than anything, anyway. Both of them. Melanie thinks you're terrific, you know. I'm hoping she'll put up with me because it gives her an in to you.''

''I'm glad you're having fun, darling.''

None of this worked out. I took the bus to Glasgow after lunch and got out to Bearsden somewhere around six o'clock. I went home first, to see to the cats and check the post and the answer-phone. There was only one message, from Melly, saying she'd be home by three and would I call her as soon as possible, so I made myself a mug of tea and dialed her number. She answered first ring, and as soon as she heard my voice she broke in.

''Who were you talking to yesterday? You met them on some steps and you went to a caff and drank Coke and talked and talked, and then you ran and got into a taxi, I think, and then . . . no, I'll leave that bit out . . . there was a restaurant. And a man and a woman. Some sort of fuss going on. No. Wait. Yesterday evening you came back to the restaurant with Trish and had what looked like a really nice meal, and champagne, and the man and the woman were there again, and the man was sitting and talking and talking to Trish, and she was playing up to him. I think they were talking French. And somebody . . . somebody brought you the meal and did the waiting and so on . . . This is all real, isn't it? I'm not making it up. Tell me I'm not making it up.''

She was pretty upset, I could hear.

''You're not making it up,'' I said. ''It all happened.

The bit you left out was looking at your own face in a wing mirror, wasn't it?''

"And rubbing some dirt in. Who is she, Keith? What's her name?''

"Melanie Perrault. We think she's your twin, only Mum says she can't be.''

"And the man's my father, then?''

"Looks as though he's got to be.''

"I thought so. Oh, God! Tell Trish to watch out for him, Keith. He's got a foul temper. What's she like, then? Does she call herself Melly too?''

"No. Melanie. Suppose you smoked a bit and swore a bit and had your hair cut ragged . . . You remember that picture you drew of how you'd get yourself up if Janice would let you? That's what she was wearing—it looks as if you'd actually seen her trying it on in the shop. But the clothes and the hair don't matter . . . Jesus, was I glad to see you coming up those steps. Notice how I stared?''

"Did I notice? A right twit you looked, Keith.''

"Thanks. OK, I'll go on from there . . .''

I settled down and did that, best I could remember, backtracking when I'd left anything out. It must have taken getting on an hour—but at least Sunday calls were cheap rate.

"How long has this been going on?'' I asked her when I'd finished. "It's when you get those dopy fits, isn't it? You've had them ever since I've known you.''

"Always,'' she said. "But not like this before. It was

just bits, and I knew it wasn't real. I mean I knew I was sitting at the kitchen table or somewhere—I mean like when you're watching TV, you can get very involved, but you know it isn't happening to you, really. This time it almost was."

"Except you couldn't hear what we were saying?"

"I can sometimes, but only when I'm not trying. It drives me crazy. You know sometimes you're reading a book in a dream and you're getting along fine until you start paying attention, and then the words won't stay still anymore. It's always been like that. When I was little, and still when I was in junior school for a bit, it used to be in some kind of circus, and I knew it was in France because sometimes I'd hear them talking French, and I'd understand what they were saying although my French wasn't really that good, but as soon as I tried to listen it didn't make any sense at all. And last night I could hear that Trish and the man were talking French but I was trying to listen to you and it was just a sort of jumble."

"We were talking about Hole and P. J. Harvey, if you want to know. Do you have nightmares about a man leading you across a field toward a sort of circus trailer, and then you running away and finding you can fly, only something's pulling you down, following you below? . . . Melly? . . . Are you there?"

"She has that too?" she whispered. "Look, I've got to talk to her. What's her number?"

I wasn't ready. I was still trying to think what to say

when she said, "No, that's no good. I can't call her at the restaurant because of him. I don't suppose you gave her my number."

"No, but . . ."

"Then what's her address? Hell, I bet he opens her letters. She's calling you up tomorrow, isn't she? Hell, I can't wait till tomorrow . . ."

By now I was getting scared. It wasn't what she was saying, it was the way she was saying it, right over the top with excitement. Melly wasn't like that.

"Hold it," I said. "Mum doesn't think it's a good idea, you two getting in touch. She told me to tell you."

"Oh, come off it—that's just Trish. Anyway, we've just got to—"

"Listen. Can't you at least wait till Janice gets home? She can talk to Trish. I'll give you her number . . ."

"Oh, great! She's still in Edinburgh! She can get a message round, can't she? I'll call her!"

"She's working tonight, Melly. She's at the theater. No! For God's sake, listen! Mum's working, and you can't ring her there. She'll be back in her hotel room—hell, the show's a long one, she said—about half past eleven. You wait till Janice gets home, and tell her all about it, and then one of you can call Mum tonight, if you still want to. If Janice wants to talk to me, I'll be round at Ken's. The number's on that card I sent you. And Mum's going to call her tomorrow evening anyway. Got a pencil? Here's Mum's number."

I gave it her and tried to calm her down a bit but it

wasn't any use so we rang off and I fed the cats and went round to Ken's. Nobody called me there. I was exhausted, but I didn't sleep that well. The way Melly had talked had really upset me.

Next morning at school I went to the library to get Mrs. McCrum to help me look up about doppelgangers. I still felt it was a crazy notion but at least it was something I could do. Mrs. McCrum likes kids using the library for their own stuff, and on top of that she's a fantasy nut, so she dug around and found some bits and pieces, but there wasn't much and they all said the same sort of thing about German folktales and gloomy German and Russian writers. Some of the stories said that doppelgangers were the ghosts of living people, haunting them, and some of them said they were fiends out to get them, but either way if you met yours it meant you were going to die, or else it happened straight off. There wasn't anything about where they came from, or it being two real people like Melly and Melanie.

When I got home to do the cats that evening I found Melanie sitting huddled in the porch. She was wearing the gear I'd first seen her in, and looked totally done in but all the same she was fizzing. Before I could say anything she jumped up and said, "I've effed things up, Keith. Real bad. You've got to help. She's here. We're both here and we can't get her back. Listen. I was in my room and having one of my fits, real strong, just yakking and yakking into the telephone. I kenned well she must be talking with you but I couldn't hear the words, only the buzz of it going through me till I was shuddering with it. I thought I was going to fly to pieces. I couldn't bear for you to be talking with her and me so far off. I was screaming for you both to stop so I could talk to her myself. There's a phone in Annie's own room. It's another number from the restaurant. I pushed the fit aside and called Information and asked them for Perraults living in Coventry. J., I told them, and there was only the one. As soon as I saw you were finished I called that number, and she answered and said 'Hi,' but before I could say an effing word myself she was there, with me, in Annie's room above the restaurant. Wait . . .''

She'd been gabbling away a hundred miles an hour while I got the door unlocked and took her into the kitchen. Now she shut her eyes and concentrated a moment and opened them and said, "I'm sorry, Keith. But I couldn't help it. It was too strong for me, and now I can't get back.''

"Jesus!" I said. "What's happened to the rest of you?''

"I don't know," she said. "This isn't right, Keith, not like this. There's still two of us . . . Where's Trish?''

"She'll be at the theater now. I can't ring her there.''

Automatically I went on with putting the kettle on and getting the teapot out. I fished Melly's mug out of the back of the cupboard and put it on the table. She grabbed it and sort of fondled it as if it was some kind of magic charm which would get her out of this.

"What happened next?" I said. "How did you make it here?''

It was Melanie who answered. She didn't sound quite so off the handle, now that she'd got the mug in her hands.

"Papa came up, yelling at me for being late down, but I was near crazed myself and I began yelling right back at him for what he'd done with me when I was a wee bairn, and when he got what I was saying he really lost it. I thought he would have killed me but Annie heard the racket and came up and tried to stop him. She couldn't hold him but I got to the door and ran down, and she must have clung on to him somehow and I was out in the street and away. I had no money. I thought of looking for your ma, but I dinna ken if she'd told him she was working in the theater, and maybe he'd come for me there. Then I poked in my pocket and found the paper where you'd written your address and I thought I'd try that. I slept on a bench, and in the morning I bummed myself a cut of bread and walked all the way to the motorway, where the hitchers hang out, and I found a fellow and a girl to hitch along with into Glasgow. I was asking my way to Bearsden, saying I'd lost my purse, and a woman gave me the money for the bus. I'd heard you saying to your ma about feeding your cats, so I kenned you'd be by. But Keith, I'm effing hungry."

"I'll fix you some scrambled eggs. That's what Melly . . . hell, I suppose you know that. For God's sake, which of you is it in there?"

I was watching her do exactly what Melly would have done about her tea. First, a great splosh of milk into the mug, and then a fiddling little half spoon of sugar, tipped

211

slowly in as if she was trying to count the grains, and then stir and stir until the tea was ready to pour.

"There's the two of us, buzzing against each other," said Melanie's voice, "and there isn't room for us both. We can't go on like this, Keith, or we'll be flying apart."

"I believe you," I said. Anyone would have spotted there was something wrong. She was obviously on a high, but it was a sick sort of high, spiky, edgy, dangerous-feeling. Her eyes glittered and her whole body seemed tense and twanging. She clung to her mug as if it was all that was keeping her from flying to pieces, like she'd said. I didn't know what to do. It wasn't any use calling a doctor. I couldn't ring Mum at the theater . . . well, I could try, if it was this important . . . Or Janice—she probably wouldn't be home, but it was worth a go . . .

I put the teapot on the table and gave Melanie her eggs. I was waiting for her to finish pouring so that I could have a cup when the telephone rang. It was Mum.

"Thank heavens you're there," she said. "I haven't got much time, but something dreadful has happened. Janice called, early this afternoon. She got home last night and found Melly in a coma, and the telephone off the hook. She rushed her to hospital but they couldn't find anything wrong. She stayed with her all night and all this morning, until she'd talked to the doctors, and then she went home to pick up things for her. While she was there she noticed a number Melly had written on the telephone pad so she called it. She didn't know who'd be there, but there was a room number and they put it through to me. By the mercy of heaven I'd had the morning off and was just getting ready to come round to the theater. I was horrified when she told me what had happened, but all I could think of was that it might be something to do with Melanie, so I explained about all that. Janice didn't want to listen—it's not her sort of thing. I had to stop, because she was getting upset, and it wasn't until I'd rung off that I worked out you were the only person who could have given her my number. I'm stuck here now till the third act's started, and then I'm going to race up to Annie's . . ."

"Don't do that," I said. "Listen. Did you tell M. Perrault you were anything to do with the opera?"

"No. Why? I did tell him I made costumes, but he seemed to think I meant I was a dressmaker. He wasn't very interested in me. He wanted to talk about himself."

"Thank God for that," I said. "I was afraid he might be coming after you."

"After me? Why on earth?"

"Because Melanie had a row with him and cleared out. She's here. And so's Melly, sort of."

"There? At Bearsden?"

I explained what had happened. She was wonderful. She just accepted it as if there wasn't anything crazy about it.

"This is dreadful," she said when I'd finished. "What on earth are we going to do?"

"The first thing I've got to do is try and get Melanie calmed down," I said. "She can't go on much longer like she is."

"Try to get her to have a nice warm bath. Not too hot. You'll have to turn the water on and it'll take about an hour to get hot. I wonder if it would be safe to give her one of my tranquilizers. They're very mild. In the pink box in the drawer by my bed. Just one. I've got to go now, but—"

"Wait," I said. "Can you ring Maisie"—that's Ken's mum—"and tell her I won't be round tonight? Say I've got a friend come unexpected, and they're not very well, and I'm looking after them."

"I'll fit that in somehow. Good luck, darling . . ."

"Hold it," I said again, because Melanie had come out into the hallway, where our telephone is, and was making signs. I nodded to her to go ahead and butt in. It wasn't Melanie, though, it was Melly.

"Give her my love," she said. "And ask her where Mum is—I want to talk to her."

I passed the message on. I think it shook Mum, and I can see why. It made Melly being in Bearsden real, somehow, in a way just talking about it hadn't.

"Sorry," she said. "She'll be at the hospital—Walsgrave. The number's in my old address book. On the shelf with the cookery books. And give her all my love back. And Melanie too. I've got to go now. Good luck, darling—I think you're doing wonders."

We rang off. I turned the hot water on and found the pills and gave one to Melanie and told her what it was. She looked at it a moment.

"I dinna ken," she said. "Hell, we've got to try something—we're just about hanging on, only."

I got through to the hospital but they absolutely refused to go and find Janice for me. I made it as urgent as I could, but my voice doesn't sound that grown-up and I got a bit upset, so I wasn't sure they'd taken me seriously. Then all we could do was wait. It was only half an hour, but it was forever.

"Hold me tight," said Melanie suddenly. "Hold on to me, Keith!"

I took her into the lounge and turned the telly on and we sat on the sofa with my arms round her. That should have been fun but it wasn't. It was like holding a wild bird, one that's got into the house and you've caught it and you're carrying it out in your hand with its wings folded so it can't flap them and hurt itself, and it lies there still and quivering—like that.

And then the telephone rang and I let go and she flew to it like the bird.

I went into the kitchen but left the door open so that I could see out into the hallway, so I could check she was OK without listening in. She'd settled down on the chair with the handset in the nook of her shoulder, the way she always does, because she can't help doing body language with her hands even when the other person can't see. She did most of the talking, and cried a bit, but it didn't make any difference her being Melly now—she still had the same twanging, fizzing jumpiness pulsing out of her . . . And then, right in front of my eyes, she sort of slumped. The phone slid out of her shoulder but she grabbed it and took a deep, slow breath and said something, and then held it out for me to come and take.

"She's gone," she said in her Melanie voice. "Tell her, Keith. I'm done for."

I took the phone and said, "Janice? This is me. Keith."

"What now, for God's sake?" she said.

She sounded really upset.

"Melanie says Melly's gone. She was here. They were both in Melanie's body . . ."

"Are we all crazy?"

"No, we're not. *It's* crazy, but . . . I mean, weren't you talking to Melly just now? Didn't she tell you what had been happening?"

"Somebody I thought was Melly was telling me something I thought was a lot of nonsense, and I don't understand it and I'm extremely upset . . . wait . . . someone seems to be looking for me . . ."

I heard voices, then Janice again, crying as she spoke.

"I've got to go, Keith. I'm in the sister's office. That was the nurse. She says Melly's woken up and she's asking for me. I'll try and call you back."

I went and told Melanie and then I pretty well collapsed, sitting at the kitchen table with my head in my hands, shuddering with relief.

After a bit Melanie said, "That was an effing close thing, Keith. Christ, I'm shattered. Is there a fag anywhere?"

I found her a pack of Mum's, and an ashtray, and took

her into the lounge, where she slumped on the sofa. She hadn't finished her eggs, but they were cold, so I took a loaf out of the freezer and defrosted it in the microwave and made her a peanut butter and red-currant jelly sandwich, which Melly had a craze for, and she wolfed it, so I made her another. When the water was hot I ran her a bath and pretty well forced her to go and get into it and while I was there I made up the spare bed, and then I put a message on the answer-phone saying I'd be back in twenty minutes and went round to Ken's to tell Maisie I really was all right, and to borrow some milk—we'd used up what I'd got for the cats.

When I got back I found Melanie had fallen asleep in the bath and I had to yell at her to wake her up. She got out grumbling and swearing, and dried herself, sort of, and staggered out in the pajamas I'd given her, tripping over the trouser ends. I pushed her into bed and tucked her in and turned the light out. When I said good-night she didn't answer.

Now there wasn't anything to do except fix myself something to eat and wait for Janice to call and worry about how I could skip school next day, let alone the rest of the week until the opera finished in Edinburgh. Janice did ring in the end. She was still upset, but differently. She said Melly was OK as far as anyone could make out, but they were keeping her in hospital for observation. And she'd told Janice everything she'd done since the phone call—everything Melanie had done, that is—being beaten up by M. Perrault, and getting away, and sleeping out, and

217

hitching over to Glasgow and finding our place and waiting for me to get home, the lot. It was the bit about M. Perrault that convinced Janice. He'd been her husband, remember, but Melly couldn't possibly have known what he was like.

"I absolutely hate this," she told me. "I find it extremely stupid and extremely frightening, and I think I'd rather we were all crazy. But I have to accept that it's happening."

I told her I felt the same, and asked her to give my love to Melly. I said I'd ring Mum and tell her what had happened.

In fact Mum rang me from the theater during the last act. I could hear the singers shrieking and bellowing away in the background. I said it looked as if Melly had got back somehow, and she was out of her coma and so on. I asked her to call my school and tell them I wouldn't be in because I wasn't feeling too good—and what about the rest of the week? She told me she'd found someone to take over the costume job, but she would have to go in in the morning to show her the ropes, and she should be home by teatime. Was I relieved! I flopped into bed and slept till the middle of the morning, when the telephone rang. It was Janice, saying Melly seemed pretty well normal and the hospital were letting her go home. I told her about Mum, and fixed that they'd talk that evening.

Melanie was still asleep, but she looked OK and was breathing easy. I had some Weetabix and was grilling bacon when she groped her way into the kitchen, all woozy and pathetic in my old dressing gown.

"That smells effing good," she said. "Do some for me?"

I told her about Janice and Melly. I wanted to talk about what had happened so that we'd know what to do next time. I mean, was it the tranquilizer, or talking to Janice, or something just snapping? I thought this was important, but Melanie wasn't that interested.

"Next time we're stuck with it," she said. "So it's effing well got not to happen."

We got dressed and watched idiot afternoon TV, and a video, and I went out and bought stuff for supper. I was almost at our road when I saw Ken coming along from the other direction, so I walked on and met up with him. He was on his way round to our place to tell me about this bird he'd seen at the weekend which might have been something crazily rare but was probably just an albino blackbird. I said I couldn't ask him back in as our friend who wasn't well was asleep now and I didn't want to disturb her. It worked out OK, but it made me realize we'd got to have a story about Melanie. We'd got to have something for her to do, and we couldn't leave her alone in the house all day, either. It wasn't just that she'd have gone crazy with boredom—she didn't feel as if it was safe to leave her alone that long.

When I got home Mum was there, so of course we started talking the whole thing through again.

"At least it's taught us a lesson," Mum said. "We don't understand what we're dealing with, but at least we know from now on that we've got to be extremely careful. You aren't going to try calling Melly again, are you?"

"Course not," said Melanie, "and neither's she—but it's going to be effing hard. Sorry, Trish. But you don't understand. Nobody can understand but us. We're each calling the other, calling and calling . . . When Keith was away just now, and before you were home, it swept over me till I was screaming inside me, shaking and sweating and holding myself down so that I didn't go running off to hitch my way to Coventry. And the same with her, and that isn't guessing. It's a thing I ken. But I dinna ken how long I can take it."

"It isn't like when you're having one of your dopy fits?" I said.

"No, nothing like. That was before I kenned for sure she was real, and in a place I could be going to—I could walk into a room and she'd be there, waiting for me. Before, I was only watching, seeing what she was seeing, and she'd not have kenned I was there. Now I can feel her. Put a cloth over my eyes and spin me around, and I'll point you where she is. I could walk straight to her, and maybe I'd weary on the way and fall asleep, but my body would go on walking to her."

Then the phone rang and I went to answer it. It was Janice.

"Melly thinks this is safe," she said. "I hope to heavens she's right. Is Trish back yet? Can I talk to her?"

Mum came and I went back into the kitchen. In spite of what Melly had told Janice I was pretty anxious. I thought any sort of connection between where the two girls were might make something happen, but when I asked Melanie she shook her head.

"It isn't that way," she said. "Just now I ken with my mind she's there, and that's our ma talking with Trish, and that's it. It's the other times, when the whole of me's aching and screaming for us to be together, body and soul, just the one body, just the one soul . . . Mary, mother of God, help me!"

She wasn't swearing either, she was praying. I'd never heard anyone do that before, not for real. I took hold of her hand and held it and she started to cry, quietly, wiping the tears away with her sleeve and swearing under her breath and crying again. This is going to sound really stupid, but I was glad she was doing it. She needed to cry, and she needed to hold my hand so that she could do it, and she trusted me enough to let herself go like that. Yes, I was glad.

The next few days were a real muddle. I'm not going to write down all the different telephone calls and so on, mostly Mum and Janice, but sometimes me talking to Melly and sometimes Melanie and Janice trying to get to know each other a bit. It was specially hard on Janice, Mum said, getting used to the idea that there was this other daughter, or other half of one daughter, depending how you looked at it, who she'd never met and who'd lived this life she didn't know anything about. And on top of that Janice still hated the idea that there wasn't some kind of ordinary, real-world explanation for what had happened. That's why I put in that bit about the other daughter or the half daughter. Melanie and Melly were absolutely set, certain, sure that they were two halves who'd somehow come apart, but Janice was just as certain they were two different people, and always had been and always would be, and what was happening between them was some kind of psychic freak.

"She thinks she might have had twins without knowing it," Mum said. "She had a perfectly appalling labor, in their caravan, with the horrible sister and a couple of old hags from the circus acting as midwives. It was extremely primitive and full of superstitious nonsense, and she passed out several times, so I suppose it's just possible. I know in some places people are very superstitious about twins, because they think one of them must have come from the devil, though I've never heard of that happening in France. But I can tell you one thing—the little boy I was looking after when I was an au pair was perfectly obviously left-handed, but when I suggested he might be, the family was very upset, and the grandmother wanted the parents to sack me on the spot. There'd never been the slightest taint of left-handedness in either family, she said. So what Janice thinks now—or rather what she seems to be trying to persuade herself—is that she had twins without knowing it and they took the left-handed one away . . ."

"You said there didn't have to be a left-handed one," I said.

"No, I don't think so, and I wouldn't have thought you could tell that small. But these are very superstitious people and perhaps they believed they could. Anyway, let me go on. . . . Then, when she ran away with the baby and they came after her and took it away, what they did was exchange it for the other one, which they'd farmed out somewhere, and bring that one back. I must say I don't believe that either. You know your baby and it knows you, however like the new one might be, though according to Janice it cried and cried and wouldn't stop for days after they brought it back."

"But you don't believe it," said Melanie. "Tell me you don't believe it, Trish. It's . . ."

She was trying not to swear when Mum was around, and sometimes it was pretty funny when she bit something back at the last moment, but not now. She was really upset.

"No, I don't," said Mum. "I can believe in somebody having twins and not realizing it, in circumstances like that, but not in people discovering at once that one of them was left-handed . . ."

"They didn't have to know then," I said. "They could just believe one of them was going to be, and take the second one away and keep it until they found out, and then do the swap. And they were just about ready to do that when Janice cleared out, so they had to come after her. And you did say the baby cried a lot, after."

223

I could have kicked myself. I'd only just registered that Melanie really couldn't cope with Janice's kind of explanation, about twins and so on, and I needn't have blurted that out, even if it made a sort of sense. Anyway, Melanie totally lost it.

"That's crap!" she yelled. "I tell you it's effing crap! We're one! I'm her and she's me, and the eff with anything else!"

"I believe you," said Mum. "You know it's so and Melly knows it's so, and that's all the argument I need. What Keith said was perfectly sensible, but what's happening isn't sensible."

"We can't go on this way," said Melanie. "I tell you, we can't go on this way!"

Another evening I was doing homework in the kitchen—you get a lot of that in Scottish schools. Mum was at the theater and Melanie was in the lounge watching TV. I was steaming along through some math when she yelled at me to come and see. I yelled back I was busy and she came rushing out and started trying to pull me out of my chair, yelling at me it was important and I'd got to come. I could see she was on one of her highs so I said I'd come for a bit.

It was a program about Siamese twins. There'd been stuff in the news about a pair who'd been born in Liverpool and they were going to try and separate, and this was some kind of documentary about other pairs. It wasn't my sort of thing. Given the chance I'd have zapped to another channel, but Melanie made me watch the lot. Some of the twins hadn't got a chance. They'd got shared livers and kidneys and things, and there was no way they could be cut apart and both of them live. The ones who were more lightly joined the surgeons could do something about, but it was always chancy. We were looking at a pair who were joined at the chest when Melanie pressed the mute button.

"That's us," she said. "That's me and Melly."

I stared at the screen. They were babies still, about a year old, I guessed. Two heads, four arms, four legs, and this body thing in the middle. It was a still photograph, not film. Both faces were screwed up, both mouths seemed to be crying, all eight limbs struggled and threshed. It was horrible.

"They canna live like that," said Melanie, "and you canna cut them free of each other."

She always sounded much more Scottish when she was upset. After a bit she pressed the button again.

". . . died at two and a half years," said the voice-over. "Even with modern surgical techniques, it is unlikely that either of them would have survived an operation to separate them."

She didn't say anything else until the program was over and she'd switched off.

"Do you see now, Keith?" she said. "It isna livers and that we share, but try and make us two, the way you and

225

my ma are trying, and one of us will be dead. Both of us, very like. We must be one, like we were when we were born. We must be *made* one."

"Made one? How?"

"I dinna ken. All I ken is when I was a wee bairn I was one, and Papa took me away and made me two, and one he gave back to my ma and one he kept for himself, but we couldn't live long like that, no more than the bairns in the program. I tell you this, Keith. If you hadn't been coming down the steps by Princes Street the morning you were, there'd have been some other thing happen to pull us together again."

"What would happen if you just met, and got it over with?"

"The one of us would be dead, and the other would go crazy past curing."

I'd never said anything to her about doppelgangers, and nor had anyone else as far as I knew. I didn't bother to ask how she could be so sure. She wouldn't have been able to tell me.

When Mum came home she called Janice, which she did most evenings. Janice said that Melly hadn't watched the TV program, but she'd described the Siamese twins to her and said almost exactly the same things that Melanie had been saying to me.

I had three weeks back at school after Edinburgh, before the summer holidays started, so we had to work out what to do about Melanie. We couldn't risk leaving her alone.

She said so too. I'd be doing homework and she'd be listening to a tape on my Walkman and she'd jerk up and stare in front of her. Or maybe she'd be watching TV in the lounge and she'd come sort of sleepwalking into the kitchen and mutter to me in a dead kind of voice, "Hang on to me, Keith," and I'd stop what I was doing and simply hold her tight, ten minutes, quarter of an hour sometimes, and she'd give a big sigh and say, "Ta, I'll do now," and I'd let go. If anyone had come in and found us they'd have got the wrong idea. OK, I was keen on her in a way I'd never been on Melly, or anyone else come to that, but what was happening to her was too serious for that kind of messing around.

Janice couldn't leave Melly alone either, but that wasn't as much of a problem, because Melly had school, and friends, and all her usual life to hang on to. Melanie didn't have any of that, nothing to anchor her down. Mum arranged to go in to the opera afternoons and evenings, and she took Melanie in with her to give her a hand. Then I'd take the bus in after school and bring Melanie back to Bearsden, though sometimes we hung around in Glasgow for a couple of hours so she could buy a few clothes and get to see a bit of life. Mum and I'd only been a few months in Bearsden, so people didn't know that much about us. Our story was that Melanie was half French, and her mum was a friend of Mum's, but her parents had split up and she was staying with us while things got sorted out. and we were being careful in case her dad showed up tried to take her away. That was all pretty well tru

I gave myself nightmares about M. Perrault somehow nosing her out, the way he'd found Janice at the hotel when she'd run away from the circus. Luckily there are pages and pages of Robinsons in the Glasgow phone book. I suppose if he'd gone to the police about Melanie going missing, and told them it might have something to do with Mum, they'd have tracked us down, but Melanie said he wouldn't because he didn't trust policemen. We didn't see anything about her in the papers or on the local news.

Mum worked in the sewing room in the theater, next door to what they called the Wardrobe, which was a regular room stacked with racks of costumes and shelves of boots and hats and shoes and gloves and sword belts and so on for all the different productions. They'd have two or three operas on the go, and maybe a couple of others being got ready, and there might be fifty or sixty people in the cast, what with the chorus and everything. That's a lot of costumes.

Usually there'd be half a dozen women in the sewing room, stitching and cutting, but with the opera on tour it was just Mum in the evenings. I got there one time and found her sitting on a pile of clothes with Melanie on her lap, rocking her to and fro like a baby. They both looked utterly exhausted.

"Thank God you're here at last," said Mum, though I wasn't any later then I'd said. "I don't know what's up, but Melanie's been having a very bad time. I haven't sewn a stitch for the last hour and I've a pile of work to do. Do ɔu think you can take her home, darling? She seems to be quieter now. You'd better take a taxi. My wallet's in my jacket pocket. Will you be all right with Keith, Melanie? You can call me if it gets bad again and I'll come straight home.''

Melanie stood up, shivering. I could see she'd been crying.

"I'll do fine," she muttered. "Sorry about that, Trish. I couldn't stop myself."

"That's all right," said Mum. "I could see you couldn't. I'm going to start sewing, but don't let Keith take you away till you're ready."

"I'll do fine," said Melanie again. "I'll just be going to the toilet."

As soon as she was out of the room I asked Mum what had happened.

"I'm not sure," said Mum. "I was sewing in here and Melanie had wandered out and after a bit I went to see where she'd got to—I can't help feeling anxious about her, you know. She'd wandered into the Wardrobe and she must have been trying on some of the costumes—she's done that before—I told her she could . . . Anyway I found her sort of stuck in front of the mirror—you know, the full-length one—wearing one of the green cloaks from *Trovatore*—far too big for her but just right for her coloring. I asked if she was all right and she didn't seem to hear me, so I asked a bit louder and she still didn't. But when I actually touched her she spun round and screamed, and stared at me as if I was some kind of wild animal. Next thing she was yelling and swearing. She didn't know me at all. And we had auditions going on so all I could do was drag her in here and shut the door and try and get her calmed down. And that's what I've been doing ever since. I'm desperately behind, darling. I'm going to be late back—well after ten, I should think. Are you sure you can cope? You'll call if you need me, won't you? The receptionist's name is Mercy. She's much less of a dragon than she tries to sound. Anyway I'll warn her you may be calling . . .''

Then Melanie came back and said thank you and sorry again to Mum, and Mum gave her a hug and we left. I started looking for a taxi, but Melanie said she'd rather walk a bit. In the end we walked the whole way back to Bearsden, which is all of seven miles. We didn't talk much at first. I didn't want to bother her. We must have been nearly halfway home when she said, ''I was blowing around, Keith, blowing around this great cold empty space. Like . . . you've seen a paper bag blowing along a street on a windy day, high up between the buildings, whirling and jinking wherever the wind tells it? Like that. And you know what was in there with me? The creature, the one in the traveling cage, like I told you about in my nightmares. And there was this wee glass door I must get to, if ever I was to come out of that place. And I could see myself standing in my green cloak on the other side of the wee glass door . . . It wasn't any dream, Keith. It was the worst thing that has ever come to me in all my days.''

It was after half past nine when we got home. Melanie had a bath while I fixed supper. She came down in her dressing gown and we ate off our knees in the lounge, watching the telly. Then I went into the kitchen to get on with my homework. After a bit I looked into the lounge to see if she was OK, and she was curled up asleep on the sofa, so I got a duvet and put it over her and went back to my homework. Somewhere around ten Janice rang and I told her Mum was still at the theater.

"Well, will you tell her Christine has confirmed she can have Melly this weekend?" she said. "So I'll definitely be coming up, late on Friday."

(She'd been going to come the weekend before. She was desperate to meet Melanie, of course. But at the last minute Christine had had something happen which meant she couldn't look after Melly, and there was no one else Janice felt it was safe to leave her with. I don't know what she'd told Christine—as much as she could without sounding crazy, I expect.)

"Great," I said. "I'll pass that on. I can't tell Melanie now because she's asleep . . . Is Melly OK?"

Janice hesitated. I guessed she'd sooner have talked to Mum about it. She's not as good as Mum is at letting me (or Melly, come to that) in on things.

"I think she's all right now," she said. "Why? Did something happen your end?"

I told her, except for what Melanie had told me. I felt that was private to Melanie.

"About what time would this have been?" said Janice.

I worked it out. Mum had said two hours.

"Around half past five," I said.

There was another pause while she made up her mind whether to tell me any more.

"I'd rather talk to Trish about it," she said. "I'm sorry, Keith, but it's all a bit private and personal. It's not that I don't trust you . . ."

"That's all right," I said, though actually I felt pretty miffed—I'd told her about Melanie, hadn't I? "Mum should be home about . . . oh, any minute now. I'll get her to call you, shall I?"

"If she's not too tired," she said, and we rang off.

I told Mum when she got in, and she rang and talked for getting on an hour, but I was still doing my homework when she finished so she came into the kitchen and told me what had happened while she made herself her bedtime tipple, which is chamomile tea and a slug of scotch.

"Melly went to a therapist this afternoon," said Mum.

"Did she actually want to?" I said. "Or did Janice make her?"

"It was Janice's idea," said Mum. "She still thinks what's happening is some kind of fixation the girls have got. But Melly thought it might help too, she says. Janice dropped her at the therapist—his name's Dr. Wilson—at five and went off to do some shopping, and when she got back—she was a bit late—she found Melly looking very shaky and dazed, and it was obvious that she'd been badly upset. Dr. Wilson was seeing another patient by then, but he came out and said he thought it was all right to take Melly home, but she shouldn't be left alone and he'd telephone as soon as he could, and explain what had hap-

232

pened. Melly insisted she was all right, but she didn't want
to talk . . .''

"Just like Melanie," I said.

"Yes, I suppose so. Well, they got home and Melly
seemed to settle down, and then Dr. Wilson rang at about
half past eight. Apparently Janice had told him what was
going on, both about Melanie now, and about what had
happened at Arles when she'd run away from the circus, so
he'd asked Melly if she wanted to talk about any of that.
She was quite open about it, he said, and was talking
without any sense of strain or unease, though just like
Melanie she tended to get upset at any suggestion that the
two of them are actually two separate people, and then all
of a sudden she regressed. Do you know what that
means?"

"Went back?"

"Well, yes. They use it in some kinds of therapy. The
therapist helps the patient go back to an earlier phase of
life, sometimes almost as soon as they could walk or talk,
and remember what it was like to be that child, and things
that had happened to them then. It's more than just play-
acting—it's as if they actually become that child . . .''

"Sounds interesting," I said.

"I believe it can be," she said. "But it's not the sort of
thing anyone should try without trained help. They probably wouldn't get anywhere, but if they did it might be
really dangerous for them. Anyway, Dr. Wilson wasn't
even trying that with Melly when it happened. Without
any warning she collapsed onto the floor and lay on her

233

back with her arms and legs flailing and screamed and screamed like a very unhappy baby. Babies cry quite differently from small children, even. It's not a noise Melly could normally make, if she wanted to. Dr. Wilson said he had never seen anyone regress so far back. And she wouldn't stop. He had great difficulty bringing her out of it. I think this must have been going on almost the same time that Melanie was having her outburst at the theater.''

"It would be," I said.

"When she did come back she was still extremely upset," said Mum. "She didn't want to talk about it, but later on she told Janice that she'd been blowing around in an empty gray place and there'd been a small door she couldn't get to . . .''

"You're going to tell Melanie about this, aren't you?"

"I expect so. Why?"

"Just tell her. Go on."

"Well, Dr. Wilson said that it looked as if something extremely traumatic had happened to Melly very early in life, and that possibly it was connected with being separated from her twin . . .''

"That doesn't work. It happened as soon as they were born."

"But not as soon as they knew each other, darling. They'd been together for nine months before they were born."

"You aren't serious, Mum?"

"I am, as a matter of fact, but don't let's argue about it now. I want to get to bed."

"And I've got to finish my homework. Go on."

"There isn't much more. Dr. Wilson said, of course, that we'd all got to be extremely careful about how we approached that period of her life. The same applies to Melanie, I should think. We don't talk about it unless she positively wants to. And he also said that we should respect what the girls say about their meeting. If they believe it's dangerous, however much they long to meet, then they're probably right. We mustn't try to push them into a meeting until they themselves think they're ready."

"He sounds as if he's got his head screwed on. I thought those types were all nutters."

"Just what your father would have said, darling. Well, I'm going to bed . . ."

"One thing, Mum. You've got to make sure Janice does come this weekend. It's important. If Christine falls through again, I'll go down and be with Melly."

"That's nice of you, darling. Let's hope it doesn't come to that."

It didn't. Janice came, no fuss, and it worked out better than I'd expected. I'd been worried because Melanie had got used to plenty of hugs and cuddles from Mum, and Janice isn't like that. Her train didn't get in till after ten, and Mum took Melanie down to meet her at the station. When they arrived we had a hot drink and chatted for a bit in the kitchen, and then Mum and I went to bed to leave them alone. I was sleeping in the attic so Janice could have my room, so I didn't hear them come upstairs, but Mum said it wasn't till almost two in the morning.

Anyway the visit went all right. They weren't actually easy with each other at once, but you couldn't expect that. It must have been extremely weird for both of them. But they got on a lot better than I'd expected, because Janice is very prim and proper and has pretty old-fashioned ideas about a lot of things, and Melanie—she'd talked to me about this—had decided not to try and pretend that she wasn't what she was. I don't mean she swore and smoked the whole time, but she did a bit, and she was—well, Melanie, not Melly. The point is that Janice accepted it.

The other thing that happened was that Janice told us she'd found a private detective who could speak fluent French and she was going to ask him to go out to Arles and see if he could find anything out about what had happened fourteen years before.

"It isn't going to be cheap," she said. "But . . ."

"I'll go half," said Mum.

"I wouldn't hear of it," said Janice.

"Well, let's talk about it later," said Mum. "Go on."

"There are two sides to it," said Janice. "The first is that we can't go on as we are, watching Melly and Melanie the whole time, worrying about them and so on. Something's going to give, and give soon. We can all feel it. Besides, Melanie's my daughter. I want her to be able to come and live with me like a normal daughter. And I'm quite sure that the more we know—the less of this beastly mystery there is—the more chance we have of getting things right. I don't know how much this man will be able to find out, but he should at least be able to look up the birth records and so on. The French are very strict about records. I'm not insisting that Melly and Melanie are twin sisters, because they're both so determined that they aren't, but it's still the only explanation I can understand. That's one side. The other side is about me. Suppose I'd always thought Melly was my only daughter, and somebody told me that actually I'd had twins but one of them had died soon after she was born, it would still be very important to me to know if that was true. And since Melanie is here, and alive and well, and what's more since she's so obviously my daughter and no one else's, I really have got to know how it happened. I don't see how we can get things right between us until we know. That's what I mean about it being a beastly mystery. I don't like mysteries anyway, but this one's going to ruin our lives if we aren't careful. Isn't it, Melanie?''

"Too effing right it is," said Melanie. "Sorry, Ma. And we're never twins, but we've got to know, still."

The detective's name was Eddie Droxeter. You'd never have known he was a detective to look at. "Some kind of third-rate poet with indigestion," Mum said. He had a long, pale face and a big mouth and sad eyes and he was tall and thin but he wore baggy clothes and stooped as if he was trying to make himself look shorter and less skinny. He was expensive, all right. Over a thousand pounds for a week, all in. Janice only had what she earned—she was a buyer for a small chain of clothes stores—so that was a lot for her. Mum told me she hadn't been able to persuade Janice to let her pay Melanie's share, and she hadn't pressed it too hard because she didn't want Janice to feel she was trying to take Melanie over, but she'd got her to accept an interest-free loan of half.

I liked Eddie. I may have made him sound a bit of an ass, but he was obviously pretty bright. He came up to Scotland to talk to Melanie about the circus, because she'd known it till only four years ago, and been part of it, while Janice had always been an outsider. To cut costs he came to Glasgow on one train and went back on the next, and I took Melanie down to meet him in the station tea room, with other passengers hurrying in and out around us and the announcements booming away overhead.

He wanted everything she could remember, especially the names of anyone who might be persuaded to tell him something.

"There's none of them will talk to you," Melanie said.

"Story of my life," he said. "Not being talked to. I'm expert at it. Seriously. This guy won't talk because he's an obstinate cuss, and this guy doesn't know anything, and this guy's scared, and this guy's got something to sell but wants to up the price, and this guy just wants another drink . . . All right, it's a circus, so there'll be acrobats. Let's make a list . . ."

It was interesting to watch how he really got Melanie going, and coaxed her on without wasting any time but without hurrying her either, getting her to talk about the people, not just the names, but what kind of character they were, and remembering always that she'd been only ten when she'd left. I'd thought a thousand pounds plus was a lot of money for a week's work and he probably wasn't going to be worth it, but now I realized he might be.

At one point Melanie went off to the toilet and I asked him if he thought the girls were really twins, or something else.

"They've got to be," he said. "I go along with the theory that the father concealed the birth of one child, for some reason, and when the mother ran off with the one he regarded as *his* daughter he came and took her away and brought back the other one."

"What about things like the scars on their arms?"

"That sort of thing happens with twins. I can't explain it. But, for instance, I was reading about twin brothers in America who'd been brought up separately, and when they finally met they were doing very similar jobs and wore almost identical clothes and their wives even had the same name as each other."

"Weird."

"There's a lot of weird stuff about twins. Now, before Melanie comes back, what can you tell me about the father? He's the obvious person for me to talk to, and barmen are used to strangers wanting to chat, but I'm leaving it till after Arles in case he smells a rat and alerts the people out there. He's not entirely sane on the subject of his daughter, right?"

"He's crazy," I said, and started to tell him, but then Melanie came back and they went on with stuff about the circus until it was time for him to catch his train.

Eddie'd come up to see us the day before end of term. It was lucky it wasn't any earlier, because Melanie went through a bad patch while he was away, and not having to go to school meant I could be with her all day long. I don't mean that she was miserable, just incredibly wired and jumpy. Twanging from the moment she got out of bed till long after midnight, when Mum and I were dropping. She said her dreams were like that too, hurtling her along, strange and buzzing. She tried another of Mum's tranquilizers but it scared her.

"I came kind of loose," she told me. "I felt I was going to slip away out of myself, and wouldn't ever come back. I'd be in that empty place, other side of the wee door."

Then sometimes she'd go into a kind of daze, for a couple of hours at a time. I took her out bird-watching with Ken once, and she had a great time making out she was a French hussy—Ken's so shy and proper he makes *me* look wild. He was interested in a pair of sparrowhawks whose brood was almost ready to fly and he wanted to see it happen, and this meant lying still on a grassy ledge, where we could see the nest, for hours and hours. I didn't expect Melanie to stick it for more than ten minutes, but she barely stirred all afternoon. I nudged her when anything interesting happened at the nest, and she looked at it through Ken's binoculars in a dazed kind of way, but I wasn't sure she knew what she was seeing.

"Where've you been?" I asked her as soon as I could talk to her alone.

"Away," she said. "With Melly."

"In Coventry?"

"Aye. No. She was here too. The place was nothing. I can't explain."

"Was that . . . safe?"

"Aye. Like that. No problem."

But mostly, like I said, she twanged, and it wore her out. When I'd first seen her she'd been exactly like Melly, and like Janice must have been when she was a kid, not fat, but a bit pudgy. Now she'd lost so much weight that you'd have said she was skinny, and her eyes were sunken and had that bruised look round them, but the eyes themselves glittered as if she was on speed or something, which she wasn't, of course.

It was a great relief when Janice rang to say Eddie was back and he'd got news.

Now that school was out and I was home all day Mum had gone back to normal working hours, so we all got together in the evening.

The first thing Eddie had done was go to the *mairie* and look up the births register. He knew the exact day, so it wasn't difficult, and he found that one baby, Melanie Perrault, had been recorded. That didn't prove anything because M. Perrault might have registered the other one under a different name and there were a couple of other girls born around then who might have been the other twin, but he did a bit more research and found that they were both real people and still alive.

Next he looked for the circus. It was on the road, so he hired a car and tracked it down in a little town up the Rhône valley. He went to a performance, and after it he asked to see the proprietor and said he was a TV researcher who was doing preliminary work for a program about traveling circuses, and could he hang around with them for a day or two and talk to people? (Eddie had cards with the name of a bogus TV company on them—he said they were very useful sometimes.) He told the proprietor there'd be money coming if the program was made, so of course he was interested. He was married to Melanie's aunt Sylvie, by the way.

So Eddie did what he'd said, and hung around, and took photographs of everything, and asked questions, and stood people drinks, and so on. He was very careful about the questions he asked, to make them seem natural, but he pretended to be specially interested in the animals, and because there weren't any lions it was OK to ask if they'd ever had lions, and then why had the lion tamer left, and where was he now, because he might be interesting to talk to. Several people told him that M. Perrault had suddenly sold his lions and cleared out, and they didn't know why, or where he'd gone.

"I was careful not to press it," Eddie said. "That first day all I was hoping to do was suss out which of them to

try and go a bit further with. It wasn't going to be easy—
I've come across professional criminals who were freer
with information than that lot. But on the whole I thought
I was getting along as well as I could hope, so I wasn't
really ready next morning when this fellow turned up. I
was having breakfast in my hotel and going through my
notes when he came up to my table and pulled out a chair
and sat down without so much as a by-your-leave.

"I said good morning, but he just sat and stared at me. I
asked if there was something he wanted but he didn't say
anything. I'd just about decided he was a nutter when he
said, 'There are these two girls, identical, now fourteen
years old. They have learnt of each other's existence and
now desire passionately to meet, but they are also afraid to
do so. Correct?'

"He'd got me right off balance, but I managed to say
something about it being an interesting story, and was
there any more?

" 'They do well to be afraid,' he said. 'They will have
their desire very soon. You cannot prevent them. And
when they meet they will die.'

"He hammed it up by snapping his fingers when he said
that, and that helped me get him placed. Melanie had
described him to me, but I hadn't made the connection
and I hadn't seen him at all around the circus. But I'd
watched his performance. He was one of the clowns, and
his act was to do bogus conjuring tricks which always went
wrong—you remember Tommy Cooper?—that sort of
thing . . ."

243

"Monsieur Albert," said Melanie.

"That's right," said Eddie, "but he called himself Albertus Magnus for his act, and at the critical moment he'd snap his fingers the way he'd just done. By now I'd got my wits about me enough to pretend I thought he was trying to interest me in a story for my TV company to produce, so I told him I'd need more, a lot more, before there'd be a hope of selling it to anyone. We beat around the bush quite a bit, and that allowed me to get a bit of a line on him. I put him down as a charlatan, but he obviously knew something and he was prepared to sell it to me if the price was right. Tentatively I decided that he had probably helped in the original abduction . . ."

"No," said Melanie. "Papa couldn't abide him."

"But Janice told me that he and your aunt Sylvie were friends," said Eddie.

"Not anymore, they weren't," said Melanie.

"That's very interesting," said Eddie. "Suppose he had helped with the abduction, he might then have tried to blackmail your father. That would account for a change of attitude. We still have to account for his knowing so much about you. Now, I think I was told that when you last saw your father you started to accuse him of what he had done to you when you were a baby. Did you actually tell him then that you knew about Melly's existence?"

"That I did," said Melanie.

"Then he will almost certainly have guessed that you learnt about it from meeting Trish and Keith," said Eddie. "And also that they must know Janice, and tell her, and that she would very likely want to know more. So he could well have written to his sister warning her that somebody might be making inquiries at the circus, in which case Monsieur Albert might also have learnt of it and decided to cash in on his knowledge. Most of what he said to me can be accounted for like that.''

''But not all of it,'' said Mum. ''For instance, how would he have known about the girls wanting to meet and being afraid to? That isn't at all obvious. Anyone would expect that the very first thing we'd all want to do was arrange a meeting.''

''I don't pretend to account for everything,'' said Eddie. ''I'm just saying that a lot of it can be rationally accounted for, so perhaps the rest can too. Shall I go on? I was still making out I thought he was trying to sell me a plot outline, and he was still ignoring that. After a while, to push the thing on a bit, I said that in any case my company wouldn't look at his story unless it had a happy ending, and was there any way in which the two girls could be brought together without some kind of tragedy?

''He sat and stared at me for a while, and then he said, 'I can do it, and I alone. It must be done in a certain room in Arles, upon the nineteenth of August, at sunset. At no other time and in no other place can it be done, and by me alone. For me, personally, it will be both difficult and dangerous. My fee therefore will be a hundred thousand francs.' That's about thirteen thousand pounds.

''Of course I said that there was no question of my company coming up with a sum like that on the basis of a

sketchy verbal outline, but I went on pretending to negoti-
ate in case he let something else slip. I didn't get very far,
I'm afraid, because he saw what I was up to, and lost
patience. He took a napkin and wrote an address on it and
gave it to me and said, 'Go back to England and talk to
your friends. If they decide to make use of my services,
come to this place at eight in the evening of the seven-
teenth of August. At this point I will explain to you what is
required. All must be agreed by the evening of the eighteenth. Upon the nineteenth I will perform the operation.
You will pay me ten thousand francs before I begin. Your
friends will then have twenty-four hours in which to decide whether they are satisfied with the result. If they are,
you will then pay me the remaining ninety thousand. That
is all I have to say.' And he walked out.

"I tried again at the circus later that morning and they
didn't want to know me. In fact they pretty well threw me
out. And that's about it."

Mum looked at Melanie and Melanie looked at the tablecloth. Mum sighed.

"We've still got to go ahead," she said.

"I was afraid you'd say that," said Eddie.

Now I'm going to go back. I knew almost all of what
Eddie had told us, because as soon as he'd come back from
France he'd reported to Janice, and she'd phoned Mum
and Mum had told me. Janice had been very upset about it
and spent hours on the phone to Mum several evenings in a
row.

"It seems quite mad," Mum told me. "In fact Eddie thinks we're being totally irresponsible, but we both believe this is something we've got to try. You've seen what Melanie's been like these last few days. Melly's been the same. We all know they're working up to some kind of crisis. We can actually feel it coming . . ."

"On the nineteenth of August?" I said. "Could be."

"Janice left the circus on the eighteenth," said Mum. "So the nineteenth is fourteen years to the day since whatever it was happened to Melly when M. Perrault took her away."

"Monsieur Albert would know that, though," I said. "If he helped, I mean."

"Yes, of course. But there are still some things he said to Eddie which I don't see how he could have known. Let me go on. You know what Janice is like. She's not the sort to go along with any kind of out-of-this-world explanation, but even so . . . You know what she said? 'I feel as if Melly was dying of some kind of galloping cancer and there was this miracle cure which somebody told me about. If I was desperate as I'm getting to be about this, I think I'd try it. It would be better than feeling guilty for the rest of my life because I hadn't.'

"And there's something else. Dr. Wilson has phoned a couple of times because he's worried about Melly, but Melly's absolutely adamant she doesn't want to see him again, and Janice daren't tell him any more than she has in case he decides he ought to get social workers in, and they'd almost certainly want to take Melanie into care, and

247

perhaps Melly too. But at one point he said that it might be just as dangerous for the girls not to meet when they felt they were ready as it would be for them to meet when they weren't.''

"I'd go along with that," I said. "Melanie would go crazy. I mean crazy. Throw herself under a bus or something. I'm serious about that, Mum.''

"Janice has been saying almost the same thing about Melly,'' said Mum.

The point about this was that Janice hadn't got thirteen thousand pounds, and she'd have needed quite a bit more, what with fares and hotels and so on, not to mention hiring Eddie again. And there was no way she could raise it. Mum could, because of my dad's insurance money. She'd bought our house outright, without a mortgage, but there was still a bit of a nest egg left. So a lot of the telephone calls to Janice were about persuading her to let Mum use it. And the reason why Eddie had come to Bearsden was so that *he* could try to persuade her not to. She hadn't paid him to come. He'd done it on his own account because he was so unhappy about it.

"I think you're making a bad mistake," he said.

"Tell me something," said Mum. "Don't you think ten thousand francs is actually rather a little for him to ask? I mean if he's simply going to lay on some kind of conjuring trick so that he can walk off with our deposit, wouldn't he be asking more? Fifty thousand, I'd have thought. Doesn't that suggest he himself believes he can do what he says, so he's prepared to wait for the full fee?''

"All it suggests to me is that he thinks his conjuring trick is going to be good enough to persuade you he's done what he promised. That's why I'm not pulling out now, which I'm otherwise very inclined to. But I'm sticking with it because I believe you'll get into a worse mess without me than you will if I'm there."

"Thank you," said Mum.

We flew out to Marseilles on separate flights. Melanie didn't have a passport, but luckily Melly had one of her own as well as being still on Janice's, and of course the photograph was spot on, apart from the hair, so that was no problem. Eddie met us at the airport in a hired car and drove us to Arles across a flat, dusty, baking plain with dingy white cattle and vineyards. While he was driving us up he told us what had been happening. After that he was going back for Janice and Melly on the next flight.

"I'm not at all happy about this," he said. "In fact I'm still hoping I can get you to cry off. I'll refund my fee, if that will make the difference."

"I wouldn't dream of asking you to do that," said Mum, "whatever else happens. You've been marvelous. But it's worse than we thought, is it?"

"You'll have to make your own minds up about that. I know what I think. I wish I could tell you this was some sort of straightforward scam, and he's just going to perform a lot of mystic passes and then pocket the fee. I could cope with that. But there's something else going on and I can't make out what. Anyway, I saw him yesterday evening. There didn't seem any point in going on with the story that I was some kind of film scout, so I told him I was acting on your behalf and you'd hired me to protect your interests. I then took up a fairly tough negotiating position—nothing he could object to if he was on the level, but plenty if he wasn't. The main point is that I've insisted on a legally enforceable contract, with all the money in the lawyer's hands until what he calls the operation is completed to your satisfaction. I was expecting him to jib at that, but he didn't.

"Then I insisted on seeing the room where it was going to happen. It turned out to be in the building where I met him, which is an old inn out in the suburbs. He took me upstairs and showed me. It's a large room on the top storey. It looks as if some kind of club or something used to meet there once, but it's almost empty now. The point is that it can be reached by two sets of stairs at opposite ends of the building, so that the girls don't even have to use the same entrance before they finally meet. I went over it very thoroughly and I couldn't find anything wrong with it.

"Now I'll come to his demands. The first seems to me pure hocus-pocus but ought to be possible. The girls have to be identically dressed, and their hair identically cut and arranged. They have to be exact mirror images of each other. That means no fastenings on the dresses, and everything else symmetrical. If there's a pocket on the left breast there must be one on the right, and so on. I didn't get it about the fastenings until he showed me on my own shirt. My shirt buttons left over right, so my mirror image looks as if it buttons right over left . . .''

"I knew it was something to do with mirrors," said Mum. "You remember what happened in the Wardrobe, darling? And that's why their scars are on opposite arms. Go on, Eddie. There's bound to be a Carrefours or a Prix Unique in Arles. I'm sure I can find something for them there. And Janice will have to take Melly to a hairdresser and get her hair cut to match. Hell, we'll need a photograph."

"That's OK," said Eddie. "I'll take one as soon as we get to the hotel. Now the next thing is a good deal trickier. Albert told me he'd be bringing an assistant. To push him a bit further I thought I might as well offer to do that myself, though I was pretty sure he'd find some kind of occult nonsense reason to turn me down. Sure enough, he asked me when my birthday was and when I told him May he said that wouldn't do because it had to be somebody born as near as possible to the cusp of Sagittarius and Capricorn, which I gather is just before Christmas—I'm not into astrology myself. Again I thought I might as well call him on that, so I told him I'd find somebody else, and very much to my surprise he accepted that at once. All he said was that it mustn't be a woman, and he gave me till this evening to come up with someone suitable. I spent an hour this morning ringing round the local agencies, but without any luck so far. It's not a big deal. We can always just tell him—"

"No," said Mum. "If we're going to go along with this

at all we've got to do it properly. That means doing exactly what he says. Anyway, Keith's birthday is the twentieth of December. Is that any good?''

"Well," said Eddie. "I have to tell you I don't trust this guy an inch. He knows something, and he's up to something. No offense, Keith, but . . . Look, Trish, give me another hour, and if I don't come up with a genuine cusp-of-whatsit candidate I'll try Keith on him this evening. I'm seeing him in any case with the contract. And if I don't find someone and if he then turns Keith down I'm going to do my damnedest to persuade you and Janice to call the whole thing off, after all."

"We can't do that now," said Mum. "Not if we can possibly help it."

"Let me tell you this," said Eddie. "I was trying to get him to agree what we meant by your being satisfied with the operation—you, Janice, and both the girls, all happy, or what? Then I realized that he was talking as if there was only going to be *one* girl around when it was over."

"That's right," said Melanie.

She and I were in the back of the car and Mum was in front with Eddie. I'd been leaning forward to hear what Eddie was saying, but she'd spoken in such an odd way that I turned and looked at her. We'd all been having a very much easier time since Eddie had come back from France and it had been settled that we were going out to Arles. Melanie (and Melly too, Janice said) had stopped her wild fizzing and calmed down almost to normal. Beyond normal, even, because she'd spent most of the time in a sort

252

of gentle daze, just waiting. "Getting myself ready," she told me. Now she was fizzing again all right. As I turned she grabbed me and whispered in my ear, "Dinna let them back out now, Keith. Please! They canna do it now!"

"Do my best," I whispered, and went back to listening to Mum and Eddie. Out of the corner of my eye I'd seen Eddie banging the side of his fist against the steering wheel, he was that upset.

"I don't get it!" he said. "I absolutely don't get it! You're responsible adults. OK, you're a bit gone on the mumbo jumbo yourself, but you're grown-up. And Janice doesn't believe a word of it. And yet you're both prepared to put these girls into the hands of this charlatan. Not to mention risking a considerable amount of money."

"Is it really like that?" said Mum gently. "I mean . . . No, look. We're upsetting Melanie. Get us to the hotel and take your photograph. And then—you've got a bit of time before you need to go back for Janice and Melly?— we'll talk about it then while Melanie and Keith are getting settled in. All right?"

Arles is roasting in August. There are shade trees down the main streets, but the heat bounces off the shabby plaster houses and the air crackles in your nostrils, and smells of dust and diesel fumes and garlic and cooking oil, and if there's a breeze you pick up wild, dry herby smells from the baking plain. Your clothes stick to you and you stick to

253

anything you sit on and you sleep under not even a sheet and you're still too hot.

Our hotel was in a quiet little back street and didn't look at all smart. (Janice and Melly were staying on the other side of the town.) Eddie took some pictures of Melanie with an instant camera, for the hairdresser, while we were still out on the pavement, and then Mum checked us in and Melanie and I waited upstairs while she talked with Eddie. We had tall, shuttered rooms with incredibly old-fashioned furniture. Mum and Melanie were in one room and I was in a sort of annex off theirs.

Melanie was extremely jumpy until Mum showed up, just as bad as she'd been those first few weeks in Glasgow.

"I hope it's going to be all right," Mum said. "I think I've persuaded him to carry on for the moment anyway, though he still thinks we're taking a terrible risk with the girls. Which we are—there's no getting away from it—but anything else seems worse. And of course we've still got to see what Janice says.

"Eddie's going to see this Monsieur Albert this evening, and he's going to tell him straight out that we don't trust him, and that we've got to be absolutely sure that there's no way he can do anything to harm either of the girls. Eddie's got it into his head that he's going to try and make off with one of them by some sort of conjuring trick—he is a conjurer after all, so he's going to insist on there being someone from our side in the room the whole time— Keith if he can't find a grown-up who fits. If the man won't accept Keith then we'll know he's trying to cheat us, because Keith's perfectly genuinely on the cusp of Sagittarius and Capricorn. I've realized what that's about, by the way. We're almost on the cusp of Leo and Virgo now, and the girls were born almost on the cusp of Aries and Taurus, and that makes a perfect triangle—I think it's called a trine, and it's supposed to be very significant—I don't remember why. So at least it wasn't something Monsieur Albert just made up as an excuse for not having Eddie.

"The other thing he's going to insist on is that we've got to be able to seal the room off completely, so that no one can get in or out from the moment it starts till it's over. Apparently there are two little rooms at the top of the two stairs—that's on either side of the big room, like lobbies. The doors lock, so we won't be able to interfere. Eddie's going to go over the whole place again this evening, and measure everything, and make sure there aren't any secret doors or compartments and so on. I must say I don't see how the man could possibly imagine he could get away with something like that. Surely the other girl . . . Anyway, if he turns us down over any of that Eddie's going to call it off . . . I'm sorry, Melanie—I think we'll have to . . . God, I wish this was over. I'm absolutely sick with worry. I don't think I want any lunch."

"I do," I said.

"Me too," said Melanie. "I'm really hungry."

It was strange. A few minutes before she'd been so jittery it almost hurt to watch, and now she'd calmed down completely. She'd barely seemed to register what Mum had been saying about calling things off if Monsieur Albert wouldn't agree, and now she lay on her bed and looked at the ceiling while Mum unpacked enough to change her shoes and so on.

"They must have landed by now," said Mum as she got her things together for going out.

"A wee while back," said Melanie. "They're in the terminal now, showing their passport. There's a bairn behind them, crying."

"If you could do that on the stage you'd make a fortune," said Mum, but she sounded cross about it.

We went out and found a store and bought long French loaves and butter and cheese and peaches and Coke, and made ourselves a picnic in the shade of some trees in a hot little square with a dribbling fountain in the middle. Then we went off to find the clothes, with Melly drifting along in a kind of happy daze, letting herself be pushed and shunted round this enormous superstore while we looked for absolutely mirror-image dresses. Everything seemed to have a little logo on one side, or a pocket, or something. At last we found two bright yellow shift things with zips at the back. Melanie just glanced at them and said, "Yuck," but Mum and I went over them inch by inch looking for some way of telling them apart.

"I suppose they'll do," said Mum. "Only I wish they weren't so hideous."

We were trying on sandals and Melanie had hold of my shoulder while she balanced on one leg getting her heel right in the other foot, when she froze. Her nails dug into me like claws.

"Ouch!" I said. "You needn't do that!"

She didn't hear me. She stuck there, except that her head turned slowly as if she was watching something extraordinary going along the next aisle. Then she relaxed.

"What was that about?" I said.

"They were driving by," she whispered. "In the road just out there."

From then on, for the rest of the day, she was a quite different sort of dreamy, quiet, smiling, doing little dance steps while she walked, breaking off in the middle of something she was saying for a few seconds and then carrying on, as if she'd just said hello to a friend who'd passed by. Mum paid for the clothing and went off to talk to Janice and Eddie while Melanie and I walked slowly back to the hotel along the shady side of the streets, turning off to look at anything that seemed interesting. Melanie too. Being interested, I mean—even more than me. It was as if she kept saying, "Look! Look!" to somebody I couldn't see was there.

We stopped at a cafe and had what was their idea of tea—in a glass, just hot water, with your own tea bag which you put into it, and no milk, but French milk is disgusting anyway. Then we got a bit lost, so we weren't back at the hotel until only just before Mum. I'd been expecting problems, in fact I thought Eddie might have persuaded Janice to call the whole thing off. I mean she saw things almost the same way as he did. But no.

Mum told me about it while Melanie was in the shower.

"She'd already told him she thought we had to go ahead," she said. "Before I got there, I mean. She says Melly might crack up completely if we don't. She's worried, of course, but she's a bit more down-to-earth about it than I am. She says the only thing that matters is that the girls are convinced this is the right way for them to meet, and it makes no difference if Monsieur Albert's a complete charlatan. In fact what would be worrying would be if he wasn't. She says he can't really expect us to believe there'll only be one of the girls left at the end of it, that's just mumbo jumbo, and of course they'll both be there and he'll claim he was talking metaphysically, or something, but it's worth letting him see he's not going to get away with trying anything like that. And tomorrow morning she's going to look for some sort of paging gadget for you to have on you, so that you can call us the moment you think there's anything wrong."

"All right," I said.

"You're sure, darling. You'd say, wouldn't you?"

"Yes, of course," I said.

Actually I didn't know what I felt. All this was making me pretty anxious. I couldn't think properly. One side of me agreed with Eddie and Janice, that Monsieur Albert was a crook, a con man, and all he was probably after was the money, though he might try something nasty with the girls and it was up to me to stop it. That's what my brain said. But another side of me—well, I'd spent so much time with Melanie, and I minded so much for her and about her, and she was so sure that this thing mattered more than anything else in the world . . . well, I believed that too. I had to.

Not just that. I was actually praying that Eddie didn't find someone else with the right birthday. I was scared stiff, but I wanted to be there. Me and no one else.

We waited for it to get a bit cooler, but it didn't, so in the end we went out and had supper at a restaurant in one of the main squares, with tables out on the pavement. Just being with Melanie now was like being on some kind of wonderful high, she was so happy, bubbling and chatting, and then going dreamy for a few minutes, and then coming back to us and telling us what Melly and Janice were up to. I could almost feel them, Melly and Melanie, swooping to and fro between their two bodies like the swifts swooping and wheeling against the evening sky.

"I don't know if I can bear this much more," Mum whispered to me at one point. "It'll be so agonizing if it all goes wrong."

"Not much longer now," I told her.

But it was. It was forever. The night was forever, and the morning longer, and the afternoon longer still, and I'd look at my watch thinking that would be another twenty minutes gone and it was maybe three. The heat made it worse. It was almost as if time had sort of melted, like a road melts on really hot days, and everything stuck to it as it went along.

Eddie came round soon after breakfast. He talked to Mum alone for a bit. Melanie seemed to have gone all sleepy. She said she didn't want to talk or think because she was getting herself ready. She seemed perfectly happy, but we didn't want to leave her alone, so I waited with her until Mum came up and told me that Eddie hadn't found anyone else and he needed to tell me what I'd got to do.

I went down feeling nervous as hell and we sat in a dark, hot little bar smelling of last night's smoke and drink while he explained.

"I saw him again yesterday evening," he said, "and I got most of what we wanted. I wasn't expecting the lot. The chief thing I didn't get was that he wouldn't hear of anyone waiting in the two lobbies at the top of the stairs. The whole of that floor has to be free of irrelevant astral influences, believe it or not. At least the bastard's consistent. But we can wait on the landings below, and we can see the top of the stairs from there, and that's pretty well as good. I've got a French colleague coming from Marseilles to give a hand, so that means there will be two each side. And I've been over the whole place again, measuring up, and I'd bet my life there's no other way out."

"He didn't mind?" I said.

"Didn't turn a hair. Amused, if anything, but he doesn't give much away. The other thing he wouldn't stand for was me taking you round there this morning to show you the layout. More astral contamination, of course. Best I can do is a sketch map. I made him take me through the whole process, as far as it concerns you. This wasn't just so that I could check it out. It's so that if he tells you anything different you'll know he's up to something. And he is. I'm still dead certain of that.''

He unfolded a piece of paper and showed me his sketch. It was not quite square, with two smaller squares on the corners on one of the long sides, leaving a space like a fat T. This was the main room. The small squares were the two lobbies, with stairs leading up to them.

"Right," he said. "There are four good windows, so there should be plenty of light. Once the proceedings have begun, Albert will be at this end here, where I've written 'A,' and you will be here at 'K,' behind the mirror. I haven't seen the mirror, but he says it's a bit under three feet wide and about five foot six high. He wanted to put you right down here by the bottom window, but I insisted that you must be able to see him throughout the proceedings. He didn't like it, but in the end he agreed on condition that once things are under way you keep absolutely still and don't do anything to distract him. By the way, I haven't told him that you'll have a pager, assuming Janice can find one.

"When you first come into the room, take a good look round. Apart from the mirror there'll be only what's already there—that's to say this stack of chairs in the corner and this table here. The tablecloth hangs down a few inches. If he's moved it or changed it so that it prevents you from seeing under it except by lifting it up, object.

261

That's the only hiding place I can see in the room, and I think it's too obvious for him to consider. There are little balconies outside the three main windows. Take a look out and check there's no one on them.

"When you're satisfied, tell him, and he'll then go through the procedure with you. I've told him that you understand simple French, provided he speaks slowly and clearly. All right? Now this is what he says is going to happen.

"Sunset is at eight-forty-six, local time. A few minutes before that he'll tell you to fetch the girls. You come to this lobby here, go to the top of the stairs, and beckon to Melanie to come up. You don't speak unless you have to. Trish and my French colleague will wait on the lower landing. Once Melanie's in the lobby you lock the outer door and blindfold her with the cloth she'll give you. You then go and call Melly from the other lobby. This way, you'll be able to see Albert from the top of the stairs all the time he's alone in the room with Melanie, and you can signal to me if you think everything's OK. You lock that door—don't worry, I'll bring a jimmy—and blindfold Melly.

"You go back into the main room and wait for Albert to tell you to bring the girls in. You do that, Melly first, and stand them back to back here, in front of the mirror, where I've put these crosses. He's seen what they'll be wearing, but he'll check them over and go back to his chair. When he signals to you to remove the blindfolds you do so, and go back behind the dotted line. He'll signal

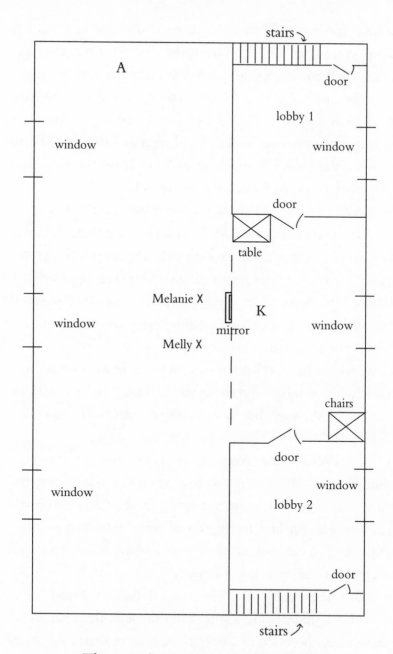

The upstairs room at the Orangerie

again, and you tell them to turn round. After that you keep complete silence. The girls will do what they are compelled to do, he says, whatever that means.

"The mirror has a leather cover, fastened with two buckles at the back. He'll ring a bell three times, twice for you to undo the two buckles, and the third time for you to remove the cover. You fold it and put it on the table and you then move to K and stay there, until—"

"Will I be able to see the girls from there?" I said.

"No, you won't. I couldn't shake him on that. This was the best I could get. He says it's not to stop you seeing the girls, but so that they aren't distracted by seeing you. They mustn't be aware of anything except the mirror. But you'll be able to see him and everything else except that narrow section of the room, and I don't see what he can get up to from where he is. That window is three storeys up a sheer wall with a busy square outside. That curtain will be closed, by the way, but he's leaving the other two open for light.

"All right? Then you stay in your chair until everything's over. He'll ring the bell again for you to put the cover back on the mirror and fasten the buckles. You don't need to wait for him to ring three times. And that's apparently it. You can unlock the doors and we'll come up and check that the girls are all right."

"Did he actually say girls? Two of them?" I said.

"No, he didn't. He's still going through this charade of pretending there's only going to be one of them. Right up to the point when you take the cover off he was talking about *les jeunes filles,* and from then on it's *la jeune fille.* I know it's nonsense, and I'm dead certain there's nothing he can do to make it happen, but it makes me bloody uneasy and I wish to hell I'd never got into this.''

After Eddie had gone we got through the day somehow. I just remember the heat, and the sweating tourists, and a cafe with air-conditioning where we had ice creams, and the way the sun slammed into us when we went outside again, and the stuck minutes. I don't think Melanie noticed anything at all. She was in a different kind of dream today, not soaring about, but sleepwalking round with us.

She actually managed to sleep after lunch. I just lay on my bed and sweated, and Mum read. By teatime I was too nervous to stay there anymore, so I decided to go out again, though it wasn't any cooler. Melanie woke up and said she was coming too, so we went back to the cafe and had Cokes. She seemed wide awake now, but very quiet and solemn, so I didn't try to chat. Time oozed by.

We were on our way back to the hotel when Melanie took my hand and said, "I've a thing to tell you, Keith. It came to me while I was asleep. But first you must promise me you won't say a word of it to Trish or Janice or Eddie.''

Once, after some mess I'd got myself into at school, Dad had told me what to do if somebody asks you this. You say, "If it's something I can promise.'' But you don't, of course—certainly not if it's someone like Melanie who asks you.

"All right," I said.

"I ken now why Papa sold his lions," she said. "He didn't want this day to come. He couldn't just leave and go to another circus, because Monsieur Albert would find him there, easy. But he thought maybe if he crossed the sea . . . Edinburgh would be a good long way . . . But it was never enough . . . Papa loved his lions more than anything in the world. But he sold them for me."

"I suppose that means he loved you more than the lions," I said. She looked at me sideways and smiled. I knew why, because I'd heard the silly jealousy in my own voice.

"Why don't you want me to tell Mum and the others?" I said, to cover up.

"Because Eddie's right. You can't trust Monsieur Albert. He'll be trying something."

"But what? I mean, if he does what we want without any cheating at all he's going to get a lot of money."

"I dinna ken. But he'll be trying something yet."

When we got back to the hotel we found that Eddie had been and left a sort of electronic gadget for me which Janice had found. I'm going to go on calling it the pager, though I don't know what it was really for. It looked like a pencil torch. There were two of them and Eddie was keeping the other one. They each had a button on them which you could press, and when you did the light on the other one lit up and it gave a buzz. Mum and Eddie had tested it, and it worked from the street outside up to our rooms in the hotel. I dug out a shirt with a breast pocket and put it in there with a couple of pens. It looked like the sort of thing a kid carries around anyway.

Then we had a bit over half an hour left before our taxi came. I felt extremely nervous again. Time went slower than ever and I kept swallowing and feeling sticky-chilly in spite of the heat, and getting up and walking around and sitting down again, and not being able to concentrate on anything for more than a couple of minutes. Mum read, and Melanie, in her yellow dress, lay on her bed with her eyes shut, but she wasn't asleep.

When the taxi came it took us a fair distance, right out of the touristy parts, past a lot of ugly modern flats, to a bit where the buildings were old again. I guessed this must have been a village right outside Arles, once, and then Arles had grown round it. We stopped in a grubby square with a church on one side and trees in the middle, where men were playing that game which is a bit like bowls, except that the balls are made of steel and you throw them through the air. The houses had heavy dark shutters and brown or orange plaster, peeling and soft-looking. The roadway was cobbles. Noisy little vans buzzed and bumped across them.

Round from the church the pavement was broad enough to hold a few tables, where men were playing dominoes and drinking beer or wine. The tables belonged to the hotel. It looked so shabby you couldn't imagine anyone wanting to stay there. Its name, Orangerie, was written in dark green paint across its front.

The men at the tables gave Mum the eye as she led the

way in. Melanie drifted along in a kind of trance. I had to hold her elbow and steer her.

Eddie was waiting for us in the lobby. He led us along a corridor and up two flights of stairs to a landing, where he introduced us to the detective from Marseilles, who'd come to help. His name was Pierre.

"All set?" said Eddie. "We've still got about twenty minutes till kickoff, but Keith should go up straight away and meet our friend. Just give me a minute to get round to the other side, Keith, then carry on up these stairs and through the door at the top. You'll find yourself in a small room with another door on the far side. Knock, and wait till he tells you to come in. After that, carry on as we've arranged, and if he tells you anything different, you do what I said. Don't argue with him. Just do it. And if there are any problems, send for me. OK? Well, good luck. See you later."

We counted sixty seconds on my watch, and then Mum kissed me and wished me luck. Melanie just smiled vaguely at me. I wasn't sure she even knew I was there.

I climbed the stairs with my heart hammering, opened the door at the top, and went through into a little square dusty room with one small window and not a scrap of furniture. I knocked on the door on the far side, waited until a voice said, *"Entrez,"* and went in.

For a moment I could hardly see. The room faced west, and the setting sun was blazing in through three tall windows which ran right down to the floor. The light from the middle one was straight in my eyes, dazzling after the darkness of the stairs, but hazy too, and the air was full of a horrible sweet oily smell. I bumped into a table and felt my way round out of the direct sun, where I could see.

The right-hand window was open and a man was standing there, looking out over the trees in the square and the jumbled roofs to watch the sun go down. He was smoking a funny short pipe with a tiny bowl. That was where the haze was coming from. It wasn't pot—I know what that smells like.

It was incredibly hot up there, in spite of the open window. It was right up under the roof and the sun had been beating down on the tiles all day. I thought I'd been sweating like a pig already, but now it really streamed off me. And the air was foul to breathe, too, with that sweet, sticky smoke mixed in with the dry, hot dust.

The man didn't move, so I took a look round. The room seemed pretty much like Eddie had told me, with the stack of chairs down at the bottom beside the far window, and the table on the corner where he'd drawn it. I took a special look at the tablecloth, which was a grubby old red thing with tassels at the corners. It hung only a little way down and I decided it must be the same one he'd seen.

He hadn't seen the mirror, but that was where he'd drawn it too, opposite the middle window. It was about as tall as I am, but all I could see of the mirror itself was a round stand of very dark wood, right at the bottom. The rest of it was covered by a sort of black leather sheath, very old and crackled, with two straps that buckled behind.

I opened the middle window and looked out. There was a tiny balcony—really it wasn't much more than a railing to stop people falling out—but there wasn't anyone hiding out there or on either of the other two, so I came back in and waited there, thankful for the outside air.

At last the man turned round and beckoned, and I went over. He looked at me for a while, so I looked back. He was short and square with big, trembling hands. He was half bald, and the rest of his hair was clipped short. His eyes seemed extra large, and soft, and deep. His face was brown but had a funny dead look to it, like your hands go when you've kept them a long time under water. (I'd seen a program about retired clowns once, and one of them had a skin like that. He said it was from the old-style makeup.)

After a bit he said, *"Bon. Eh bien, tu t'appelles Keet?"*

His voice was quiet and flat, and came a lot through his nose. He sounded tired and bored.

"Oui, Keith," I said.

He nodded and took me through my instructions in French, in the same order as Eddie had done. I was shuddering with nerves inside, and I thought the easiest thing was to act a bit dumb. We looked into the two little rooms I was going to bring the girls through. The other one was no different from the one I'd already seen. He showed me where he wanted me to make the girls stand, and the signals he'd give me to take the blindfolds off and then to tell them to turn round. Then he took me behind the mirror and unfastened and refastened the top buckle, and made me do the same. He told me to wait and fetched a small handbell out of his bag. I think it may have been silver, but it was almost black.

"*Je sonne une fois,*" he said, and shook the bell, holding the clapper with his other hand so that it didn't actually ring. "*Tu défais la première boucle.*"

He mimed undoing the top buckle, and looked at me. I nodded. He shook the bell again.

"*Au deuxième coup, la deuxième boucle,*" he said, and mimed undoing the other strap. This time he waited a bit before he shook the bell.

"*Au troisième coup, tu ouvres l'envelope et tu l'enlèves.*"

He put the bell on the table, still making sure it didn't ring, and mimed sliding the cover off round the mirror from behind.

"*Exactement comme ça,*" he said, and made me stand where he'd stood and do what he'd done.

With his finger he drew an imaginary line from the corner of the table across the room behind the mirror.

"*Tu ne dépasses jamais cette ligne,*" he said, speaking even slower than he'd been doing. "*Et tu ne regardes jamais dans le miroir. Jamais, jamais, jamais.*"

"Right," I said, miming it all again as I went through it. "The first time you ring the bell I undo the top strap. The second time I undo the bottom strap. The third time I take the cover off. I mustn't cross this line and I absolutely mustn't ever look in the mirror."

"*Bon,*" he said, and went and fetched a chair from the stack and put it behind the mirror.

"Alors," he said, *"tu plies l'envelope et le mets sur la table, et tu t'assieds ici. Puis tu ne bouges plus jusqu'à la fin."*

I went and sat in the chair to check how much I could see. I wasn't slap up against the mirror, so the only bits of the room which were hidden were a wedge of space in front of the mirror and two narrow triangles round the corners on either side of me. But the chair where Monsieur Albert would be sitting was well in sight, and so were both the end windows, while I could just see the top of the middle one above the mirror. The windows themselves were double and opened inward, so even when the curtains were closed I didn't see how anyone could come in that way without moving them enough for me to notice.

"I get it," I said. "I fold the cover and put it on the table, and then I come and sit in this chair and don't move till it's all over."

"Bon," he said, and went back to his window and his pipe. I got up and checked the back windows, including the two in the lobbies, but they didn't seem to open at all, so I went back to the chair and sat there looking round and trying to think if there was anything else I could do.

The sun was almost down and streaming flat across the room when Monsieur Albert knocked out his pipe on the window frame and came and closed the center window and drew the curtains, darkening all that part of the room but leaving the two shafts of light streaming in at either end, golden in the dusty, smoky air. I was all tensed up, peering for the slightest sign that he was trying to trick us, and I knew that something had bothered me, some other movement I'd seen out of the corner of my eye as he'd closed the curtains. Then I spotted what it must have been. He'd left his window open, and the far half of it was at an angle to the room with its dark curtain hanging behind it, so what I'd seen was the reflection of the central shaft of sunlight being blanked out. It wasn't important . . .

Yes it was—it might be! What I could mainly see was the reflection of the blaze of light across the other end of the room, striking the two walls of the lobby as far as the door on my left, but right at the edge of it was the beginnings of a dark shape which I realized was the very edge of the mirror. There was nothing else it could be. The reflection was a bit wavy because the glass was old, but the bit of the mirror was surprisingly clear against the brightness beyond. Please, please don't let him shut the window, I thought as he went back that way, and he didn't. He settled into his chair, opened his bag, checked through the stuff inside, and looked up.

"On commence," he said. *"Fais entrer les deux filles. Uniquement les deux filles."*

I went through the lobby on my right, opened the far door, and beckoned to Melanie. Mum kissed her and she climbed slowly up the stairs, looking calm and serious. I held the door for her and locked it behind us. She waited in the middle of the room and gave me a red scarf, which I folded into a loose roll and tied over her eyes.

"Good luck," I whispered, and she smiled, but as if she wasn't sure what I was talking about.

When I crossed the room on my way to the other lobby

Monsieur Albert was sitting with his hands folded and his head bowed, as if he was praying. I went to the top of the stairs and beckoned to Melly and gave the thumbs-up to Eddie, to tell him that so far it had all gone as he'd fixed. But when Melly came climbing toward me I stood and gaped and almost forgot everything, because she wasn't Melly, she was Melanie. The room and the stairs were the other way round, and it was a green scarf she gave me, not a red one, and I knew with my mind that this was Melly because it had to be, but I still couldn't make myself believe it, especially when she smiled exactly the same smile when I wished her luck. I thought I'd known how like they were, but now that they'd got their hair the same I realized I hadn't, the likeness was so amazingly exact. I don't think even Janice could have told them apart. I'd finished tying the blindfold before I remembered to check back through the door and see what Monsieur Albert was up to, but he was still where I'd left him, huddled on his chair with the bald top of his head glistening with sweat. He looked up when he heard the door close and put his finger to his lips. I nodded to tell him everything was ready.

He pointed to the other lobby, so I went and fetched Melanie, leading her by the hand to the exact place he'd shown me. Then Melly. When they were back to back in front of the mirror he got up and went into each of the lobbies in turn and tried the outside doors to make sure I'd locked them. Then he came back and looked very carefully at the two girls, starting at their shoes and working up. He adjusted the shoulder of Melly's dress, and then spent some time comparing their hair. After a bit he took a small pair of scissors out of his pocket and snipped a wisp of hair off the back of Melanie's head and another by Melly's left ear. He was careful not to drop the stuff he'd cut, but took a brown envelope out of his pocket and popped it in. He was putting the envelope back when he seemed to change his mind and handed it to me. I put it in the back pocket of my jeans.

He pointed to tell me to go back behind the imaginary line on the floor, so I did that, checking over my shoulder that he was going back to his chair. He sat down and started to fish things out of his bag, first a piece of cloth which might once have been white but now was a sort of brownish cream with darker stains on it. He spread it carefully on the floor in front of him and then one at a time took several little packages out of the bag, unwrapped them, and arranged what was in them on the cloth. One was a small brass cup, which he placed upside down. Another looked like a chicken's foot, but very old and dried. There was a dark blue stone and a lump of something wrapped in a yellow bandage, like a mummy. I couldn't see what the other things were. I think there were seven of them. He put them in a circle and drew with his finger in the air between them, in the shape of a star, finishing where he'd begun over the cup. He took some powder out of a small tin box, shaking it into the palm of his hand, and dribbled it into the center of the circle in a thin stream, moving his hand so that it made some kind of pattern on the cloth. He sat staring at it for a while before he looked up and gave me the signal to remove the blindfolds.

I did that and went back to my place.

He raised his hand and made a circle with his finger in the air.

"You can turn round now," I croaked.

They turned, opposite ways, moving exactly together as if they'd rehearsed and rehearsed it. They looked at each other just as if each of them was seeing herself in a mirror, and they each put up the same hand to fiddle with the same bit of hair, the way girls do when they spot themselves in a window or something. They smiled and put up both hands and touched, palm to palm. Their happiness was beautiful. It filled the room. I forgot my nerves and the stink of smoke and the awful dusty heat and just stared. Now at last I understood what Melanie had been telling me all along. She and Melly weren't two girls who happened to look amazingly like each other—they were one girl, only there happened to be two of her.

I didn't come to until I heard the bell ring. That reminded me that I'd got Monsieur Albert to keep an eye on as well, so as soon as I'd got the top buckle undone I looked to see what he was up to. He was crouched forward over the cloth, concentrating on it as if it was the only thing in the world, streaming with sweat and muttering under his breath.

When I looked back to the girls they had taken hold of each other's hands and were circling slowly round, face to face. I didn't know how many turns they'd done so now I really couldn't say which was which. They were still smiling, but now it wasn't simply and peacefully, like somebody waking from a good dream, but—I don't know—as if they were sharing a secret they knew, and no one else did.

Out of the corner of my eye I saw Monsieur Albert ring the bell again, reaching out and picking it up and shaking it without stopping his muttering or looking away from the stuff on the cloth. I undid the second buckle and waited with my hands on the top of the cover ready to slide it round and off. It seemed to be quivering slightly under my touch, but that was probably only my nerves.

The girls were circling faster now, swinging each other round with their feet almost touching and their bodies leaning apart and their heads thrown back, laughing aloud too and circling faster and faster so that if either of them had made a mistake they'd have fallen in a heap, but they went on speeding up till they seemed to me to be moving faster than they could have possibly swung on their own, as if something had hold of them and was spinning them like a top till their shifts were a yellow dizzying blur . . .

The bell rang, long and loud. The cover was heavier than I'd expected and I thought for a moment that I was going to knock the mirror crooked but it stuck where it was as if it was bolted to the floor. I laid the cover on the table and began to fold it by feel, looking over my shoulder to watch the girls. They were slowing down, slowing down. They ought to have been too dizzy to stand, and they did look dazed, lost, but they were held. I could actually see that. Something was holding them, controlling them. I remembered what Monsieur Albert had said to Eddie, that they'd "do what they were compelled to do."

I didn't like it. It scared me. Up to now I'd been nervous about the girls meeting because we'd built it up into such a big thing, and I'd been doubly nervous about it being up to me to spot whatever kind of trickery Monsieur Albert might get up to. But those were ordinary sorts of nerves. Now for the first time I really felt—I *knew*—that something was happening which there wasn't any kind of ordinary explanation for. Besides that, it meant that Monsieur Albert had actually known what he'd been talking about, and I'd better do exactly what he'd told me, or everything might go wrong.

I looked down and saw that I'd managed to fold the cover into a neat roll—it could almost have folded itself, because I hadn't been noticing what my hands were up to. I'd even fastened it with one of its buckles. I went back to my chair and sat down, hitching it forward a couple of inches as I did so—the way you do, but I did it on purpose, because it meant I could see a scrap more of the mirror in the reflection from the windowpane. I couldn't see the actual girls at all from where I sat, but they were right in the middle of the reflection, a bit wavy and hard to make out, but there all right. They were turning very slowly now, close together, with their hands under each other's elbows and their bodies almost touching.

As I watched, the light in the room changed. It seemed to happen almost in an instant as the sun went down and the golden shafts of sunlight at either end of the room went dim. I glanced at Monsieur Albert. I didn't want him to catch me staring at the reflection in the window, but he wasn't. He seemed to be in a sort of trance, stiff but quivering, with his hands held tense in front of his shoulders, cupped, palms forward, fingers spread, while he gazed unblinking at the girls. He wasn't seeing me at all, so I looked back at the window reflection.

I could see the girls better now. Before, I'd been looking through one shaft of dusty sunlight and they'd had the other one behind them, so they'd just been a couple of dark outlines. Now I could just about see their faces, both in profile because they'd stopped turning and were standing one with her back to the mirror and the other facing her. They looked solemn but not sad, like dancers in a dream.

Moving exactly together, they raised their hands and touched palms, the way they'd started their dance. Slowly they moved toward the mirror until the nearest one had her back right against it.

She didn't stop there. She went on, into the mirror. I'd only seen it with the cover on it, and even then it wasn't more than a couple of inches thick, but she slid right into it, slowly, her arms and hands going last of all. I could just see her left hand in the bit of mirror at the edge of the reflection, with the other girl's right hand resting on the glass. They stayed there and didn't move.

Monsieur Albert gave a sort of shuddering sigh, which reminded me again that I was supposed to be watching him too. He was leaning back in his chair with his eyes closed and gasping like a runner after a race. The sweat was dripping off the tip of his nose, his face glistened, and his shirt looked as if someone had turned a hose on him.

I looked at the reflection in the pane, and saw that the girl who was still in the room was backing slowly away from the mirror, still in her open-eyed dream. She stopped, and I watched her beginning to wake up. Her hand went up to her hair and fiddled with it, just like at the beginning. She smiled. She was happy. It had worked. It was all right.

She stayed like that, gazing at the mirror. I guessed she had to, that she couldn't look away until it was covered up, so I turned to Monsieur Albert, waiting for him to ring his bell, but he was busy with his things on the cloth again. He took the cup and put it, right way up this time, in the middle, and moved the other objects closer in around it. He took an envelope out of his pocket, shook something from it into his palm, and carefully poured whatever it was into the cup. He tucked the envelope into the bag. Then he took a small stone bottle out of the bag, uncorked it, and dripped two or three drops of liquid onto the other stuff in the cup.

He held his hands out over the cloth as if he was warming them at a fire, and concentrated. I could feel the effort of his concentration. I think a little smoke came out of the cup—I'm not sure . . .

And then I saw him relax. He straightened, and looked up, and smiled.

I don't know how to describe it, but it was obvious. He was watching something really nasty happen, and he was loving it.

I looked at the windowpane to see what he was seeing.

The whole of the middle of the room seemed much darker now—I'm not sure about that either, and anyway night comes quickly that far south. The girl was still there, in front of the mirror, just her shape against the light from the other window. She had her arm thrown up in front of her face as if she was fighting not to go on looking in the mirror but she couldn't help it. She was held, com-pelled . . .

I don't mean I could see anything holding her, but I could see *how* it was holding her, how it was stopping her getting her arm over her eyes, making her look, and then beginning to force her in toward the mirror, though she was leaning away from it, with her other arm up now, pushing at nothing, fighting not to get any nearer, but all the time being forced slowly in . . .

I didn't think. I just knew it was wrong. There wasn't any time for the cover. I jumped up and tried to knock the mirror over but it was like hitting a house. Monsieur Al-bert was screaming at me. I grabbed the tablecloth with both hands and swung it over the mirror. It floated out as if there'd been a wind underneath it, but I tugged it down my side and rushed round and took the girl by the arm and yanked at her.

For a moment she didn't budge, but then a flapping end of the cloth got in front of her face and she came with a rush and we both went sprawling back behind the mirror. As I fell I saw the girl's hand going out and grabbing the tablecloth to stop herself from falling, and pulling it clear just as Monsieur Albert came rushing across . . .

He stopped. No, he didn't. He *was* stopped. Dead. I was on my back and beginning to scramble up and I saw it happen. One moment he was going full tilt and the next he was stuck. He ought to have fallen flat on his face but he didn't, because he was held. Compelled.

Slowly he turned to face the mirror. He stared at it. His face was gray under the tan. He took a deep breath, squared his shoulders, gave a little nod, and walked steadily into the mirror. It didn't take long. I don't know—ten seconds . . .

Then, far too late, I remembered the pager and fished it out and pressed the button. I finished scrambling up and knelt by the girl. She was lying on her front with her head turned sideways and her eyes closed. I could hear Eddie starting to break his way in through the door, but I couldn't leave her alone to go and unlock it. I felt I had to get her as far away from the mirror as possible, so I rolled her over and took her under the arms and dragged her down to the bottom of the room. I'd just got her there when Eddie and Mum came bursting in.

Eddie took a quick look round and ran to the other room. I heard him unlocking the door. Mum rushed down to where we were.

"Where've they gone?" she said. "Where's . . . Oh, God, what's happened to her? Which is this one?"

I just stood, shaking my head. I was shuddering, and sopping with sweat, and my head was pounding. I had a horrible sick feeling that I'd ruined everything, barging in like I had. Janice was there now, kneeling by the girl and sobbing, "Melly! Melly, darling! Is it you . . . ?" And Eddie and the other man, Pierre, were talking, arguing behind us.

The girl's eyes half-opened. We all hushed.

"I'm here. It's me," she whispered. Melly's voice.

"Where's Melanie then?" said Mum.

Dreamily the girl smiled.

"I'm here. It's me—together, I'm telling you." Melanie's voice.

There was a noise on the stairs, somebody running up, several people. Quickly Eddie and Pierre moved out into the lobby to meet them. Men's voices then, loud, arguing in French, too fast for me. Eddie came to the door and beckoned to me, so I went over.

There were three of them. I think I'd noticed them at one of the tables outside the hotel when we'd arrived. They looked pretty tough and determined.

"These appear to be friends of Monsieur Albert's," said Eddie. "They want to know what happened to him."

"The mirror took him," I said.

Eddie translated. The men looked at each other. One of them shrugged.

"*Et alors son miroir a fini par le manger,*" he said.

"*Il le devait une âme,*" said one of the others.

We stood out of the way and they looked through the

door, but wouldn't come into the room. Two of them crossed themselves. They went back to the top of the stairs, talked a little in low voices, and left.

I turned back to the room just in time to see Mum going round to the front of the mirror.

"For God's sake don't look in it!" I yelled, but she'd already done so.

"Sorry, darling, but it's just a mirror," she said. "Have I done something wrong?"

I suppose it must have been the final straw. I vaguely remember registering that Melly/Melanie had come to and Janice was hugging her down at the end of the room, and that was why Mum had gone wandering off, to leave them alone together, and the next thing I remember was waking up and knowing I was in a hospital even before I opened my eyes, because of the smell. I don't remember this either, but according to Mum the first thing I said was "Get the cover on the mirror. Somebody's got to get the cover on the mirror."

They said it was shock, though I tried to tell them it was just the heat. I expect they were right, but I was ashamed of just passing out like that, when it was all over. Every time I thought about what had happened and how nearly it had all gone wrong I got the shudders, so in the end they gave me a sedative and kept me in hospital all night. Melly too . . .

(Don't bother from now on whether I say Melly or Melanie—it's the same person. A lot of people have two names, anyway.)

Mum and Janice had told the doctors that we'd had some kind of terrible shock when we were alone together, and they didn't know what it was, and we'd both passed out. Actually Melly seemed pretty well OK, but she couldn't remember anything that had happened in the room, so they kept her in hospital too, but they let us out next morning.

Janice had insisted on staying with Melly, and Mum felt the same about me, so they'd slept in chairs by our beds, and Eddie came and picked us all up in the morning, and we went and had breakfast together in the most normal, touristy restaurant we could find. We got a table with a big umbrella out on the pavement in one of the squares, and I told the others what had happened.

Eddie hated it. He really fought against having to believe it. Even with Melly being so obviously Melanie as well, and so happy about it, he still wanted to find some way of thinking that Monsieur Albert had somehow hypnotized us all, me and both girls and both mums and him and the other detective, Pierre, and somehow stolen out with the missing girl, but in the end he gave up.

"All right," he said. "Provisionally, and with a lot of misgivings, I'm prepared to act on the assumption that what you say happened actually did so. It is still an unholy mess. There is a missing kid I should have reported last night, as far as anyone outside is concerned, and I bloody nearly did so, in spite of Janice and Trish begging me not to. One reason I didn't was that Pierre had found those three types who barged in on us having a drink outside and talking it over, and he managed to settle down at the next table and listen in. They certainly appeared to think that our friend had disappeared into the mirror in the way Keith has described.

"And here is another reason . . ."

He took an old book out of his briefcase and showed it to us. Its cover was some kind of pale leather, the color of an old dinner-knife handle. He flipped through the pages so that we could see that it was full of a spidery sloping handwriting.

"I found it in the man's bag," said Eddie. "I threw the other stuff into the river but I thought I'd better take charge of this in case it told us anything. I was up half the night trying to make head or tail of it. I think it's about three hundred years old. It's mostly in French, with some Latin and a bit of Italian, I think. I thought I might be able to read the French, at least, but it's full of magical jargon and the writing's hell to make out. Almost the only bits I could make sense of are the various headings, which are in capital letters. Look."

He showed us a page. Even I could read the words at the top. *POUR PREPARER LA CHAMBRE.* To get the room ready.

"What happened to the mirror?" I said. "Is it safe? Have you got it covered up?"

"In a minute," he said. "Let's finish with this. There isn't a title or anything, it just starts straight in. It's a sort of instruction manual for various operations. . . ."

He leafed through and read out some of the headings.

"To call out of the mirror one who is trapped in it. To return one to the mirror. To make two from one. To summon from afar the phantasm of one who is trapped in the mirror. To make one enter the mirror and bring out the phantasm—"

"Hey! Wait a sec. What's that?" I said, because something, a brown envelope, had fallen out of the book as he turned the page.

"Just a bookmark he was using," said Eddie. "Nothing in it except a few bits of hair. Well—"

"No, wait," I said, and scrabbled in the back pocket of my jeans. Mum hadn't managed to get back to the hotel for clean clothes for me, so I was wearing what I'd had on yesterday. At least they'd dried out.

I fished out the envelope Monsieur Albert had given me and looked inside. There were some short dark hairs in it.

"Sorry," I said. "It's all right. But you remember I told you about him snipping bits off the girls' hair. I just thought . . ."

"Let's have a look," said Janice, so I passed her the envelope. She shook the hairs out onto her hand and looked at them.

"No, that's not Melly's," she said. "It's much too coarse. May I see the other one, Eddie? . . . Yes, that's hers . . . Oh, my goodness . . ."

"That's what he was putting in the cup," I said. "I should have remembered he was a conjurer."

Nobody said anything for a bit. More than anything else

that had happened this gave me the cold shivers. I don't know why.

"I wish I knew what the hell he thought he was up to," said Eddie. "And even more how the hell he thought we were going to let him get away with it. But at least it bears out what I was saying. My other reason for not insisting that he has somehow tricked us all is that everything goes to suggest that the man himself believed in the genuineness of what he was trying to do. He was going to do what he'd promised us, though he was also going to cheat us in the end."

"And he did it," I said. "What he'd promised us, I mean. Right, Melly?"

She nodded. It was much easier for us, of course. I'd been there. I'd seen it. I knew it was true. And Melly knew she'd got what she wanted, though she still couldn't remember a thing about how it had happened. It wasn't that hard for Mum either, because she's so good at putting herself in your shoes. When I'd been telling the story she'd practically been in the room with me, living it. But it was much tougher on Janice. It wasn't her kind of thing at all. (I'll put this in here, though it comes later, and I wasn't actually there. Mum told me. It was at the airport. We were going home together because we'd had to change our tickets anyway. I'd gone to look at the bookstore while Mum cruised the duty-free and Janice and Melly stayed with our bags. Mum got back to find Janice alone, because Melly had gone to the toilet. She was crying. "I keep remembering my other daughter," she told Mum. "It's all right when she's here. Then I know I've got them both. But when she's not . . .")

Eddie wasn't so involved, of course, but he still hated it, like I've said, and you can't blame him.

"We're all going to be in very serious trouble if anyone finds out that we've failed to report a missing child," he said. "I'm going along with this for the reasons I've told you, but I'm risking my job and my license to do so. We've all got to get out of here and back to England as soon as we can fix fresh flights, and till then Melly will have to show her face at both hotels, so that questions don't get asked. You'll have to think of a story about why only one girl's flying home—the other one's gone to stay with friends and will be coming home by car with them, or something. And I don't know what the lawyer's going to say about the money he's holding—we'll just have to see. And God knows what I'm going to put in my report."

"Well, I think you've done wonders," said Mum. "I'm sorry we've landed you in this mess, and thank you for being so good about it."

He shrugged and smiled.

"At least it makes a change from watching people's wives," he said.

"You were going to say about the mirror," I said.

"I don't think there's much we can do about that," said Eddie. "After I'd got you to hospital I went back to settle with Pierre. I'd left him to see if he could find anything out, and as I've told you he did pick up a bit by listening to

289

the talk outside. But as soon as he went in and tried to ask questions and they realized he'd been with us, they threw him out. He was waiting for me in the square. I went back in on the excuse of wanting to pay for the damage to the door and they threw me out too. It was a woman. She was furious, and frightened, and she wouldn't take any money, and that's all I know. Pierre, by the way, is aware that something pretty rum was up, and he doesn't want to know about it. As far as he was concerned he'd only seen one girl.''

Well, I hung around with Janice and Melly while Eddie and Mum went off to see the lawyer. Luckily he'd already decided for himself that Monsieur Albert was a crook, and though they couldn't tell him the whole story, anything like, they told him enough for him to agree that if Monsieur Albert hadn't shown up in a month to claim it, he'd send the money back to Mum. Then we drove around with Eddie and did touristy things and had an amazing meal in the evening to celebrate, and though it was still roasting hot and we ought by all rights to have been dead with exhaustion, not to mention nervous as hell that a lot of French cops were going to show up and start grilling us about what we'd done with the missing girl, we didn't bother about any of that. We just talked and laughed and had a really good time.

It was because of Melly. She wasn't wild with high spirits, or anything, but there was this great glow of happiness flooding out of her, so strong that you felt nothing could ever shake or change it. I'd only got to look at her for the stuff that had happened in the Orangerie to sort of fade out and lose its grip. Yes, it had almost gone horribly wrong, but it was never going to, because it had to end like this. This was fixed.

The last thing Eddie said to me when we said good-bye was, "I'd still like to know how the hell the bastard thought he was ever going to get away with it."

We all flew back to Birmingham because Mum had a fortnight off and that meant we could go and stay with Melly and Janice at Coventry, and catch up on old friends. When Dad had died Mum had said she never wanted to set foot in Coventry again, but now she really enjoyed herself, and even talked about him sometimes as if she was getting used to the idea that he wasn't around anymore.

The thing I found really hard to take was the idea that Melly and Melanie were one person, not two people who happened to be living in one body. I think I could have coped with that. It was easy for Janice once she got home and settled in to all her usual ways. As far as she was concerned she'd got Melly back, happy and full of life, and Melly helped by just being Melly for her, not smoking or swearing, and by hanging around with her old crowd. She kept her Melanie hairdo, but she'd been nagging for months to be let have it cut like that, and Janice might have given in anyway.

It wasn't hard for Mum, either, though she'd got fond of Melanie at Bearsden. The business about this being both of them didn't seem to bother her. That's how it was, and if Melly was happy with it, she was too.

It was different for me. I'd always been fond of Melly. I'd missed her when she wasn't there, and if she'd come up to visit us in Bearsden I'd have been glad to have her around and sorry when she left. But when Melanie had been living there with us I'd been a lot more than just glad—there'd been something about her which really got me going, something—I don't know—dangerous. (Actually I think there must have been about Melly too, only she didn't let you see it.)

I used to nag away at this when we were alone together. I couldn't help it. I wasn't going to tell her straight out how I felt, but I kept noticing little things that reminded me, and saying something about them. For instance, we were washing up and I passed her a cup to dry and she'd switched hands since the last cup—she was good as ambidextrous now—and I said something about that as if I was joking but she didn't answer. Then, when I was doing the next cup I realized she'd stopped drying so I looked up. She was watching me half sideways, smiling that Melly smile.

"I ken weel what you're effing thinking, you poor wee laddie," she said.

I felt myself blushing like a beetroot. She laughed and kissed me on the cheek but my hands were all covered with soapy water and I couldn't grab her, and then she was back to being Melly.

———

She came up to Bearsden for her half term. (Janice was working and stayed in Coventry.) Scottish half term wasn't the same as English, so the first two days we only got the evenings together, and the first of them Mum was there so we just sat around and talked. She was different in Bearsden, not just Melly or Melanie, but somewhere between, and older-seeming, very sure of herself without having to prove it to anybody, the way you felt Melanie had needed to.

The second evening Mum said she had to work late. Melly'd got tea ready by the time I was home and she put it on a tray and took it into the living room so that we could sit on the sofa and pretend to watch telly and have a really good cuddle. That was great. God, I was happy.

After a bit she said, "You remember that dream I told you?"

"The nightmare, you mean? About the man taking you across a big field toward a traveling cage with some kind of monster in it?"

"Aye. I had it again."

"Oh . . . That sounds bad. Does it mean . . . ?"

"No. It was just the once, and I won't have it anymore. I'll tell you. I was a bairn again, and watching Papa feed his lions, and I went wandering off but there was nobody with me. There was this big field, and over the far side one of the traveling cages, so I went to see. The door was open, so I climbed the step and looked inside, but there was nothing there except this old mirror with its glass all broken. I looked at it awhile, and then I said to myself, 'I must go and find Papa and show him.' That's what I'll be doing tomorrow.''

"Going to Edinburgh?"

"Aye. It's a thing I must do, and I didn't need the dream to tell me. Do you ken how old I am?"

"Trick question. Not fourteen, anyway?"

"Twenty-eight years I've lived in my two bodies, and I'm not shutting any of them away, or it'll be like having a room in my house I'm scared to go into because there's a ghoulie in it."

"Can I come too?" I said. Next day was Saturday, and Sunday she was off back to Coventry.

"I was hoping you'd say that," she said. "We'll tell Trish we're going to Edinburgh, and she'll get the wrong idea, think it's for a sentimental visit to where we met up."

"She doesn't know anything."

"She does, too. Got eyes in her head, hasn't she? Bet you couldn't sit still, last few days before I showed up. Why do you think she stayed away tonight?"

"Anyway it isn't the wrong idea," I said.

"Maybe not," she said.

Then, later, I said, "Are you going to tell him what happened at the Orangerie? You still don't remember any of that?"

"Nothing. I'll just tell him what you told me."

"I've worked out a bit more, if you're interested."

We hadn't talked about this hardly at all since we'd left Arles. She hadn't wanted to know. But I'd been over and over it with Mum and I'd been down to the main library in Glasgow and read everything I could find about doppelgangers and magic mirrors and so on.

"All right," she said.

"It isn't about what actually happened," I said. "It's about what Monsieur Albert thought he was trying to do. You remember Eddie reading those bits out of the book while we were having breakfast? And then I interrupted him by asking about the envelope with the hair in it?"

"Yes—but I wasn't paying a lot of heed."

"Well, one of them was 'To make two from one.' That's what he did when you were a baby, and I bet there was something in it about how it only lasts for seven years, or fourteen, or whatever, and then the two have to come together again. And there were two others. One was about summoning the phantom—no, the phantasm—of someone who's trapped in the mirror, and one about making someone go into the mirror and bringing out the phantasm. That's what he was doing when I stopped him. You'd have been in the mirror and your phantasm would have been outside, and he'd have passed the phantasm over to us and we'd have thought it was you. It would have been just like you and talked like you, and it might have been a bit dopy but we were used to that, and it wouldn't remember anything, like you don't, and I wasn't supposed to have seen anything that mattered. And then Mum would have paid him the money and we'd all have gone home, and after a bit he'd have called your phantasm back. I don't think it would just have disappeared. I think it would have died, and we'd have buried it and all been very sad, but if we'd dug down and opened the coffin there wouldn't have been anything in it. I found a story like that in the library."

She thought about it.

"Aye," she said. "And that's why Papa took me away. And that's what Monsieur Albert would have been doing so late of a night in his caravan, calling his toys out of his mirror, and playing with them any way he wanted. Oh, Keith, it was lucky for me you were in the room with me!"

She was leaning against me, very cozy, but I took her by the shoulders and pushed her away and held her.

"Now, listen," I said. "OK, it was lucky, and OK, you're grateful, but this isn't anything to do with that. I'd have done that for anybody, for Ken, for somebody I didn't know at all. It's over, and you're grateful, and that's OK. But this is because I really like you, and I'd feel the same if none of that stuff in Arles had ever happened. But if you're just doing it because you think you owe it to me, then I'm not interested."

She grinned at me.

"Dinna fret yourself, Keith," she said. "I like you fine. This evening."

The coach was just getting into Edinburgh when she said, "If this goes right, I'll be coming back here."

"Leaving Coventry? What will Janice . . . ?"

"No, I get along fine with Mum," she said. "In fact I

was wrong when I told you she didn't feel like a ma—or maybe she always knew inside her there was something missing between us, and now we've found it. She's great, and I wouldn't change her for Trish, even. But still I'm not letting go of Edinburgh, and Annie's and all. I'll be having as much of that as I can fit in, maybe only a couple of weeks of waitressing in the holidays, but that will do fine.''

''What about your dad? Won't he still . . . ?''

''Not if today goes right, he won't.''

I didn't try to tell her she was mad. I didn't even think that. If anybody could do it, she could. And maybe she'd arrange to come to Edinburgh by way of Bearsden. And maybe . . .

''Can Annie use an extra waiter?'' I said. ''OK, I'm way under age, but so are you.''

We got in in the middle of the morning and went straight to Annie's, so as to be there before it was busy with customers. It wasn't much of a day for tourists, anyway, in spite of it being Saturday—November, and a thick chill drizzle falling.

M. Perrault was the only person in the restaurant when we went in. He had his back to the door and was polishing his glasses and putting them on the shelf, but he turned to see who it was and stood there, staring. I stayed by the door while Melanie walked between the tables and waited in the middle of the room.

He finished the glass he was holding and put it carefully with the others, and then came out round the bar. His right hand was clenching and unclenching by his belt. His face was almost white. I could see a blue vein on the side of his head bumping in and out as he walked heavily toward her. She looked him in the eyes and took a pace to meet him. I heard her say something in a low voice.

His eyes widened. He stopped. His hand dropped to his side, but the blue vein went on pulsing.

He said something—a question. She answered, only two or three words.

He turned and put his arm on the bar and bent his head, shaking it slowly from side to side.

I must have been holding my breath all this while, because now I noticed I was letting it go. I should have known it was going to be all right, I thought. She is the lion tamer's daughter.